W9-AXK-075

PRAISE FOR
KATHY HOGAN TROCHECK AND

CRASH COURSE

"Fast reading [with] interesting twists and ironies."
—*Naples News* (Naples, FL)

"Best of all, *Crash Course* has the incomparable sexagenarian Kicklighter. . . . A zany plot . . . [that] offers a wry peek at retirement, Florida style. It will send you scurrying for Hogan's first Kicklighter caper, *Lickety-Split*."
—*Buffalo News*

LICKETY-SPLIT

"On the surface [Trocheck's] clever plots are sheer entertainment [with] witty dialogue and sassy characters. . . . Trocheck brings a keen sense of St. Petersburg's retirement community to *Lickety-Split*, capturing not only the sights of the city but also its smells."
—*Chicago Tribune*

"Trocheck packs her brisk tale with plenty of plot and pizzazz. . . . The payoff's worth waiting for."
—*Orlando Sentinel*

"Unswervingly suspenseful and carefully plotted, with an appealing cast. . . . One can only hope that Trocheck . . . will bring this entertaining curmudgeon back very soon."
—*Atlanta Journal-Constitution*

BOOKS BY KATHY HOGAN TROCHECK

Featuring Truman Kicklighter

Crash Course
Lickety-Split

Featuring Callahan Garrity

Strange Brew
Heart Trouble
Happy Never After
Homemade Sin
To Live & Die in Dixie
Every Crooked Nanny

Published by HarperPaperbacks

ATTENTION: ORGANIZATIONS AND CORPORATIONS

Most HarperPaperbacks are available at special quantity discounts for bulk purchases for sales promotions, premiums, or fund-raising. For information, please call or write:
**Special Markets Department, HarperCollins Publishers,
10 East 53rd Street, New York, N.Y. 10022.
Telephone: (212) 207-7528. Fax: (212) 207-7222.**

CRASH COURSE

A TRUMAN KICKLIGHTER MYSTERY

Kathy Hogan Trocheck

HarperPaperbacks
A Division of HarperCollinsPublishers

HarperPaperbacks

A Division of HarperCollins*Publishers*
10 East 53rd Street, New York, N.Y. 10022-5299

If you purchased this book without a cover, you should be aware
that this book is stolen property. It was reported as "unsold and
destroyed" to the publisher and neither the author nor the
publisher has received any payment for this "stripped book."

This is a work of fiction. The characters, incidents, and
dialogues are products of the author's imagination and are not to
be construed as real. Any resemblance to actual events or
persons, living or dead, is entirely coincidental.

Copyright © 1997 by Kathy Hogan Trocheck
All rights reserved. No part of this book may be used or
reproduced in any manner whatsoever without written
permission of the publisher, except in the case of brief
quotations embodied in critical articles and reviews.
For information address HarperCollins*Publishers,* Inc.
10 East 53rd Street, New York, N.Y. 10022-5299.

ISBN 0-06-109172-3

HarperCollins®, 🏛®, and HarperPaperbacks™
are trademarks of HarperCollins*Publishers,* Inc.

Cover illustration © 1998 by Marc Burkhardt

A hardcover edition of this book was published in 1997
by HarperCollins*Publishers.*

First HarperPaperbacks printing: May 1998

Printed in the United States of America

Visit HarperPaperbacks on the World Wide Web at
http://www.harpercollins.com

❖ 10 9 8 7 6 5 4 3 2 1

This one is dedicated with love to
Andrew Rivers Trocheck,
who daily gives us a one-man crash course
on raising a son.
What a joy!

ACKNOWLEDGMENTS

The author wishes to thank the following for their advice and assistance: John V., Victor J., and Dean J. Economy of Economy Auto Sales in Decatur, Georgia; Chris Russell of County Recovery; Charles E. Guthrie, Allen J. Genaldi, and Edward S. Guenther of the Florida Department of Law Enforcement; Bill Pronzini, M.D.; and as always, my intrepid research assistants and legmen, John and Sue Hogan and Alice Barchie.

CHAPTER

ONE

TRUMAN KICKLIGHTER FROWNED AT THE MIRROR on his bureau. A thin, reddish-brown trickle weeped off the end of each of his eyebrows, giving him a clownlike appearance. Not what he had in mind. Not at all.

He blotted each eyebrow with a tissue. Now the ends were gray again, and the red-brown stain was soaking into his skin. It was the heat. August in St. Petersburg, Florida, and the air-conditioning at the Fountain of Youth Residential Hotel had once again gone on the fritz. He was perspiring so profusely that the Nice 'n Easy was melting as fast as he combed it into his hair and eyebrows. Now it was trickling down his forehead, and into his ears.

Management, meaning young Mandelbaum, was making feeble excuses about how there was a problem with the wiring, which would be fixed just as soon as the electrician could get to it. In the meantime, temperatures hadn't dropped below ninety since Labor Day and the old yellow-brick hotel was hell on earth.

The window air conditioner Truman had invested $199.95 for was useless now. Every time he plugged it in, all the lights on his floor winked on and off and then off. So now the unit sat on the floor, an expensive end table, while he propped open his only window with a brick.

He was waving a handheld hair dryer over his eyebrows when he heard the loud knocking on the door.

"Mr. K? It's me, Jackie. Can I come in?"

"Just a minute, Jackie," he called. Quickly he opened the top drawer of the dresser and swept in the Nice 'n Easy, the toothbrush he'd used for application, the hair dryer, and the used tissues. One more hasty blot with the tissue. He scowled. Now it looked like he'd developed liver spots. He slipped his short-sleeved white sport shirt on top of his undershirt and buttoned it.

There was one chair in the room, a high-backed wooden number he'd brought from the old house after Nellie died. He sat down and picked up the paperback copy of *Sense and Sensibility*.

"Come on in," he said, trying to sound casual.

Jackleen Canaday was feeling the heat, too. After working the Saturday early dinner shift, she'd gone to her own room at the hotel and stripped down to cut-off jeans and a white tank top. She came in carrying a newspaper.

"You weren't at dinner," she said accusingly. "Chicken croquettes and cream gravy and pickled beets. Mrs. Hoffmayer had two helpings."

"It's too hot for cream gravy," Truman said, fanning himself with the paperback. "Besides, it's my Great Books discussion group night. I'll eat there."

Back in the winter and spring, they'd had twenty members, a real lively bunch. But now they were down to only seven members, and he was the only man in the group besides old man Drewry.

They'd read *The Odyssey*, *Remembrance of Things Past*, *Ivanhoe*, *David Copperfield*, and *War and Peace* over the winter. He'd nominated *Lady Chatterley's Lover* for this time, but the women, especially Elvida Hamm, a former librarian, had block-voted against "that smut." Old man Drewry voted both ways.

Now they were plodding through *Sense and Sensibility*. He would quit, Truman had admitted to his friend Ollie, except that the refreshments served at this book group were of the highest quality he'd experienced anywhere. Each woman tried to outdo the other with her covered-dish offering: creamy, crumb-topped macaroni and cheese, garden-fresh vegetables, salty-sweet Coca-Cola–glazed hams, lemon icebox cakes, towering chocolate layer cakes. It was beyond description.

"Great Books," Jackie said, waving a hand dismissively. "Bunch of old ladies reading poetry. There's a car listed in the classified ads. I was hoping you'd give me a ride over to this car lot, Bondurant Motors up on U.S. 19 to check it out. It's only six hundred dollars, and that's exactly how much I have saved."

"What kind of car?" Truman asked. "I didn't know you could buy cars anymore for that kind of money."

"A 1970 AMC Gremlin," Jackie said, pointing at an ad circled on the classified page. "Says it's a cream puff. Low mileage, radio, the works. What do you think?"

"I believe the part about low mileage," Truman

said. "Those cars only went a couple times around the block before they quit running. You don't want a Gremlin, Jackie. Those cars were so bad they quit making them after just a few years. Hell, AMC went out of business. A Gremlin's a joke."

"It's only six hundred dollars," Jackie said. "And I've got to get a car. I can't stand riding that bus or begging rides another second."

"We'll go out tomorrow, see what we can find," Truman offered.

"Never buy a used car from a dealer. That's my policy. Besides, we're reading *Sense and Sensibility*. I can't miss Jane Austen."

On the first Saturday night of each month, Great Books night, he was always greeted at the door of the Mirror Lake Adult Recreation Center with a chorus of glad cries and gratitude. Each month, he managed to slip enough leftover food into his canvas book bag (specially lined for the occasion with tinfoil) to snack on for a week.

"Come on, Mr. K," Jackie pleaded. "This car sounds perfect for me. Besides, you hate Jane Austen. You told me Harold Robbins and Ian Fleming are a hundred percent better than her."

"Well, if we're talking contemporary novelists, sure," Truman said. "You ever read *The Carpetbaggers*? How about *From Russia with Love*? Anyway, I happen to know that Maggie McCutcheon is leading the discussion tonight."

It was nearly time to go. He got up, went to the bureau, and got his bottle of Old Spice aftershave. If there was anything that could cool him off, it was a splash of Old Spice on his face and neck. He rubbed a little extra on the Nice 'n Easy stain, which had faded to a dull purple. Then he ran the comb through his still damp hair. Was it a darker red than usual? Maybe he'd gone overboard this time.

"Which one was Maggie McCutcheon?" Jackie demanded. "The one with the hearing aid that buzzes?" Truman had dragged Jackie along to Great Books group once. Talk about boring. You might as well sit home and watch PBS.

"Miss McCutcheon happens to have perfect hearing," Truman said, picking up his car keys. "She is a prodigious researcher. And, she's promised homemade peach ice cream and sour-cream pound cake tonight. Sorry, Jackie."

She sighed a martyred sigh and stood up. "Guess I'll just have to take that nasty old bus."

"Guess you will," Truman agreed. He liked to get to his meeting after the discussion was started, but in plenty of time to plan his attack on the buffet table. Refreshments were served from eight-thirty till nine. He always left at nine. Sharp. Any later than that, the widows would be inviting him home to help finish up their leftover food—and maybe take a look at why their cable reception was so poor or their dishwasher made a funny thudding sound during the spin cycle.

CHAPTER

TWO

JACKIE REACHED UP WITH BOTH HANDS AND jerked hard at the upper sash of the metal window, grunting out loud with the effort. It squeaked and the window slid open maybe five pathetic inches.

"Have mercy," Jackie said, slumping back in her seat. Of all the days to catch a city bus with a malfunctioning air conditioner. First the hotel and now this.

Was there any place cool left on the face of the planet?

The sweat had soaked through her shirt, and now the front of her shorts were damp, too.

August. Supposed to be off-season in Florida. Tell that to the college kids. Forty of them, must be. All of them staying at the Fountain of Youth. It was old man Mandelbaum's idea to make the place a youth hostel. After the church deal went sour last year.

That was the idea, make the place a youth hostel for the summer, once the snowbirds had gone back up north for the year. Just a handful of regulars stayed there year-round. The regulars, most of them retired, like Mr. Kicklighter and Ollie and that nasty Mrs. Hoffmayer, groused about the college kids, but it wasn't like they could afford to live anyplace else. Her either, for that matter. She'd moved into a one-bedroom efficiency at the Fountain of Youth in May. Her own personal Independence Day.

Jackie bent down and rubbed her aching shins. Jesus. The college kids packed the place, two and three to a room, for twenty-five bucks a night. Ran up and down the halls all hours of the night, even though the front door was supposed to be locked and lights out at eleven. And they could eat like there was no tomorrow. Breakfast and lunch was what they liked. Cheap and filling. Pancakes, eggs, sausage, grits, hamburgers, french fries, pizza. Pie. Anything salty, greasy, or sweet. She had to keep an eagle eye on her tables. Some college kids were okay. But others thought being poor was a game. Cute or something. They liked to ditch a check, sneak out without paying. Let one of 'em try it on her. She'd jerk a knot in their tails all right.

She had her face pressed up against the open bus window, looking for the right street address. Suddenly the bright red-and-yellow Bondurant Motors sign loomed up ahead.

At the same time she pulled the cord to tell the driver to let her off, she saw something red out of the corner of her eye. Candy-apple red. Devil red. Jackie caught her breath and stared. The bus lurched to a stop at the curb and she stumbled off. She knew this place now, but had never paid attention to its name. It was the same tired old used-car lot she'd passed a million times on her way up U.S. 19. The same old pink car, some kind of Chevy probably, an old one, fifties, maybe, with gigantic sharklike fins, spun lazily around a shaft mounted on the flat roof of the concrete-block office building, its headlights blinking in the purple-dusk sky.

But it was the red car she couldn't take her eyes off of. It shimmered in the glow of all those red and yellow lights strung around the edges of the lot. It was like a bolt of fire, positively ablaze. It was her dream come true. A red Corvette.

God, it was hot. Worse than the Fountain of Youth, and here it was nearly eight o'clock in the evening. The street was hotter than the bus. This part of U.S. 19 was nothing but concrete and asphalt and endless streams of cars and exhaust fumes. She felt like a wet, woolen blanket had been thrown over her—in a steam bath.

Enough. She walked toward the Corvette. Her 'Vette.

She circled it three times, not daring to look at the price sticker until her third time around. The price was beside the point. It was her car. White leather upholstery. Tinted T-top, gleaming chrome wire wheels. She shivered despite the heat. Somebody had painted on the windshield with yellow paint "Do Ya Think I'm Sexy?"

Her favorite Rod Stewart song. It was an omen. Fate.

"Want to take her for a ride?" The voice in her ear was lazy, drawling. Wintergreen scented.

She whirled around. He was tall, maybe six feet. Brown, wavy hair lightly moussed, a golden tan, deep cleft in his chin, funny gold-green eyes. He wore black walking shorts, sparkling white Nikes, a red golf shirt with "Bondurant Motors" embroidered over the left breast.

"I'm Jeff," he said, sticking his hand out to shake. "Jeff Cantrell."

She shook his hand briefly, trying to take it all in. The red 'Vette. The price tag. $10,000. Jeff. He looked like the car. Sexy. Dangerous. Fun. The $600 Gremlin was forgotten.

"I'm Jackie. Ten thousand," she said casually. "That price firm?"

When he smiled, you could see a little chip in his front tooth. And his upper lip pulled up into a bow, like the Kewpie doll her aunt kept on a shelf in her parlor. He winked and pulled a set of car keys out of the pocket of his shorts. He tossed them to her. She reached out and caught them one-handed. She could be as cool as him.

"We can talk while you drive," Jeff said. "I'm supposed to close up at eight, but what the hell. Think you can handle a five speed?"

"I can handle a lot more than you think," she said slyly.

Jesus. Where had that come from? It was the car. It had sucked her in, changed her from a hard-working, bus-riding waitress to a two-bit, trash-talking party girl.

He winked again. "Let me just get a copy of your driver's license. For the insurance. Ronnie's rules. Ronnie Bondurant. He's the owner. He's real particular about letting people drive this 'Vette."

"I should hope so," she said.

He showed her how to crank the 'Vette. It took a couple of tries, and she nearly died the first time the car stalled out on her. But the radio worked as soon as she turned the key in the ignition. She flipped the dial to her favorite station. Urban classics. Motown.

Jeff was smiling, running his hands over the sparkling white-leather dashboard. "Cherry, huh? Hard to believe it's an '86."

Jackie flipped some switches on the dash, hoping one of them was the air conditioner. "Cherry. What's that mean?"

He guided her hand toward a knob and helped her slide it all the way to the right. Air poured out of the vents. Hot at first. But his hand was cool.

"Cherry," he repeated. "In the wrapper. Like, brand new. Give it some gas now, so it doesn't stall out again. It's okay. See, the car hasn't been driven in a couple of weeks. Ronnie won't let just anybody drive this particular car. We get kids, teenagers, they see a red sports car, they just have to drive it. Ronnie says, 'No way. No cash, no flash.' But you, I can tell, a car like this is definitely in your future."

"Maybe," Jackie said. She put the car in reverse and put her foot down firmly on the gas. The 'Vette leaped backward and stalled again.

"Shit," she said, so frustrated she could cry. She felt sweat beading down her back, down her neck, on her upper lip. Her legs stuck to the leather upholstery. He'd think she was some sweathog, probably make her get out of the car so she didn't stink it up.

Jeff laughed at her. "Don't be so nervous," he said. "You're doing fine."

Ten minutes later, the sweat had dried and she had goosebumps from the AC. She was maneuvering the 'Vette gingerly through the thick Saturday night traffic on U.S. 19. And Jeff had explained everything. The car had belonged to a doctor in Clearwater. Actually, his wife. When the doctor found out his wife was screwing her tennis pro, he'd picked up the car at the country club, driven it right over to Bondurant Motors, and sold it on the spot. That's why the price was so cheap, Jeff explained. Another ten minutes of hearing that sweet drawl and he'd explain her right out of her panties.

"Nine thousand," Jeff told her as they glided back into the parking lot at Bondurant Motors. He had his arm thrown casually over the back of her seat. "And I'll have to do some fast talking with old Ronnie. But I can handle him."

"The bank," Jackie said, a catch in her throat. "I had some credit-card problems a couple years ago. My old boyfriend took off with my card and was charging things . . ."

"Buy here, finance here," Jeff said firmly. "Jackie, do I look like a banker to you?"

She shook her head no.

"Besides," he said smoothly, "we're not interested in old history. We're interested in putting people on the road. Everybody makes mistakes, Jackie. So what happened to that old boyfriend, if you don't mind my asking?"

"Gone," she said. "Good riddance. What about the payments?" She could feel her resistance flagging. Numbers. She needed to talk numbers. Now he would surely let loose of her, tell her to take her sorry, sagging butt out of this beautiful red Corvette, and get it into that $600 car she'd planned on.

"Girl like you needs a special set of wheels," he said. He tapped his upper lip with the tip of his tongue. "Six hundred down? How would that be, Jackie? Think you could come up with that much?"

"Six hundred down?" She couldn't believe he'd said that. It was a sign. Jesus wanted her to have this car. For six hundred dollars down she could kiss that hot, stinking bus good-bye forever. She could picture herself already, driving up to her mother's house, the T-top open, her hair whipping around her face in the breeze. She'd get a long, fluttery chiffon scarf and a pair of expensive sunglasses, like those girls, Thelma and Louise, in the movie. Only she wouldn't be driving off no cliff. No, sir.

Jeff was saying something else now, something about weekly payments, and then he wanted to be sure she had been on the same job for a year now, hadn't she? And could he call her landlord to verify her address?

"No credit check," he said hastily. "It's just another of Ronnie's rules. Come on in the office, Jackie, let's get this paperwork taken care of, get you on the road in this fine car of yours."

Jackie got out of the car and the heat swallowed her up. Her knees were all wobbly and the asphalt in the parking lot was soft and sticky, like chewing gum under her work shoes. The pink Chevy wobbled crazily on the roof. She wanted to ask Jeff how they got that car up on the roof. But the heat and exhaust fumes made all the cars a blur of color and vague shapes. All except the red Corvette. She ran her fingers lightly over the hood as she trailed Jeff Cantrell into the office of Bondurant Motors.

CHAPTER

THREE

SENSE AND SENSIBILITY WAS ONE OF THOSE BOOKS Truman had always meant to read. He'd even borrowed the Cliff's Notes from Cheryl, who was supposed to read it for an English lit class she was taking toward her Master's degree.

But Jane Austen didn't have quite the zip he was looking for these days.

He sat in the back of the brightly lit meeting room, drowsily enjoying the air-conditioning and the mixed smells of cologne and baked goods. He only half listened while the ladies chattered away about the predicament of the Misses Dashwood and the conflicting themes of desire and conservative moralism.

That the two sisters in the book were named Elinor and Marianne he had detected from the Cliff's Notes. And Cheryl, who had earned a B in the lit class, informed him that Jane Austen's work was critically hailed because of her satirical powers of observation of the mores of eighteenth-century gentry.

But his attention wandered now from English lit

to English trifle. There was a large cut-glass bowl of the stuff on the refreshment table, layers of cake and peaches and raspberries and fluffy clouds of whipped cream. Right beside it was a dish heaped high with something like chicken salad. One of his favorites. But didn't you have to use mayonnaise in chicken salad? Wasn't there some kind of food poisoning issue if mayonnaise got left out in the heat? Salmonella was nothing to mess with.

"And Truman?"

He jerked his head around. All the ladies were staring at him. Old man Drewry was working a crossword puzzle. Margaret McCutcheon seemed especially amused. Had his eyebrows started bleeding again?

"Uh, yes?" Truman said.

Mildred Davis coughed gently. "We were just wondering if a man could truly appreciate Elinor's predicament in the book. What do you think, Mr. Kicklighter?"

Truman thought it *was* mayonnaise in the chicken salad, and he was already regretting the chicken salad sandwich he would *not* be enjoying for Sunday lunch tomorrow.

He coughed, examined the tops of his brown shoes, and pulled his glasses down to the bridge of his nose to give himself time to stall.

"Well," he started. "Of course, those were different days, weren't they? Who among us can say they really understand any fictional character's predicament?"

There. Profound but not prolonged.

"I think the next book we pick ought to have snappier pictures and bigger print," old man Drewry said, standing up so fast his metal folding chair fell to the linoleum floor with a clatter. "Now let's eat."

"But we haven't voted on next month's book," Elvida Hamm protested. "And Margaret hasn't finished reading her remarks."

"I've finished," Margaret said, snapping her folder shut.

"I move we read *To Kill a Mockingbird*," Truman said loudly. Cheryl had just finished writing a paper on *To Kill a Mockingbird*, and the movie with Gregory Peck had always been a favorite of his.

"Excellent," Margaret said, beaming. "A contemporary Southern female author. Girls?"

Daizye Belle Fletcher waved her hand for recognition. "Is it in paperback?"

"Large print?" Pops Drewry demanded.

"Both," Margaret said. "You can even listen to it on an audiotape checked out from the library. We're adjourned."

Truman picked up his foil-lined book bag and headed for the refreshment table. There was a system to his buffet browsing. The gooey things, like the trifle and some pineapple cheesecake, he wolfed down as quickly as he could, at the same time scooping up the more stable items, such as oatmeal-fudge bars, sausage-cheese balls, and finger sandwiches, to be deftly transferred to his waiting book bag.

The fried chicken was a bonanza he hadn't anticipated. It was hidden away behind a large tray of cubed purple meat skewered together with canned pineapple chunks and cocktail onions.

"Try one." Mildred Davis held out the tray to him, her plump little hands fluttering with excitement. "Spam Kabobs. They're my specialty."

Truman nearly dropped his drumstick. Damn, these widows were sneaky. He hadn't even seen her coming.

"Oh no," he said, waving the kabobs away. "Pineapple and I don't get along at all. But I'm sure they're wonderful."

"Too bad," she said as she set the platter aside. "But Truman, I hear that you are somewhat of a home-repair expert. Maybe you'd be interested in seeing my lawn irrigation system. It's very complicated, with all these pipes and dials and gauges. There's this one sprinkler head that's not working at all properly. It gurgles, but it won't spit. And I thought, since you're an expert—"

"Excuse me," Margaret McCutchen said, boldly moving between Truman and Mildred, forcing Mildred to take a step backward. "I'm sorry, Mildred," Margaret said, tugging gently at Truman's shirtsleeve. "I need to borrow Truman to help unload my cooler of ice cream from the car. We won't be but a minute. All right?"

"But," Mildred said, her rouged dewlaps quivering unhappily, "I was just explaining about the pipes."

"And I'm sure Truman is dying to find out about that," Margaret said in that refined Southern drawl of hers. Not a rural kind of grits-and-gravy accent; more like bourbon and branch water. Biloxi, maybe, or Charleston.

Truman allowed himself to be steered toward the kitchen door. But he was puzzled. Despite her refined manners, Margaret McCutchen was no weak sister. She was as tall as he, skinny as a whip, with the weather-beaten skin of the lifelong amateur sailor he'd heard she was. Unlike most women her age, Margaret didn't seem to fuss much about things like casseroles or flowery dresses or pictures of her grandchildren. He didn't know if he'd ever heard her mention any grandchildren.

"The coast is clear," she said when the kitchen door swung shut behind them and they were alone. The laugh lines around her intelligent dark eyes deepened. "You can go out the back here. Run like hell, or before you know it, Mildred will have you on a leash for sure."

"What about the cooler?" Truman wondered. He had no intention of being conned into examining Mildred Davis's pipes, aboveground or otherwise, but by damn, not many people went to the trouble to churn homemade ice cream these days. He didn't want to miss out.

"There is no cooler in the car," she said. "The ice cream's out there under the table, packed in a tub of dry ice. I brought it in earlier. Do you really think I look that helpless?"

"Well, probably not," Truman admitted.

Margaret shook her head. "Never mind. My fault. It's a bad habit of mine. Trying to throw a lifeline to a man who's only testing the water. Go on back in there. Mildred's probably sent out a search party for you by now."

"I'm full," Truman said. "In fact, I was trying to leave gracefully when Mildred ambushed me. So I do thank you for the rescue."

"Full?" Margaret said, hooting. "Leaving? Oh, please. You were loading up that bag of yours with food to take home. That's the only reason you come to these meetings, isn't it? Not that I blame you. I was only wondering. How did you plan to brown-bag the ice cream?"

Truman blushed furiously.

"I'm an avid reader," he said. "Read all the time. Just not Jane Austen. And if you must know, I was actually holding back on the chow tonight, saving room for that ice cream of yours."

She reached for the book bag, which he'd been trying to hide behind his back. He let her take it, feeling both foolish and a bit relieved.

"Guess you caught me," he said. "Red-handed. I didn't know I was being so obvious. That's sort of embarrassing for somebody like me. I'm a journalist, you know. We pride ourselves on not being obvious."

Margaret smiled widely and he could see the pale pink skin in the folds of the tanned laugh lines.

"I'm a busybody. We pride ourselves on noticing everything."

She handed the bag back to Truman.

"I've got another whole quart of peach ice cream in the freezer at home," Margaret offered. "And my car is parked just outside."

It sounded good, but Truman didn't like the feeling that he was being buttonholed. Or that she would have the impression that he had nothing but time on his hands. Or that he was just out to mooch free meals.

"The Braves are playing a doubleheader on the coast," he said. "Thought I'd go get a beer, see how L.A.'s new manager is doing."

She nodded that she understood. "Another time, then."

A tray of plastic bowls and spoons was sitting on the stainless-steel kitchen countertop. She picked it up. "Good night, then."

He held the door open for her. It seemed the thing to do.

"Margaret?"

She caught the door with her hand. Her nails were as short as his, scrubbed bone white.

"Yes?"

"How's your air-conditioning?"

"Excellent," she said. "I have a ten-year service contract. And I never allow gentlemen callers to see my pipes."

It was her broad wink that caught Truman off guard.

Ollie wasn't supposed to work Saturdays at the newsstand. There were no office workers or post office customers or passengers waiting around to catch a bus at Williams Park across the street on Saturday evenings. Especially not in August, when anybody with any sense or money had escaped up north for the summer.

Bored, he'd wandered over to Chet's some time after seven. He read some professional wrestling magazines, straightened the dusty rack of postcards, ate a package of Cheez Nips washed down with an orange soda, and busied himself uncreasing the dog-ears of the foldouts in *Playboy* and *Hustler*. It had gotten dark outside, past nine o'clock, when he shut off the lights and locked up.

He was crossing Central Avenue toward the hotel, minding his own business, not even jaywalking for once, when a flashy red sports car roared up to him and slammed on its brakes, sending Ollie flying sideways to avoid ending up as a hood ornament.

BEEEEP. The driver, a woman wearing a flowing white scarf, laughed hysterically.

"I'm hit," he screamed, dropping to the pavement. "Christ, lady, you killed me."

BEEEEP.

"Scared you, didn't I?" Jackie said, standing up with her head sticking out of the open T-top of the red Corvette.

Her laugh, not like any laugh he'd ever heard from Jackie, scared him almost as much as nearly being splattered all over the blacktop.

Ollie got to his feet. "Jackie? You tried to kill me? On purpose?"

"Check it OUT!" she yelled. "What do you think of my new wheels, Ollie?"

"My knees are bleeding," he pointed out. "And look. I got tar on my good new shorts."

The crotch of the baggy orange shorts hung to his knees, which were indeed slightly scratched up. And his high-topped white cotton crew socks were streaked with tar and dirt, his thick-lensed glasses askew.

"I'm sorry," Jackie said. "I guess I got carried away. What do you think? Isn't it cool?"

Ollie straightened his glasses and stepped up to the Corvette, running his finger down the glistening red hood, whistling in admiration.

"You can make it up to me," he told her. "Let me drive."

CHAPTER

FOUR

AT BREAKFAST SUNDAY THE YOUTH HOSTEL KIDS pushed their tables together and were noisier, sloppier, and ruder than usual.

Or so it seemed to Jackie. Her feet hurt. She and Ollie had walked all the way back to the hotel after the Corvette broke down while they were joyriding out on the beach. Neither of them knew anything much about the way cars worked, they'd had only a dollar in cash between them, and Jackie had been too proud to call anybody to tell them her brand-new used car wouldn't crank. If she'd been alone she might have tried hitchhiking, but Ollie was sure that the only people who picked up hitchhikers were homicidal maniacs.

So they'd walked. And walked. And arrived back at the hotel around two A.M. And she'd had to get up at six to work the first breakfast seating at seven.

She slammed plates caked with maple syrup and egg smears into a bus tray and snarled at anybody who asked for seconds of anything.

Ollie never came to Sunday breakfast, which cost a dollar more than weekday breakfast because you got bacon and ham, plus hash browns and a lot of other stuff. He usually slept late, had peanut butter crackers and orange soda in his room, and showed up starved at dinnertime.

Truman didn't materialize until the second sitting. Nearly eight o'clock.

He'd gotten in late, too, around one, but unlike Jackie, he was beaming now with energy and conviviality.

"Hello, Sonya," he said, passing Mrs. Hoffmayer. She was so shocked by this sudden show of friendliness that she coughed and sputtered bits of french toast all over her chin.

"Hello, KoKo," Truman said to the small dog whose head poked up from Mrs. Hoffmayer's lap. The dog pricked up its ears and bared its teeth, remembering the last time Truman had shown him any attention. The incident had involved white paint and necessitated an expensive and unattractive new grooming style for KoKo.

"Don't touch him," Mrs. Hoffmayer screeched.

Truman smiled and made his way to the corner table.

He had to signal Jackie twice to get her attention. Finally she trudged over with a tray of steaming food, and slid the bowls of food noisily onto his table.

"You're late," she said.

Truman eyed the offerings with frank disappointment. Only one biscuit in the bread basket, two shriveled strips of bacon, and an anemic-looking slice of ham. He touched his finger to the grits. They were cold. The eggs, too. And Jackie was obviously in a foul mood.

"Coffee?" he asked.

"It's brewing," she snapped. "And don't say nothing about the food, 'cause those damn hostel kids came through the first seating like a horde of locusts. You're lucky to get this."

Truman took a biscuit and slathered it with butter. She hadn't brought any of his strawberry jam, but he was in too good a mood to let her sour his morning.

"You seen Ollie?" Jackie asked.

"No," Truman said. "Why?"

She shrugged. "I thought maybe he told you about what happened last night. About my new car. How it broke down." She glared at him reproachfully. "We tried to call you for a ride. Spent all the money we had. Then we had to walk home. All the way from the beach. Where were you so late?"

"I went out with a friend after Great Books," Truman said. "We watched the ball game. It was a late one. The Braves were playing on the West Coast."

That much was true. After they'd left Mirror Lake, Truman had suggested they might watch the game at the El Cap. He was still apprehensive about wandering into widows' lairs.

It turned out that Margaret McCutcheon had never been to his favorite watering hole, the tiny sports bar on Fourth Street that was the nearest thing to a hangout Truman had.

He had introduced Margaret to Frankie, who was running the place now that Steve and Rose were retired. They ordered a pitcher of Budweiser, and Margaret insisted on paying for half.

This was a woman he could like, a woman who drank real beer and didn't mind paying her share. She knew about baseball, too, although she was an American League fan due to growing up in Boston. She could cook, too.

After the game, she'd invited him over to her place, and he'd gone.

Margaret lived in a very nice condominium in the old Detweiler Hotel, which had been renovated and was now quite upscale. As promised, her air-conditioning was cool and efficient. They'd talked and laughed and gotten to know each other.

He'd learned that she'd been divorced only six months before her wealthy husband had died, while they were both in their fifties. So, Margaret told him firmly, she was not technically a widow at all. There were no children or grandchildren. She'd been a college physics professor before retirement, liked to sail and travel, had her own money and a late-model Nissan.

They'd talked until quite late, enjoyed large dishes of her delicious ice cream and healthy slabs of her home-baked pound cake. In fact, a good chunk of that pound cake was upstairs, wrapped in foil on his dresser. He would have it for his late-afternoon treat.

"A friend?" Jackie said. "Like, a date?"

"It wasn't a date, damnit," Truman said. The eggs were cold and greasy, and his biscuit was burned on the bottom. "But what if it was? Anything wrong with that?"

"None of my business," Jackie said. She went over to the coffee station and got the pot of coffee that had finished brewing. As a peace offering, she went in the kitchen and grabbed some biscuits that had just come out of the oven, and tucked Truman's strawberry jam in the basket, covering it with a napkin.

When she got back to the table, Truman had his head buried in the sports section. She poured his coffee, but didn't leave.

"Brought you some more biscuits. And some jelly. Aren't you going to say 'I told you so'?"

He took a sip of coffee. "I told you so. Where's the car now?"

"Ollie helped me push it into a gas station," Jackie said. And then her words came out in a torrent. "I couldn't help it. That car and me were meant to be. A red Corvette, Mr. K. And I got a great price on it. You should have seen me driving around, guys looking at me, women giving me the evil eye 'cause I looked so hot. Until it started making a funny noise and it stopped dead where it was."

"A Corvette?" Truman dropped his newspaper on the floor. "I thought you told me you were going to look at a Gremlin. A six-hundred-dollar AMC Gremlin. What happened?"

She told him everything. About how hot and smelly the bus had been, and how the salesman, Jeff Cantrell, made her such a good offer, and how they'd financed it right there, and how they didn't even do a credit check because they were in the business of helping people buy cars.

"Ollie said maybe it was something simple that went wrong, like a spark plug or something," she said.

"He wouldn't know a spark plug from a bathtub plug," Truman said ungraciously. "Have you got a contract, or anything like that?"

"In my purse. In the kitchen," Jackie said.

"Better let me take a look," he said.

He perched his reading glasses on the end of his nose. The print on the contract was tiny and faint, a carbon of a carbon. He'd been thinking about going to the VisionMart to get some new prescription glasses. He had a coupon—$14.99, including the eye exam.

As he read, Truman frowned. And sighed. Jackie kept busy with the hostel students, who were shoveling down pancakes and hash browns as fast as she could bring them out, but every few minutes she came by and stood next to his shoulder, anxiously watching his expression.

"Well?" she said when she could stand it no longer.

"These people ought to be run out of town," Truman said, flinging the contract aside like a soiled napkin. "Goddamn con artists."

"What?" Jackie said. "What's wrong? You haven't even see the car yet. Wait till you see my 'Vette, Mr. K. It's cherry. Jeff said so. You can even ask Ollie. I was gonna see if you'd give me a ride out there after breakfast, to pick it up. Maybe the battery just needs charging. That happens sometimes, right?"

"Sometimes," Truman said. "If the car even has a battery."

"Jeff's a good guy," Jackie protested. "A lot of people, they see a black chick getting off a bus, they wouldn't give them the time of day. But Jeff was real polite and nice. And Mr. Bondurant doesn't let just anybody drive that Corvette. Don't be so negative, Mr. K. Just because they run a used-car lot doesn't mean they're dishonest. That's a stereotype, you know.

"Here comes Ollie now," Jackie said, looking toward the door from the lobby. Ask him, he'll tell you it's a good car."

The college kids were sniggering to each other as the dwarf with the thinning, uncombed hair trudged through the dining room toward them. He still wore the baggy, tar-stained orange shorts from the night before, but today's shirt was an acid-green tank top that exposed his pale, hairless chest.

Ollie collapsed into the empty chair at Truman's table. "You're buying me breakfast," he told Jackie. "After last night, you owe me at least that much."

"I'll buy you breakfast," Truman said. "I've seen the contract for that car of hers. She's been cleaned out, my friend."

Ollie rubbed his eyes. "Maybe it's just a spark plug."

Jackie turned his coffee cup over and filled it up. "Mr. K thinks I've been ripped off. But he doesn't know Jeff like I do. He let me write a check for the down payment, because the bank was already closed and I couldn't get cash. And after we'd done all the paperwork, he was real excited for me. He says he loves to put beautiful women in beautiful cars. He was going to take me to dinner, but he couldn't leave because Mr. Bondurant and his assistant manager are out of town and Jeff is acting sales manager. Does that sound like a crook to you?"

"It's a great car when it's running," Ollie said, helping himself to a biscuit. "She let me drive it."

"You don't have a driver's license," Truman said. "You're both crazy."

"Cherry," Jackie repeated. "That's what Jeff called it."

"Does cherry translate to rip-off?" Truman asked. He could tell Jackie didn't like hearing the truth, but it couldn't be helped.

He didn't know anything in particular about this

Bondurant Motors outfit, but buy-here, pay-here lots were as big a scourge in Florida as cockroaches and hurricanes.

The way it worked was like this: The used-car lot would sell you a car, a piece of crap, probably, and at a price that was two or three times what it was worth. They didn't run credit checks because they didn't need to. They milked you for as much down payment as they could, then they set up an "easy payment plan" biweekly or even weekly, sometimes, at indecent interest rates.

And if you missed even one payment, legally they could come after your car, keep any payments you'd made, and even charge you wildly inflated towing and storage fees. The next day, the same lot could sell the same car all over again.

It was a beautiful system, if you owned the car lot.

Like most of the other scams that flourished like mildew in Florida's tropical splendor, the easy-pay lots catered to people without any other options. Poor people. Immigrants. People with no credit, bad credit, minimum-pay wage earners.

Every year the Florida legislature promised to change the laws that allowed the easy-pay lots to exist. Every year, the car dealers' lobbyists reminded law-makers that poor people don't make campaign contributions.

"That paper you signed obligates you to pay $77.10 a week for three years," Truman said. "That's 156 payments. You're paying twenty percent interest, Jackie, and $12,027.60."

"Is that legal?" Ollie asked. "That ain't legal, is it?"

"Florida doesn't have any usury laws," Truman said. "It's a wonderful state, my friend."

Jackie was sitting down now, too, looking even glummer than when she'd started the morning.

"For that you could get a new car," Truman said. "A good one."

"Not a 'Vette," Jackie protested. "See, that's how much you know about cars, Truman. You're out of touch, no offense. And that car is the prettiest thing I've ever owned. I don't care what it costs. It's worth every cent."

"If you miss a payment, it's history," Truman said. "So's your investment, your equity in the car."

"I'm not gonna miss a payment," Jackie said heatedly. "I'm a hard worker, Mr. K. I've wanted a car like that my whole life. Nobody's going to take it away. It's mine. And as soon as I get it fixed, you'll see how fine it is."

Truman knew he had pushed her too far. It was time to back off a little and try some tact. He didn't want to see her cheated. Nellie always did say you caught more flies with honey than vinegar.

"You are a hard worker," he soothed. "You're smart and decent and good-hearted. If anybody deserves something good, it's you, Jackie. Would you mind if an old friend made a suggestion?"

"What kind of suggestion?" she asked. She knew Mr. K was trying to look out for her, but she was an adult, wasn't she? And she knew what she was getting into, didn't she?

"You've got a cousin who's a mechanic, right?"

"My cousin's husband," Jackie said reluctantly. "Milton."

"Let this Milton take a look at the car. See what the problem is, and if there's anything else wrong. He can tell you if you got a good deal or not. If the car's as good as you say, I'll shut up."

"What if Milton says it's a good car? Then will you believe me?"

"Absolutely," Truman said. "That's all I'm saying."

CHAPTER

FIVE

MILTON TUTEN WAS A MAN OF VERY FEW WORDS. He towed the Corvette into one of the bays at the garage where he worked, and while Jackie watched, he opened the hood and peered over it, like a scholar studying some ancient writings. He put it up on the hydraulic lift and walked around underneath it, peering up at its underbelly with a flashlight and muttering under his breath.

When he was done, he wiped his hands on a rag and put the greasy rag in his back pocket, giving Jackie a look of utter disbelief. "You telling me somebody got you to pay nine thousand dollars for this thing?"

Jackie nodded glumly. She didn't dare tell him what Truman had said about the car's true cost. Milton would tell his wife, Sonya, and she would tell her mother, Jackie's aunt Louise, and it'd get back to her mother, and Jackie would never hear the end of it. Not until the day she died.

"Something wrong with my car?" She was already

regretting asking Milton for his advice. She felt defensive and protective toward the 'Vette, like it was her own child or something, and folks were telling her it had buckteeth and knock-knees and no telling what else.

He walked around and opened the driver's-side door, peering in at the dashboard. "Odometer's been messed with. Sixty thousand miles. Hah! More like two hundred sixty thousand."

She felt a little twist in her belly. "Low mileage in a car like this, that's rare," she could hear Jeff telling her about the doctor's wife.

"It's still a good car though, right?" she said pleadingly. "Maybe you could work on it. I could pay you a little bit now, and some more when something goes wrong."

"What's wrong with this car you and me can't fix," Milton said grimly. "This here car's been wrecked. Totaled out. Maybe more than once, all the welding seams under there. Frame's all bent to hell."

He put his big, greasy hand on the hood of the nice, shiny car and Jackie shuddered involuntarily.

"This T-top rattles like my grandma's dentures. You didn't notice that when you drove it?"

She'd asked Jeff about that noise.

"That's just the way it goes with these 'Vettes," Jeff had said reassuringly. "What you call an idiosyncrasy. Just do what I do."

"What's that?"

He flipped the radio volume knob up three turns.

"See," he'd shouted. "Now you don't notice the rattle at all."

Milton reached in the car again and with his stubby outstretched index finger, he jiggled the steering wheel like a loose tooth. "How about this steering wheel? It's fixing to come off of this steering column."

"Tilt steering?" She was quoting Jeff Cantrell again.

"Nah, man," Milton said, slamming the door shut, walking away, leaving her standing there with her baby diagnosed as a terminal case. "That car salesman seen you coming, Jackie. He picked you clean."

Funny. She hadn't noticed the water stains on the roof liner before. Or the cracked vinyl on the dashboard, or the way the passenger-side window wouldn't close all the way because the rubber gaskets had rotted out.

Now, not even the complimentary wild-cherry car deodorizer, the one that said "Bondurant Motors," could hide the smell of rot. She turned the key in the ignition and stalled the car. Three times. She took a deep breath and started the car, listened to the belching motor, and turned the stinky red car in the direction of Bondurant Motors and Jeff Cantrell. She'd see about this piece of crap. Yes, sir.

Jeff Cantrell had a couple of live ones. A young Mexican couple. They were gesturing and yammering in nonstop Spanish over the powder-blue 1979 Cadillac Eldorado he'd pulled into the slot vacated by the red Corvette.

Ronnie had taught him all the Spanish he needed to clinch a sale.

"*Trabajo*," Jeff said loudly. "*Ustedes trabajo?*"

"*Sì*," said the wife. She had a long braid hanging

down her back and was doing most of the talking and gesturing. She jabbed the señor in the side.

He reached in the pocket of his faded jeans and offered Jeff a creased and wrinkled pay slip. The pay slip said his name was Joaquim Morales. It was issued by the Hernando County Public Works Department. They'd driven all the way down here to St. Pete just to look at cars.

Perfect. Ronnie loved to sell cars to greaseballs. "If they can't *habla*, they can't bitch about nothing," he said. Even more than greaseballs, he loved to sell cars to guys with government jobs.

It was impossible to fire anybody who worked for the city or the county or the state, according to Ronnie Bondurant. And if the greaseball got slow on payments, all Ronnie had to do was make a call to a supervisor, threaten to show up to collect his money, and the greaseball would be there on Friday with the *dinero* in hand. Cash money.

"*Cuanto?*" Mrs. Joaquim was saying. Her husband was already sitting behind the steering wheel of the El-Dog. That's what they called Eldorados here on the lot—El-Dogs. Ronnie bragged that he'd sold every pre–1980 El-Dog in Pinellas County, hell, make it Central Florida, at least once.

"*Ven aca,*" Jeff said, pointing across the lot toward the little concrete-block sales lot. It was as hot as blue blazes out here. Now he'd get them in the air-conditioning and get the money. He felt great. Sunday afternoon and here he already had four burning gas. Wait till Ronnie got back in town.

They were under the red-and-yellow-striped aluminum awning that stretched over the driveway in front of the office when Jeff heard the familiar sound of a Corvette in need of shocks, struts, a lube job, and probably a whole new engine mount. The red 'Vette came hurtling toward him, not slowing down, coming right at him and Mr. and Mrs. Morales, must have been thirty miles an hour. Suddenly, before they were sidewalk sandwiches, the driver slammed on the brakes. Rubber squealed. Mrs. Morales screamed.

"Jesus H. Christ," Jeff hollered. The brakes on that 'Vette were shot. He could have been killed.

"*Madre de Dios!*" Mrs. Moralies was making the sign of the cross over her ample bosom.

The cute black waitress, Jackleen something, shot out of the 'Vette before the engine had quit knocking.

"Hey, you," she said, running up to him, getting right up in his face. "This car's been wrecked. The frame is bent. It's a piece of shit. I want my money back."

With each sentence she spoke, she jabbed a long fingernail into his chest.

"Hey, now," Jeff said, flashing his dimples. "Good to see you, Jackleen. Just let me slip into the office, finish up with Mr. and Mrs. Morales here and I'll be right with you."

"No way, you son of a bitch," Jackie said. "I'm going into the office with you right this minute and you're going to give me back the money I gave you yesterday and take back this crapmobile you sold me."

He took a step away from the jabbing fingernail and the shrill demands. He'd have to get this chick calmed down and shut up in a hurry.

Too late. Out of the corner of his eye he saw the Moraleses shuffling in the direction of the battered Toyota they'd driven up in.

Jeff could feel the sale slipping away and he did

something he rarely did, because he was an even-tempered, happy-go-lucky kind of guy. He got mad. Really pissed off.

Jackie saw what was going on. "That's right," she called after the Mexicans. "Run for your life. This son of a bitch is as crooked as a dog's hind leg."

"You have fucked me over bad, lady," Jeff said through clenched teeth. "Who do you think you are, coming on my lot, chasing off my customers? You got a problem, you come in here and we handle it. You don't come in here and fuck up my sales."

"Problem?" she shouted, hands on her hips. "Yeah, I got a problem. Like that 'Vette's been totaled. My mechanic looked it over. He says the frame's cracked and the odometer's been turned back and the steering wheel could fall off the first time I take a hard left."

Jeff shrugged. His dimples were gone now and he'd set his face in stone, the way he'd seen Ronnie and Wormy do when they were getting hassled by a customer.

"'All sales final,'" Jeff said. "'All merchandise sold as is.'" He pointed to the words painted on the glass door of the sales office. "It says so right there. Says so on your contract, too. Your payment is due next Saturday. Feel free to drop it in the mail. Long as it's here by Saturday."

He straightened his shoulders and pulled his shirt away from his back. He turned his back on her.

"I'm not giving you another cent," Jackie said, running after him. "I'm getting a lawyer. I'll sue you people."

Jeff stopped dead and wheeled around to face her. She was going to be a pain in the ass now, he realized.

And it was a shame. Here he'd been looking forward to seeing Jackleen again, seeing her every Saturday, marking off the payments, maybe having some drinks and some harmless recreational sex. He'd never screwed a black chick before.

"You're not getting nothing back," he said with eerie calm. "And believe me, Jackleen, you don't want to fuck with Bondurant Motors. And you definitely do not want to fuck with Ronald Xavier Bondurant."

CHAPTER

SIX

TRUMAN DECIDED TO SKIP HIS SUNDAY-AFTERNOON walk. The heat in his room made him drowsy, but trying to nap on his narrow iron bed, drenched in perspiration, made him feel like he was being mummified. The only really cool place in the hotel was probably the big walk-in refrigerator in the kitchen. He decided to settle for the lobby.

Jackie was just coming in as he settled into the wicker armchair nearest the door. Her tear-streaked face and slumped shoulders confirmed his suspicions about her "new" car.

"Bad news, huh, kid?" he asked.

She leaned against the door frame and fanned herself. "Grandmama said if it looks too good to be true, it probably is," she said.

"Funny. My grandma said that, too," Truman said. "You want something cold to drink before you tell me about it? I'm buying."

Jackie gave him the key to the kitchen, strictly against the restaurant manager's rules. Truman found a plastic gallon jug of iced tea in the refrigerator, got some glasses, and filled a bus tray with ice from the ice machine. When he got back to the lobby, Ollie was there, too, trying to cheer her up.

"Come on," he was saying. "Let's play gin rummy. I'll let you win this time."

When Ollie saw Truman with the iced tea, he began to feel guilty.

"I've got a six-pack of Rolling Rock in my room," he began, "I guess I could spare a couple, but . . ."

"Go get it," Truman said. "This is no time for tea."

Jackie went into the dining room and got a heavy chair to keep the front door propped open wider, and Truman remembered having seen somebody lug an old circulating fan into the coatroom near the reception desk. He angled it in front of the door, and pushed the three wicker armchairs into a circle around the fan.

It was about as quiet as a Boeing 707 and as effective as a screen door in a submarine. Truman opened his beer and took a long drink, holding the cold green bottle against his forehead. "How the hell did anybody ever live in this damned swamp before air-conditioning?" he said.

"Thought you said everything in the old days was better," Jackie answered. She'd taken off her shoes and her bare feet were propped up on the big, peeling, rattan coffee table.

"Everything, except we didn't have air-conditioning," Truman said.

"My 'Vette has air-conditioning," Jackie told them sadly. "It's the only thing that works on that vehicle."

She looked over at Truman. "You were right. The transmission is all messed up. That's why it quit running last night. Milton had to put a whole quart of transmission fluid in it just so I could drive it back here. That car's been wrecked, too. Milton said it's no good. You were right about that Jeff being a crook, too. He won't take the car back, and he won't give me my money back."

"I wish I had been wrong," Truman said. "Did that Jeff fella give you any satisfaction at all? Sometimes if you squawk loud enough, these people will offer to buy the car back. They'll charge you a little more than you paid, but at least they'll take it off your hands."

"He told me to get lost," Jackie said bitterly. "He told me I better not mess with Bondurant Motors."

"TK, why don't you go down there and get the goods on these crooks?" Ollie asked. He'd wrapped his own beer bottle in a brown paper sack. Liquor was strictly forbidden in the lobby or other public areas of the hotel, and unlike Truman and Jackie, he usually went strictly by the rules. If Sonya Hoffmayer caught him with a beer she'd go screaming to the management, and they might kick him out.

"What goods?" Truman asked.

"You know," Ollie said. "Write an exposé on this used-car racket."

Ever since the year before, when Truman had uncovered a Texas televangelist's plans to turn the Fountain of Youth into high-priced Christian condos, Ollie had been urging Truman to write exposés of everything from the high markup on magazines to the true nature of professional wrestling.

"I'm retired," Truman reminded Ollie.

"Yeah, but that guy at the newspaper loved that story you did about the kids shooting the pigeons in Williams Park. And how about that story about that mailman who was spending all afternoon drinking beer down at the pool hall instead of delivering the mail?"

Truman had done some minor freelancing for the *St. Pete Times* and had handled a couple of local stories for one of his old buddies in the AP bureau over in Tampa. The one he'd run before his retirement. It was penny-ante stuff.

"Hey!" Jackie said, sitting up. "Maybe you could go over there to Bondurant Motors and tell them you're a reporter. Like that Answer Man on TV. Like a consumer advocate or something. Maybe they'd do right if you got after them."

Truman took a swig of his own beer. "I'll go down there with you tomorrow, Jackie. Not as a reporter. As a friend. These places take advantage of a woman by herself. Maybe if an old geezer like me starts raising hell, they'll see things differently."

"Maybe," Jackie said.

The big gray Lincoln sailed into the parking lot at Bondurant Motors at precisely six P.M.

Wormy Weems, assistant sales manager, was behind the wheel. Wormy was tall and skinny, with deeply tanned skin and a perpetual squint from being out in the sun on the car lot all day. Ronnie didn't like him to wear sunglasses on the lot because he said people liked to see a salesman's eyes. See if they could trust him.

Ronald Xavier Bondurant, president of Bondurant

Motors, was dozing in the soft leather front seat of the car. It had been an eight-hour drive from Atlanta. Four days of nonstop partying packed into forty-eight hours. That Ronnie, Wormy reflected. What a party guy. He'd never met anybody who could stay on the go like Ronnie Bondurant. They were good partners, Wormy and Ronnie. Wormy was good at details. Ronnie was an idea man. Ronnie was the straight man, Wormy fed him the goofy lines. They were the Martin and Lewis of the Tampa Bay used-car industry, a two-man Rat Pack.

When the Lincoln glided to a stop, Ronnie must have sensed they were home. He woke up, yawned, stretched, peered out the window at the lot, taking inventory, checking the action.

The cars gleamed in the late afternoon sun, and overhead, the 1957 pink Chevy mounted on a motorized rod on the roof of the lot spinned and dipped; an eye-catching symbol, Ronnie thought with satisfaction. The grass strip near the curb had been mowed and the sprinklers were spitting water on the pretty swath of green. No cigarette butts or beer cans in his flowerbeds, either. Ronnie liked a clean lot. And something else. Cantrell had moved the cars around. The big powder-blue Eldorado was in the hot spot near the street.

"Jeffy boy has been busy," Ronnie said, nodding his head in approval. "The kid might work out."

"Might," Wormy said, noncommittal.

Ronnie got out of the Lincoln and left the unpacking to Wormy.

Jeff Cantrell met him at the door to the office.

"Ronnie!" he said, flashing the trademark dimples. "How was 'Hotlanta'?"

"Not bad," Ronnie said. "How many?"

"Three on the street," Jeff said proudly. "And I got a Mexican couple hot to trot for the El-Dog. They'll be back Friday, Ronnie, you wait and see."

"You couldn't close on the El-Dog?" Ronnie's right eyelid twitched. Once. Twice. "A couple of spics got money in hand for a clean Caddy and you couldn't close the deal?"

"It wasn't my fault," Jeff started to explain.

Wormy pushed open the glass office door with his bony hip because both arms were full of suitcases. "Hey, Ronnie," he announced, dropping the bags to the floor. "The red 'Vette is gone."

"That's right," Jeff said, grinning. "I moved it yesterday morning. Nine thousand. Not bad, huh?"

Ronnie's eyelid was twitching violently. "How do you mean, moved it? What's that supposed to mean?"

"I bet the stupid jerk sold it," Wormy said, sneering. "You sold it, didn't you?"

"Hell, yeah," Jeff said. "For nine thousand. The blue book on it is seven. Not bad, huh?"

Ronnie sighed. His eyelid went still, dropping shut. It did that sometimes, when he was tired or tense. He slapped Jeff hard across the chops, open-handed.

The kid reeled backward, grasping at his face. Shocked.

No more dimples, Wormy noticed with satisfaction.

"Where's the 'Vette?" Wormy said, grabbing Jeff's arm.

"Enough," Ronnie said.

He tilted his head a little and gave Jeff a sad, knowing smile. "You didn't know about the monkeys, did you, Jeff?"

Jeff Cantrell shook his head dumbly, wondering whether Ronnie Bondurant was drunk or stoned or just plain crazy.

"It's a side business." Ronnie Bondurant set Jeff down in the chair in his private office and sent Wormy back out to the Lincoln to bring in the cooler.

"I was just thinking, on the way back here today. We should let Jeff in on this deal, 'cause he's all right. You like to make money, don't you, Jeff?"

"Yeah," Jeff said. "Sure."

"You did a good thing, hustling cars over the weekend, to prove to me that you can handle business. That was a good thing," Ronnie said. "But now, selling the red 'Vette, especially without consulting me—that was a bad thing."

Wormy came into the office and put the cooler down on the floor by Ronnie's chair. Ronnie reached in, took out two peach-flavored wine coolers and handed them to Wormy, who unscrewed the caps and wiped the ice water off the sides of the bottles. He handed one to Ronnie and kept one for himself.

"We gotta get that 'Vette back," Wormy said. "I'm supposed to take it to the adjuster tomorrow afternoon, Ronnie. And Joe says he's real backed up already."

"Jeff's gonna go get the 'Vette back tonight," Ronnie said. "As soon as I tell him how this thing plays out."

Wormy scowled and sipped at his wine cooler.

"It works like this," Ronnie said. "I buy a Corvette, out of an ad in the paper or one of those *Auto Trader* magazines they sell at the 7–11. Always a Corvette. You know why?"

Jeff sensed this was a test. "'Cause you like Corvettes?"

"No, asshole," Wormy broke in. "Corvettes got an all-fiberglass body. No metal at all."

"Anyway," Ronnie continued, "I got some guys, they do side jobs for me. Wormy here, he came up with calling them monkeys. Monkeys, get it? 'Cause they do what they're told and they don't ask any questions."

"Sure," Jeff said. He didn't have the slightest idea what Ronnie was talking about. He was beginning to wish he'd never quit that bartending job.

"I fix the monkeys up with junker cars, some old piece of shit Ford or Chevy. And I buy an insurance policy on the junker. Collision only. You getting my drift?" Ronnie asked.

"Collision," Jeff said dully.

"Right. Then we have ourselves an accident."

"Between the monkeys and me driving the 'Vette," Wormy said, unable to stay quiet. "Only we don't even have to really have accidents no more. Not since Ronnie found Joe."

"That Joe. Guy's an artist with an air knife," Ronnie said. "Give Joe an hour, he can carve up a Corvette like a Thanksgiving turkey. Door panels, grill, hood, whatever you want. Once he's carved up the 'Vette, he gives me an estimate, tells me how much it's gonna take to fix what he just did. Then the monkey calls his insurance agent. Tells him the bad news. He's been in an accident, and he's bashed up some guy's Corvette."

"Soon as the claim's filed, I take a spin over to the claims adjuster," Wormy said. "We just love those drive-up claims windows, man. They're the best thing since the quarter-pounder. Guy comes out, looks at the car, looks at Joe's estimate, maybe takes a picture or two, goes back inside and types out a check for ten thousand."

"Corvette repairs can be very expensive," Ronnie said.

"But not too expensive. Not more than ten thousand," Wormy cautioned. "Or they can't handle it at the drive-up."

"After we got the check," Ronnie said, "the monkey gets paid, Joe solders the car back together, we take our cut, and we're all set to do business again. Nice, huh?"

"You can do this more than once?" Jeff asked in amazement. "Doesn't it ruin the car?"

"Who cares?" Wormy said. "Eight or ten wrecks, we made a nice profit. Works great, unless some asshole sells the 'Vette before we get done using it."

"I'm sorry," Jeff said.

"Don't sweat it," Ronnie told him. "I know a way you can make it up to me. And when we got the 'Vette back, we can talk about you helping out on some deals. How'd you like that?"

"Great," Jeff said. He wished he was dead.

At two in the morning, the streets around the Fountain of Youth were absolutely quiet. The city buses that ringed Williams Park had quit running for the night. The pigeons were roosted up in the eaves of the buildings surrounding the park. The street people, the Dumpster divers, dopers, and winos, had all dropped off to sleep, in the alleys and the park benches and the twelve-dollar-a-night hotel rooms.

Wormy Weems and Jeff Cantrell circled the block three times to make sure everything was set. Finally, Wormy pulled a black Ford Explorer borrowed from the lot up beside the red Corvette. It was parked at the curb on Fourth Street, right in front of the entrance to the Ponce de Leon Restaurant.

"That's the place she works at," Jeff said, hoping he could stall things. Maybe a cop would cruise by. Anything at all.

"Good," Wormy said. "She won't miss the car at all. Do it. Now."

"I'm going," Jeff said. He got the spare key to the Corvette out of the pocket of his shorts. Bondurant Motors kept keys to all the cars they sold, just in case of the need for a quick repossession. He stepped out of the Explorer and before he had even unlocked the 'Vette, Wormy had pulled off and sped down Fourth Street, leaving Jeff alone.

Alone to commit grand theft auto, Jeff thought, wondering what kind of sentence first-time offenders could get for that kind of thing.

CHAPTER

SEVEN

THE RED CORVETTE HAD VANISHED.

"I parked it right here," Jackie said, pointing to the curb where an ugly, bronze-colored Pontiac was now parked. "It was right here . . ." The mailman, his spindly white legs visible beneath his summer-uniform shorts, was half a block away, wheeling his three-legged canvas cart down the sidewalk, and even he could hear the keening note in Jackie's voice.

"Maybe you parked it around the other side, over on Fourth Street," Truman said nervously. "Let's look there."

"I know where I parked my own car," Jackie said. "I would never park over there. Those pigeons from the park poop on everything over there. I parked my car right here, right in this spot. I swear it!"

Truman strolled down to the end of the park, surveying the cars parked across the street. Jackie was right. A red Corvette would have stuck out in this neighborhood like a crow in a parakeet cage.

"It's not there," he said when he arrived back at her side. "Guess it's time to call the cops."

The police cruiser pulled up in front of the Fountain of Youth, its lights flashing and siren wailing. The driver stepped smartly out of the cruiser, his hand on his black leather holster, his dark eyes darting back and forth, alert to unforeseen dangers or rampaging auto thieves.

"Rookie," Truman muttered.

The cop was maybe twenty-four. His skin was the darkest black Truman had ever seen, his head shaved nearly bald. His face was already sheened with perspiration in the 90-degree heat and 100 percent humidity.

"Are you the complainant?" he asked Truman, who took a step back.

"No," Jackie said, stepping forward. "It's me. My car was stolen."

The cop's metal nameplate identified him as T. Carter. His face brightened at seeing Jackie. "Fourth car theft of the morning," he said importantly.

He fetched a clipboard from the cruiser and started taking down the complainant's complaint.

His eyebrows shot up toward his scalp when Jackie told him the car was a Corvette.

"Corvette?" He pressed his lips together in disapproval. "Parked down here?"

"What's that supposed to mean?" Truman asked. "What's wrong with her parking where she lives? Don't you cops patrol our streets like the rest of town? We pay taxes, too, you know."

"I locked my car," Jackie added. "And I checked.

It was right here at eleven last night, before I went to bed."

Officer T. Carter nodded knowingly. "Sounds like Midnight Auto."

"What's Midnight Auto? One of those gangs?"

"Just some teenagers. Punks. Nothing so organized as gangs," Carter said. "They cruise the streets looking for a fun ride. Corvettes look real good."

He finished writing on the form and handed it over to Jackie to sign. "You want my advice? File the insurance and take that money and buy yourself something ugly." He thumped the hood of the Pontiac lightly. "Like this baby here." He jerked his hand away quickly, the hot metal nearly searing his hand. "Once you get a new car, don't park it on this street no more. We can't be everywhere at once."

Jackie scrawled her name at the bottom of the form. "That's it? That's all you're going to do?"

"We'll put your tag number and VIN on the computer. A car like yours, these kids might take it joyriding. Maybe they'll do something stupid and we'll get them on a traffic stop."

He took out one of his business cards and printed his home phone number on the back. "Cheer up. There's lots of cars out there. And call me if you want."

"Yeah," Jackie said, dispirited, not caring that he was trying to flirt. "Whoever took that car—they already did something stupid. They should have stolen a car that would run."

After the cop left, Jackie sank down to the curb, put her head down on her knees, and boo-hooed like a baby. Truman sat down beside her and patted her back.

"Oh, man," Jackie said, raising her head. "What do I do now?"

Truman asked the question even though he dreaded hearing the answer. "You didn't have insurance on the Corvette?"

"N-n-no," she said, sniffing. "Jeff gave me a card for an insurance guy he knew. But it was too late to call him Saturday night. And I knew I'd have to borrow the insurance money from my mama because I'd spent all of my money on the car. I was gonna call her yesterday, but after I found out the car was no good, I decided I'd just make Jeff take the car back."

She stood up and kicked the rear tire of the bronze Pontiac. "Why me?" she wailed. "Why can't something bad happen to somebody else once in a while, instead of me?" She pounded her fist on the trunk of the Pontiac, and a can came rolling slowly out from beneath it. She kicked the can, too, sending it spinning toward the sidewalk.

Truman had been sitting on the curb, feeling bad for Jackie. Now he noticed a puddle of fluid on the asphalt. It was dark blackish red. He got up and fetched the can Jackie had just kicked. It was silver and green. Transmission fluid.

He took another look at the puddle. Tire marks were crossed through it, leading out into the street, and there were more drops of the same fluid, trailing up the street toward the light.

"Did you say your cousin had to put transmission fluid in the Corvette just to get it going?" he asked Jackie.

"Yeah," she said. "He gave me another can to put in the back, just in case it all leaked out before I got back here. Made me watch how he put it in."

Truman held up the empty transmission can to show her. "Was it this kind of can?"

"I don't know," Jackie shrugged. "Maybe not. I think the can Milton gave me was red and black. Why?"

"You didn't put any fluid in it when you got back here, did you?" Truman asked.

"No," she said. "Why are you asking me all these questions? What's that can got to do with anything?"

"I think whoever stole your car knew it was leaking transmission fluid," Truman said. "So they brought some along when they came to steal the car. Doesn't sound like teenage gang members to me."

"Not Midnight Auto like that cop said?" Jackie asked, bewildered.

"More like Bondurant Auto," Truman said. "But why?"

Truman made her call that cop, that T. Carter. But the dispatcher said he'd gone off shift, and she'd have to wait until Tuesday morning to call him back. "Can't I talk to somebody else?" she asked. "It's about my car, a Corvette that was stolen. We've got a clue. We know who stole my car. Can't I talk to a detective, somebody like that?"

"You'll have to talk to Officer Carter," the dispatcher said. "I can leave him a message if you like."

"Never mind," Jackie said, slamming down the phone.

"They won't do nothing," she told Truman. "I gotta get my car back myself."

"Let the police handle this," Truman said. "We've got the can of transmission fluid. They can finger-print that, check to see if Bondurant uses the same kind. It should be easy to prove. But you let them do their job. You hear me?"

After the lunch shift was over, Jackie counted her tip money out on a bus tray. It was mostly silver, quarters, nickles, dimes. There was a New York Transit System subway token and a Canadian dime.

"Goddamn college kids," Jackie said, flinging the token across the room. Altogether, her tips for the day came to $12.67.

Her savings were gone. Payday wasn't until Friday. And now her dream car was gone. She started to get steamed. And then her anger made things seem very simple. First, she'd go out there to Bondurant Motors and straighten a knot in their tails—like her grandmama would say. She wasn't coming home unless she had her money or her car. Second, she'd have to find a part-time job if she was gonna be able to save up for a decent car. No way she could buy something good with a handful of loose change.

On the bus, Jackie folded and unfolded the papers. Her copy of the sales agreement, her temporary title, and the police report. She was sure Truman was right. It wasn't kids who had taken her car. It was that Jeff Cantrell—slimy bastard.

The slimy bastard was looking good this Monday. His hair still had the comb marks after his shower and his tan dazzled against the white golf shirt and the tight khaki shorts. And nobody who earned an honest living had tennis shoes as white and spotless as Jeff Cantrell's.

He was stroking the hood of a maroon Cutlass, talking a mile a minute to an older woman who stood beside the open passenger door, a squirming toddler balanced on her hip. A younger woman—the baby's mother, maybe, sat in the car with the motor running.

Jackie marched right up to them. Jeff was so busy feeding the woman a line of bullshit he never heard her coming.

"Excuse me, ladies," Jackie said loudly. Jeff pivoted and when he saw who it was, his dimples vanished. "I need to talk to you, Jeff," Jackie said loudly. "Somebody stole my car last night. My no-good, hunk of junk car you sold me on Saturday."

The old lady set the toddler down. Her daughter cut the Cutlass's engine and got out of the car quickly. She took the toddler by the hand. "Uh, well, we'll think about it," she said, glancing uneasily at Jackie.

"Wait now," Jeff said, feeling his sale slipping away. "We haven't even talked about financing. Or the rebate. We got a special two-hundred-dollar rebate going today." The $200 was his margin on the crappy Mogan David–colored Cutlass. But he needed that sale.

"My husband might come and look at it," the older woman said. "Maybe tomorrow." Clearly, it was Mama and Daddy's money that would pay for this car. And if Daddy knew anything about transmissions, he'd walk away from the Cutlass.

Wormy Weems was buffing the paint on a silver Ford Explorer two cars over. He heard the young black chick, saw Jeff's hot prospect wriggle off the hook and swim away.

He tucked the chamois cloth in his back pocket and strolled over to the sales office. A minute later,

Ronnie Bondurant was on the scene. Good old affable, easygoing Ronnie.

"You people came out and stole my car back," Jackie said, shaking the police report in Jeff's face. She'd gotten a little unnerved when the other two guys showed up, especially the tall one with the forearms that looked like Popeye's, but now she was mad again.

"We found the can of transmission fluid you put in it, 'cause you knew you wouldn't get far without it. It's got your fingerprints all over it. You think because I'm black and I'm a woman you can do me any which way, but I'm telling you, you can't get away with this mess you're pulling. I already called the cops on you and . . ."

"Whoa," Ronnie said, laughing easily. "Hey, now, miss, calm down and let's talk about this. How about we go in my office, sit in the air-conditioning, have us a cold beverage. I'm sure you've had a misunderstanding here."

"I didn't misunderstand," Jackie said, narrowing her eyes. "I know a crook when I see one."

"My name is Ronnie Bondurant," Ronnie said, ignoring the remark. "I'm president of Bondurant Motors. Now if you've got a problem—"

"You bet your ass I got a problem," Jackie said. "This salesman of yours, Jeff. Sold me a lemon. A red Corvette. I took it to my mechanic and he says it's been totaled out. The frame is bent, the odometer has been messed with. That's against the law in Florida, mister." Emboldened, she stepped up to Ronnie Bondurant and thumped him on the chest. "And it leaks transmission fluid."

She pointed to the front of the lot, at the spot

where the red Corvette had been parked only two days earlier. "Bet it leaked fluid all over this lot, too. Bet the police find it when they come over here to put all y'all's asses in jail."

Ronnie swatted her hand away, but Jackie kept talking.

"I came over here yesterday to tell Jeff I wanted my money back. He tells me no. Then he threatens me. This morning my car is gone. You think I'm stupid? I know he stole it. And I can prove it. Now I want to know what you're gonna do about it."

"Jeff here sold you a bad car?" Ronnie looked amazed. He was shorter than the others, at least three inches shorter than Jackie, and she was five six, but somehow, with his barrel chest, thick neck, and broad shoulders, he looked bigger than life. He had thick, curly dark hair, an uptilted, slightly feminine nose, and lips nearly hidden by a bushy black mustache.

"Jeff," Ronnie said, turning to his salesman. "Is any of this true? Did you steal this lady's car?"

"Hey, man," Jeff said, turning from Ronnie to Wormy, then back to Ronnie. "She's nuts. That car was cherry. She gets it stolen and wants to blame me? No way!"

"I can prove he stole it," Jackie said hotly.

"I know that car," Ronnie said. "And Jeff is right. That was choice merchandise. As for the car's condition, if you'll look on your sales contract, you'll see that we sell all cars on an 'as is' basis. If it had a problem with the transmission, that is something we were not aware of. We just sell the cars, miss, we don't take their life histories."

"Yeah," Jeff said. He'd heard Ronnie use that one a million times.

"Tell you what," Ronnie said, winking at Jackie. "You bring the car back here today, same condition you bought it in, I'm going to make an exception to company policy and buy it back. We can't have uhappy customers, now can we?"

He glanced from Jackie to Jeff to Wormy, an impromptu opinion poll.

"Suits me," Jeff said, shrugging.

"I don't *HAVE* the car," Jackie said, her teeth clenched tightly. "It was stolen last night. By him."

"Stolen?" Ronnie said, like he was hearing it for the first time. "That's a rotten shame. Damn shame the crime problem we got in this town. No police protection. And with all the taxes we pay, too."

Ronnie shook his head, saddened at the sudden upswing in crime in the quiet retirement town. "Least you got insurance—right? Hey," he said, brightening. "You get that insurance check, come back here, I'll personally fix you up with the sweetest deal ever. I got a '86 Toyota Tercel. Loaded."

Jackie was fighting back tears. She'd been flim-flammed good.

"You people ripped me off," she shouted. "This place is a damn nest of thieves. And I'm gonna prove it. The cops are gonna get after you. And I'm getting a lawyer and I'm calling the State Department of Motor Vehicles and reporting you for messing with odometers. And I've got a friend, he's a reporter. He's gonna blow this thing wide open."

Ronnie's eyes took on the hooded look of a reptile about to strike. He reached in his pocket and brought out the ledger page he'd taken out of the files when Wormy had informed him about the trouble on the lot. Jackie's name was at the top of the page, and there were spaces marked off in weekly increments.

"We don't have to steal cars, young lady. We run a reputable business. You bring around all the police you want. But if you start making unsubstantiated charges against me, I'm going to make you regret it. Now this here's your payment book," he said softly, letting her get a good look. "And this here column is the day your payment is due. This Friday. You got until then to come up with what you owe on the Corvette. Because on Friday, we're going to want our money. And if we don't get our money, and if you no longer have the car, we're gonna be very, very unhappy with you." As he tucked the ledger page back into the breast pocket of his banana-colored sports coat, Jackleen got a brief but convincing look at an ugly black pistol nestled in a holster at his waist.

CHAPTER

EIGHT

"**H**E HAD A GUN, MR. K," JACKIE REPEATED. SHE was too mad to get back on that bus, not when she'd sworn off bus riding forever just two days ago. So she'd walked to a convenience store across the street, picked a quarter out of her dwindling supply of tip money, and called to ask Truman to come pick her up.

Now they were sitting in Truman's car. Jackie pointed out the sales office for Bondurant Motors.

"They're inside that office," she said, near tears. "Jeff and that Ronnie Bondurant and some other guy who works there. I know they stole my car. Stole it, and they're gonna sell it again. I'll bet all those cars over there are stolen."

"Maybe so," Truman agreed. "But if they're like most of these car lots, they don't have to resort to common auto theft. The law lets them rip folks off with huge interest rates and sales contracts that mean people will be paying for junky cars like your Corvette for years after they quit running. I still can't figure out why they'd steal your car back. It doesn't make sense."

"It's a crock of horseshit, is what it is," Ollie said, leaning forward from the backseat. He had insisted on coming along to rescue Jackie. "And I don't think we should let these guys get away with it, stealing from an honest, hardworking girl like Jackie."

"She says the man has a gun," Truman said. "You want to argue with a pistol-packing used-car dealer, be my guest."

"So we just let them get away with it?" Jackie asked, not believing what she was hearing. "And I go back to that stinking bus?"

Truman rubbed the bridge of his nose. When it was hot like this, his glasses rubbed a raw spot on it. "Did you call that cop who left his card? Tell him about the can of transmission fluid we found?"

"He was gone," Jackie said. "Won't be back till tomorrow morning. By that time they'll have my car painted purple and sold to two or three more people."

"No they won't," Truman said. "Anyway, you can't just go busting back in there, accusing them of stealing the car. Let the police handle it."

"Like they did today?" she said. "How come that cop didn't find the can of transmission fluid? Or the tire tracks? All they do is take reports and then throw them away."

"Tell you what," Truman offered. "Tomorrow, you call that cop back. In the meantime, I'll make some phone calls. Find out what I can about this Ronnie Bondurant. I used to know somebody in the state attorney's office. I think they've got a consumer affairs complaint division, something like that."

"Red tape," Jackie muttered.

"Bureaucrats," Ollie agreed.

"It's the best I can do," Truman said. "This is a police matter. Can we go now?"

Jeff Cantrell sat very still. Maybe, he thought, he was having an out-of-body experience. He'd done enough drugs in his time, had the ticket stubs from a couple of LSD trips.

Ronnie Bondurant was right up in his face, not screaming, but whispering.

"You left a can of transmission fluid? Right there? Can this be true?"

He slapped Jeff hard with the flat of his hand, the big ring tearing at the flesh on Jeff's cheek.

"Did you know this, Wormy?" Ronnie asked, turning to look at his sales manager, who was perched casually on the edge of a chair, rather enjoying the spectacle of Jeffy boy's humiliation.

"Shit, no," Wormy said. "Even a retard can steal a car without leaving a track. I thought he was smarter than a retard."

"Tracks leading all the way back to Bondurant Motors," Ronnie said, his hot, wine-soaked breath making Jeff's eyes sting. "That black chick puts it all together for the cops, they start looking at our operation, what do you think that means for Ronnie Bondurant? Huh?"

"I didn't mean . . ." Jeff, said, gulping, searching for words. "To leave the can . . . Wormy came back and honked the horn. I was afraid somebody would catch us . . . I forgot to take the can."

"You forgot," Ronnie said, nodding. With his left hand, he slapped the other side of Jeff's face, catching him on the jaw with such force that Jeff fell off the chair.

"Ronnie? Where y'at, dude?" The voice came from the outer office.

Wormy stood up, and with the brass-capped toe of his ostrich-skin cowboy boot, kicked Jeff squarely in the crotch. "Get up," Wormy said. "That's Boone. We got business."

Somehow, oozing blood from both sides of his face, Jeff managed to stumble out of the inner office and collapse on his desk chair. He would have run, but he knew already it was no use. People having out-of-body experiences never escaped.

Hernando Boone was used to turning heads, had been since his linebacker days at the University of Florida. Half black, half Miccosukee Indian, he kept his kinky dark hair in a plait, strung with colored beads, that hung down his back. The Gator press guide had put him at six three, 240. It was really more like six two, 275. He had high, broad cheekbones and long, droopy earlobes and no facial hair to speak of. His eyes drooped at the corners and were the same flat black color as a water moccasin's. The fact that he'd been expelled his sophomore year, for selling steroids to his Gator teammates, had never turned him against the U. of F. His truck, a jacked-up Chevy, was Gator blue, with Gator orange stripes down the side and a strutting Wally Gator decal on the driver's-side door.

The truck was fine for some things, but Hernando had been thinking about getting something a little sportier, something the ladies would like. Ronnie Bondurant had mentioned something about a nice Corvette, low mileage, in the wrapper.

Hernando parked his truck well away from the

shitty-looking heaps Ronnie sold to the greasers and losers he usually did business with.

He saw the bleeding kid come crawling out of Ronnie's office, but so what? Ronnie Bondurant didn't take shit off people. Bondurant told him that himself. When he walked into Ronnie's office, he plopped a bulging brown paper sack down onto the desk.

"Grade-A prime," Hernando said, pulling out a two-inch-thick porterhouse steak. "These suckers are the same ones they're selling for thirty-five dollars apiece over there at Bern's in Tampa. Same exact steaks."

"And you're selling them for what?" Ronnie asked. He put down a sheet of paper he was reading and picked up the steak. He opened a corner of the plastic wrap and sniffed delicately.

"That there is part of my Beefeater's Special," Hernando said. "You get two porterhouses, four rib eyes, ten pounds of ground round, and a four-pound chuck roast, fifty-nine ninety-five, wrapped and delivered right to your door."

"That's good?" Wormy asked. The only time he ventured into a grocery store was to pick up beer or the occasional sack of fried pork rinds. The rest of the time, Wormy ate out.

"You shittin' me, man?" Hernando asked. "For home delivery? We're talking close to a hundred and twenty dollars' worth of Grade-A beef, man. You don't gotta leave the house. All you gotta do is answer the phone when my girls give you a call, tell you about the week's specials."

"It's a sweet deal," Ronnie told Wormy. "Especially on account of Hernando here has a brother works at the Publix central distribution warehouse over in Lakeland. This meat here never even got to fall off a truck. Beautiful, huh?"

Hernando smiled modestly. "I got overhead, you know. My brother, he likes living large. Then I got the rent on the boiler room, my phone girls, my drivers, gas, trucks. Like that. You're lucky, Ronnie, not to be in telemarketing. With telemarketing, you wouldn't believe the shit people try to pull."

"I could believe," Ronnie said sadly.

"No shit," Hernando continued. "Today, I caught a guy, he orders three hundred dollars' worth of T-bones and sirloins, my Beefeater Deluxe package, and puts it on an American Express gold card. Right away, I'm suspicious. 'Cause the delivery address is some apartment over on the double deuces at 22nd Street and 22nd Avenue. I get over there, it's some little woolhead from Ethiopia, someplace like that. Right off the boat. Him and some of his tribesmen, they been Dumpster diving for credit card carbons. Six of 'em living in two rooms."

"And they tried that shit on you?" Ronnie laughed. He looked over at Wormy, who was eyeing the steaks hungrily. It had been a long day and he still had to finish with that fuck-up Jeff Cantrell before they could lock up and go get dinner.

"It's taken care of now," Hernando said. "I took care of it right there. Can't have some woolhead cocksuckers runnin' around telling people they ripped off Hernando Boone. Giving the brothers ideas."

"You beat 'em up pretty bad, huh?" Wormy asked approvingly.

Ronnie had warned him not to mess with Boone, and he had taken the advice to heart. All those steroids had obviously turned what little brains the dude had into tapioca. He was big and mean and ugly. Ronnie as much as said he already regretted mentioning the Corvette to Boone while they were partying at the strip club where they'd met. Wormy could tell Ronnie was afraid of Boone, afraid he'd get pissed off and come after him. That's how crazy Hernando Boone was. He even scared Ronnie Bondurant.

Hernando tugged thoughtfully at his braid, toying with one of the beads.

"Beat 'em?" Hernando repeated. "No. I never laid a finger on the cocksuckers."

He reached into the bag of steaks and pulled out a semiautomatic pistol, the kind you always saw Colombian drug dealers brandishing in the movies and on TV. Hernando had gotten his gun from a Colombian cocaine cowboy out in back of a bar over in Ybor City. A trunk full of ribs for the pistol. And he was well on his way by the time the cowboy took a good look at the ribs and their two-week-old expiration date.

Hernando pointed the pistol at the wall behind Ronnie's desk. BOOM. A plaque naming Ronnie Bondurant "Honorary Big Brother of the Year" exploded into splinters.

Hernando swung his arm slightly to the right and squeezed the trigger again.

BOOM. Ronnie's gold-plated putter, the one he got for making a hole in one at the 1992 Tampa Bay Area Auto Dealer's Tournament was clipped neatly in two.

"Die, cocksucker," Hernando screamed. He was laughing like hell, his head thrown back, his mouth stretched into a lunatic's grin.

"Jesus," Ronnie shouted. The room filled with

blue smoke and concrete dust. There were two big craters on the concrete-block wall.

"The third little bastard went out the window with the credit card machine," Hernando said. "I'll say this. Now I know why those Ethiopians are always winning the marathons. Little bastard was gone before I got a shot off."

"You hear that, Wormy?" Ronnie said. "Boone here's an action man. Maybe we need that kind of action for our boy Jeff out there. Whatya say, Hernando?"

Just then the door to Ronnie's private office flew open. Jeff Cantrell stood, wide-eyed, in the doorway, a toylike .22 pointed at Boone. He'd seen the big, crazy-looking Indian go inside, heard him shooting up Ronnie's office. It was a holdup! Now was his chance to fix things with Ronnie, prove that he could be trusted.

Jeff glanced over at Ronnie, looking for some thanks. Instead he was looking down the barrel of Ronnie's pistol. Hey, wait! And Wormy, he'd drawn his gun, too.

What the hell? Jeff couldn't think what to say. Out of body again?

A strangled "Hah!" emerged from his throat. And then a bullet ripped through his right cheek, knocking him backward into the door.

"Hey, Ronnie?" Jeff's voice was weak. "What'd you shoot me for?" He dropped the .22 and held his shattered face with both hands. Another bullet ripped into his groin and he slid to the floor, his brilliant white tennis shoes splattered with blood.

Boone was the first to speak.

"Who was that asshole?" He put the semi back in the paper bag with the steaks.

"A former employee," Ronnie said grimly. He gave Wormy a discreet nod.

"Is that red 'Vette still hooked up to the wrecker?"

"Yeah," Wormy said. "It's gonna make a hell of a mess on the upholstery."

"Put down some plastic garbage bags or something," Ronnie said. "But wait until it gets dark. That black chick could still be hanging around, trying to make trouble. Take the car, get rid of all the transmission fluid we got around here, drop the kid some place good, then drop the 'Vette back by your place till tomorrow."

"Which insurance company we dealing with this time?" Wormy asked.

Ronnie checked the sheet of paper he'd been reading. "Gulf States Casualty. Up in Largo, on Ulmerton Road."

Hernando Boone was getting impatient. "Hey. What about my car? I thought you had a car ready for me. And I got all this meat here." He poked the paper bag, which was getting soggy on the bottom. "Man, my meat's starting to thaw."

"Sorry," Ronnie said, "but you can see, Hernando, we gotta take care of this right now."

"Fuck," Boone said. He hefted the bag a little higher and stepped over the body in the doorway. He stopped and poked Cantrell with his toe, wrinkling his nose in distaste. "Some mess. Call me later. I want that car."

Ronnie followed Boone to the door, locking it after him. He came back into the office, avoiding looking at Cantrell. Then he pushed his swivel chair away from the desk, pulled up a piece of burnt-orange carpet, and with his thumbnails, removed a section of plywood flooring. The safe was recessed beneath the old oak flooring. He swiveled the lock, opened it, and dropped in his .45. Wormy came over and handed Ronnie his .38. Ronnie dropped it in, got up, paused, then walked quickly across the room. He got the .22 Cantrell had dropped and added it to the arsenal in the safe.

When everything was put back in place, he dusted his hands on the seat of his pants. "I need a drink," Ronnie said. "Fuckin' Hernando Boone. Get some spackle, get those holes fixed up." He picked up the ruined putter, threw it in the trash and shook his head. His gold-plated putter.

CHAPTER

NINE

TRUMAN WOULD NOT BE BUDGED ON THE MATter of a stakeout at Bondurant Motors. Not with bribery: "Double desserts, and eggs cooked to order, advance notice about the salmon patties," Jackie had promised. Not with threats: "You'll never drink hot coffee in this town again," she said ominously. Nor would he be moved by more tears, pouts, or silent stares. After all, he had been married for forty years and had raised a daughter. He was resistant to such tactics.

"It's a matter for the police, not for Nancy Drew and her chums," he said, looking pointedly at Ollie, whose cooperation could be bought for the price of a pack of gum.

In the end, Jackie and Ollie double-teamed him so mercilessly that he finally agreed to let them use his car for their caper, and then only on the condition that they watch—from a distance.

At seven P.M., Jackie piloted the Nova into the parking lot of the Taste of Saigon restaurant. Buying dinner for Ollie had been part of the stakeout package.

When she came out with two cups of Coke and an order of spring rolls, Ollie was still fuming about her choice of location.

"This is no good," he complained. "Across the street would be better."

Jackie pointed at the line of cars waiting to turn into the parking lot at the garishly lit strip club across the street. A brawny man stood at the entrance to the lot, taking money from each driver before allowing him to turn in. The cinderblock building was painted shocking pink, with a huge painted silhouette of a girl's behind painted on the front. The Candy Store, it was called. Disgusting.

"That bouncer over there is collecting money to park," Jackie said. "Admit it. You just want to sneak in there and peek at those skanky old strippers shaking their booties and their big, floppy titties."

"That's not it at all," Ollie protested. He pointed at the side of the Bondurant Motors lot, which abutted Taste of Saigon. "We can only see half the car lot from here. And those girls over there are not skanky. They're stylish nudes."

"Whatever," Jackie said, taking a sip of Coke. "This is the best we can do. We can see most of the car lot, and the front door to the office. That's Jeff's car," she said, pointing. "When he comes out, we'll go over there and look around. It's after seven. Quitting time, right?"

Ollie ate a spring roll. It was cold and greasy, with a lingering shrimpy aftertaste. Just the way he liked them. He chewed and Jackie sipped and they both watched the small patch of asphalt and cinderblock at

Bondurant Motors. The inside of the Nova was hot and airless. It got so boring finally that Jackie switched on the ignition so they could listen to something besides the traffic on U.S. 19.

Ollie kept his neck craned so he could see above the dashboard and across the street. He was hoping someone would leave the front door open at the Candy Store so he could catch just a glimpse of stylish nudity. Just a glimpse, that's all he asked.

Jackie blinked to keep her eyes open. It had been a long day, and the heat made her sleepy. "Hey," she said, sitting suddenly upright. "Look at that."

Ollie reluctantly turned his head toward the Bondurant Motors lot.

A powerfully built dark-skinned man with a long beaded braid stalked out of the office of Bondurant Motors. He got into a gaudy blue-and-orange pickup truck and went screeching out of the parking lot and onto U.S. 19, making the right turn without even slowing down. Moments later, the lights in the office snapped off.

"Now what?" Jackie wondered. Five minutes passed. Ronnie Bondurant came out the front door. He glanced quickly around.

"Duck," Jackie ordered. They both slumped down in the front seat of the Nova.

Bondurant took out a huge metal key ring, fit a key into the lock, picked up a briefcase, and walked quickly over to a gray Lincoln parked in the space nearest the door.

"That was the boss. Mr. Bondurant," Jackie said. "Looks like they're closed. But then, why is Jeff's car still there?"

"Maybe he's driving another car today? I knew a

guy once, he worked at a Ford dealership. Never drove the same car two days in a row."

"Yeah," Jackie agreed. "I never thought of that. I'll bet that car he took me to the bank in wasn't even his. Probably stolen," she added.

She opened the car door and stepped out. "Let's do it."

"Now?" Ollie held up a spring roll. "I'm still eating. And look at all those people over across the street." He waved the spring roll in the direction of the Candy Store. "Somebody might see us and call the cops."

"We'll act like we're car shopping," Jackie said. "What's wrong, Ollie? You wimping out on me?"

Jackie's own stomach had started to burn, and it had nothing to do with the spring rolls. She kept thinking about Ronnie Bondurant's gun, his threats. Until now, she really hadn't believed she would go through with this.

"I'm no wimp," Ollie protested. He pitched the remains of his spring roll out the open window of the car. "Let's roll," he said, doing his best imitation of Jack Lord. Or was it Jack Webb?

They moved cautiously onto the Bondurant Motors lot. Jackie felt different. Jazzed. Her heart raced and she felt the tendons in her calves tighten with every step. The balls of her feet seemed to bounce inside her Nikes.

"Go over near the driveway, okay?" she told Ollie. "Keep a lookout."

While they'd been sitting in the car, Jackie had noticed a long, low, metal building jutting off the back of the office building.

"I want to check out that garage thing," Jackie

said, nodding toward it. "See if maybe they've got my car in there. They're too smart to leave it out here where I might spot it."

"Why can't I check out the garage?" Ollie asked, his face crumpling. "You keep lookout."

"There's only that one window," Jackie said meaningfully. The window was a horizontal slit in the metal door. High up off the ground. Too high.

"What's the signal?" Ollie asked, getting her meaning. "In case somebody shows up?"

She thought about it. "Just holler my name. And meet me back at the car."

Even standing on her tiptoes, Jackie could only manage to bring her eyes up to the window ledge. It was too high up, and anyway, it was dark in there. She walked over to the roll-up door and tugged at the handle. It wouldn't budge. Damn. She just knew her car was inside.

She turned around to see where Ollie had gone. But the rows of cars had swallowed him up. He was nowhere to be seen. "Better not be over at that nudie club," she muttered to herself.

Trying to look casual, she walked around to the side of the metal building and turned the corner. This side of the lot was enclosed by a six-foot chain-link fence. On the other side of the fence was Bondurant Motors's very own dump site. The area was littered with junk; rusting fifty-five-gallon oil drums, stacks of tires, a huge Dumpster, mounds of asphalt roofing tiles, paint cans, discarded car parts. Why would somebody fence in junk, Jackie wondered?

Then she spotted something through the mounds of discards. There was a door into the garage thing and it was open. A shaft of light leaked out into the darkening lot and she saw a flash of bright red paint. Devil red.

"I knew it," she said smugly.

Getting up the fence was surprisingly easy. But once she was at the top, the trip down looked a lot scarier. She closed her eyes and climbed down, feeling for a grip with her foot rather than looking.

It was dusk, probably a little after eight. Who was inside that building? Jeff, maybe? If he was there, she'd catch him, red-handed, with her car. Ream him a new asshole. She crept between a row of tires, hoping to get the jump on him, heading for the open door.

When she got closer, she ducked down behind what looked like the passenger seat to a van. The leather had rotted in the sun and foam rubber was bursting from the seat and the back. The door to the garage was maybe ten feet away. The red she'd seen was definitely a car. Her Corvette?

Her hands stung and her calves burned and ached from her fence-climbing stunt. What had happened to her jazzed feeling? She was this close, and she was scared. Might pee in her pants, she thought, immediately pushing the idea aside. Nobody was moving inside the garage.

Jackie bit her lip. Screw 'em. It was her car, wasn't it? She made a quick dash to the door, stopping just outside, poking her head cautiously around the corner.

There was her Corvette. Her very own lemon.

She darted inside. The front end of the 'Vette was hooked up to a black tow truck.

She knew it! They were getting ready to move it, hide her car now that Cantrell and his boss knew they couldn't get away with stealing from Jackie Canaday. That she had the goods on them. They wouldn't take any chances with it breaking down on them again. That's why they had it hooked to a tow truck. Only now that she looked closer, she saw that the back end was all bashed in, the taillights busted out, a big hole gashed there.

What the hell? They'd stolen her car and then wrecked it? She stepped closer and looked in the rear window.

There was something in the hatch.

The body was curled up, like somebody who was asleep, with black plastic garbage bags sort of wrapped around it. But the head was all wrong. The neck was twisted awkwardly, so the face was toward her. There was a hole in the face and a lot of blood, but she wouldn't forget that dimple. Or the carefully moussed hair.

She jumped, back-pedaling fast, and collided with a silver van.

Its alarm whooped and echoed in the metal building. "Warning!" a stern voice boomed. "Step away from this vehicle."

She didn't just step, she ran for her life.

When she was on the other side of the fence, it occurred to her that her hands were cut and bleeding. As she rounded the corner of the garage, she felt a draft from the seat of her jeans, and the knee, too, where she'd snagged her pants on the fence.

Ollie met her at the corner. His face was beet red and he was breathing hard. "Christ," he whispered. "Let's get out of here. A cop car just pulled in."

CHAPTER

TEN

"**W**E'RE GOING TO JAIL," JACKIE SAID, BREATH-less, diving headlong into the backseat of the Nova. "Prison. There've been Canadays in trouble before. I'm not saying different. But nobody ever went to prison till now."

"Be quiet," Ollie hissed, pulling the driver's door closed. He raised his head up slowly until it was level with the window.

"Here comes the gray Lincoln," Ollie said. "It's that boss. He's getting out now, going over to talk to the cops."

"Ronnie Bondurant," Jackie said. "Jesus. Jesus. He killed that boy."

"What are you talking about?" Ollie said, whipping his head around to look at her. "What boy?"

"Jeff," Jackie said. "He's dead. I saw him. In that garage. In my car. The 'Vette. Shot in the face, wrapped up like garbage. Oh, Jesus. I never want to see something like that again." She shivered even though it was probably ninety degrees inside the closed-up car.

"He was dead? You're sure?"

"Oh, yes," Jackie said soberly.

"And it was my car. They had it hooked up to a tow truck in there. Ollie, I touched it. My fingerprints are all over that car. What if they try to make it look like it was me that killed Jeff? People saw me yelling at him yesterday. And today. What if they try to say it was me? They could do that. Make it look like I broke in. Shot Jeff, 'cause I figured out he was the one who stole my car."

"Nah," Ollie said. But his voice somehow lacked the ring of conviction.

"What's Bondurant doing?" Jackie asked. She couldn't bring herself to look.

"He's checking the lock on the door. Now they're walking around to this side. Stay down. Hey. Now they're walking back toward the front. Hey! He's showing the cops a car."

"A car?"

Now Jackie sat up to look for herself.

Sure enough, Ronnie Bondurant had the door of a midnight-blue Gran Torino open. The taller of the two cops, a skinny white guy, walked around and slid behind the wheel. Ronnie bent down to show him something. He stood up, brought out the key ring, selected a key, and handed it to the cop.

They heard the motor start. Saw the other cop laugh, shake his head, then get in the passenger's seat. The headlights came on and the Gran Torino glided out of the Bondurant Motors' car lot at a sedate ten miles per hour. After all, they were cops, and they were on duty.

Jackie stared at the disappearing red taillights. "They're going for a test drive. There's a dead guy in that garage, and those goofballs are going for a test drive."

Ronnie Bondurant beat it toward the office. He wasn't running, but he was making good time. He unlocked the door and stepped inside. They saw lights switch on.

"We've got to do something," Jackie said. "By the time those cops get back, anything could happen."

"What can we do?" Ollie asked unhappily. He'd been more than willing to eat Vietnamese food and go along with the charade of a stakeout. It was exciting. But now, things had gone too far. He hadn't counted on finding a body or breaking and entering or getting mixed up with police and heavily armed used-car dealers.

"Let's just leave," Ollie suggested. "Right now, before that Bondurant guy comes out and spots us." He turned the key in the ignition and started the Nova. The gas pedal was going to be a problem. As would be seeing over the steering wheel.

"We can't just leave," Jackie said, tugging at his arm. "Jeff's dead. And he's in my car. We've gotta call the cops. Or they'll find him and think I did it."

"You? You couldn't have killed him. I was with you all night. You don't even have a gun. I'm your alibi."

"They might not believe you," Jackie said. "That's why we've got to be the ones to tell them about the body. I'll go back inside the restaurant and call 911. You stay out here and watch, okay?"

"Okay," Ollie said reluctantly.

Jackie was gone for a long time. Ollie watched the front door and the side of Bondurant Motors so hard that his neck got a cramp and his eyes started to water.

He glanced across the street toward the Candy Store, just to rest his eyes. Cars were still streaming into the parking lot and people were lined up to get inside. But now the short bald bouncer he'd seen before was gone.

In his place was the woman of Ollie's dreams. She was statuesque and slender, with long, jet-black hair that streamed over her shoulders and skin the color of lightly toasted almonds. She appeared to be wearing nothing more than a pair of sneakers, a gold lamé bikini top, and a matching thong. When she bent over to talk to the driver of a car and take his parking fee, he saw that the tan was all over, and what with the light from the colorful strings of bulbs around Bondurant Motors and the dancing spotlights of the Candy Store, he could see very well indeed.

He was trying to decide if the girl was Japanese, or maybe Polynesian, when his reverie was broken by the shrill blaring of a police siren. Two cruisers came speeding down U.S. 19. Ollie saw the girl look up with alarm. When she spotted the cars with their flashing blue lights, she seemed to disappear right before his eyes. Like a frightened doe, vanished into the mist, Ollie thought sadly.

Jackie came bustling out of the Taste of Saigon.

"Thank God," she said. "Come on. We've got to go over there and give them a statement."

"A statement?" Ollie was alarmed. "Why do I have to give them a statement? Can't I just be an anonymous bystander? I didn't see anything."

"You saw what was going on over there," Jackie said, beginning to lose patience with him. "There's a dead man over there, you know."

Ronnie Bondurant was standing outside talking

to the officers by the time Jackie walked up, trailing the reluctant bystander.

"You again," Bondurant said when he saw her. "What the hell is this woman doing here, officers?"

Just then, the Gran Torino came screeching into the parking lot. The driver, who had been gnawing on a drumstick from Kentucky Fried Chicken, put the half-eaten leg back in the bucket with the rest of his supper.

"Uh-oh," the driver told his partner. "We're screwed."

Jackie was taking deep breaths, trying hard not to sound like an hysterical female. It was difficult—she could feel the hysteria welling up inside her, like those Fizzies you put on your tongue when you were a kid. The panic and fear were there, fizzing just below the surface.

"There's a man inside that garage back there," she said, pointing toward the metal hangar. "He's dead. I think he was shot in the face. He's inside a red Corvette."

She glared at Ronnie Bondurant. "My red Corvette. They stole it from me last night. I called the cops and filed a report. You can check the records."

"Dead man inside a Corvette." One of the cops, a heavyset black man with thick glasses, was writing in a notepad. He acted like he was in charge. "Any idea who the deceased was?"

"His name is Jeff," Jackie said. "I don't know his last name. But he works here. He's the one who sold me the Corvette. On Saturday. He ripped me off. Sold me a lemon. I told him and Mr. Bondurant here that I was gonna get a lawyer, call the police, and maybe get a story in the newspaper. Mr. Bondurant has a gun," she said, pointing to Bondurant's jacket.

"What?" Ronnie Bondurant sputtered. He threw open his sport coat. The only thing beneath it was his knit sport shirt, the fabric strained against his thickened waist. "This girl is crazy. A troublemaker. I don't know what she's talking about."

"Look in the garage," Jackie repeated. "You'll see."

The two test-driving cops drifted up to the knot of people standing around outside the office.

"What I see," Bondurant said, turning to the cops, "was that we had a break-in here earlier. A car alarm went off, and these two alert officers were here right away. Ask them. They'll tell you there's no murder here. Just a break-in." He glared right back at Jackie and at Ollie, who was wishing intensely that he could be somewhere else. Maybe across the street, discussing Oriental belief systems with the parking lot attendant.

The tall cop, the test driver, had the grace to blush. "Uh, actually, we didn't check inside, Mr. Bondurant. Remember? We got to discussing cars."

"Well, you can check it now," Ronnie said quickly. "This girl and her partner here—I think they may have broken in earlier. I heard a noise back in the garage, but I didn't see anybody. They must have jumped the fence."

"He's lying," Jackie burst out. "Jeff stole my car, and I can prove it. That's why he killed Jeff. Ask him who stole my car. If he didn't steal it, how come it's inside in that garage? Who put the body in my car? Ask him that."

"Deranged," Ronnie said. "Drugs, maybe. You see that a lot in my business, kind of clientele I'm forced to deal with. I'd suggest a drug test. But first I want these two off my property."

"Mind if we check the premises?" the black cop asked. "We've got a report of a possible homicide. We need to check, get the paperwork taken care of. Before the homicide detectives get called out and all that kind of thing."

"Go ahead," Bondurant said, crossing his arms defiantly across his chest. "But she's not going in there. In fact, I want her removed right now."

The cops all looked at each other. Finally, the black one who was in charge stuck his writing pad in his hip pocket.

"Sorry. She's a witness. She called in the complaint. He stays here," he said, nodding toward Ollie. "She shows us what she thinks she saw."

It was fully dark now, and the back part of Bondurant Motors, the part the public did not see, was not all lit up and flagged and shiny like the front. It was dark back here, and the asphalt was broken and uneven and the air smelled sour, like rust and motor oil.

"Right in there," Jackie said, pausing in front of the chain-link fence. "The door's closed now. It was open before."

The black cop, whose nameplate said "Hilley," played his flashlight over the fence, letting it linger on the top. "How'd you get in there, ma'am?"

He was nice, calling her ma'am.

"She broke in," Bondurant said, catching up with them. "Trespassing, they call it."

"I could see my car through the door," Jackie retorted. "My car was in there. They had my car."

"Bullshit," Bondurant said. "This girl is crazy. First she comes around, complaining we sold her a lemon. She made a disturbance, caused us to lose a couple sales. Then she comes back, says somebody stole her car, accusing me, us, of stealing the car we just sold her. She was probably doped up and wrecked it somewhere. Just wants to get off the hook for the payments."

"You got a key to this gate?" Hilley asked.

Bondurant unlocked the gate. With Hilley leading the way with his flashlight, they picked their way through the debris. At Hilley's request, Bondurant produced yet another key. He unlocked the door to the garage, pulled it open, and reached around inside. He fumbled a bit before finding the light switch.

Then he stepped aside, bowed low at the waist, and swept his arm out wide in a mocking invitation to enter.

"Be my guest."

Hilley had his hand on his holstered gun as they walked inside the garage.

The silver van was there, its headlights and blaring alarm gone silent. There was a sizable work area, a red metal Craftsman tool chest, more stacks of tires, and on the wall, a calendar with a generous-busted girl whose cleavage spilled out of an unzipped Snap-On tool jumpsuit.

In the same exact spot where Jackie had seen the red Corvette barely an hour ago, now stood a tired-looking two-tone olive green and wood-grain station wagon, its hood raised, more tools littering the floor around it.

"Where was this car you mentioned, ma'am?" Hilley asked, turning to her.

Jackie's mouth hung open.

"Ma'am?"

"It was right here. The Corvette. Jeff was stuffed inside the hatch. Part of his body was covered with garbage bags. Black ones. It was right here," she said, thumping the door of the station wagon.

Hilley turned to Ronnie Bondurant.

"Do you know this Jeff she's talking about?"

"Absolutely," Ronnie said easily. "Jeff Cantrell. Hell of a salesman. He used to work for me. Hated to lose the guy."

"He quit?" Hilley said. "When was this?"

"This afternoon," Bondurant said. "He said he had a business opportunity over on the east coast, Lauderdale or someplace. Nothing personal. You know how they get when they're young. The guy was single, no attachments. He moved on."

"What about his car?" Jackie asked. "That's his car out in the parking lot. Why didn't he take his car if he quit?"

Bondurant raised one eyebrow. He did it well. "*His* car? You mean the Mustang? That belongs to me. Inventory. We always let our salesmen drive the inventory. It's good for business."

"He's lying," Jackie said quickly. "They must have moved the car and the body. While those two goof-off cops were out joyriding. It was right here under their noses and they didn't even look inside. It was right here."

Hilley had been writing in his pad again. He looked up at Ronnie.

"Mr. Bondurant? Okay if I ask the other officers to step inside here and take a look around?"

"Fine with me," Bondurant said, sticking his hands in his pockets. "Lot of fuss all on the say-so of a hophead girl like this. Somebody in the habit of breaking into a business. A burglar, you might say."

Hilley looked up sharply. "You want to file charges? She admits she came in here."

"I'll look around, see if anything's missing," Ronnie said. "If I find anything missing, you can lock her up."

"You're the thief," Jackie said fiercely.

"That's enough," Hilley said, still polite. "I think you can go wait outside with your friend now."

They left the tall, skinny cop, the joyrider, to wait with Ollie and Jackie. He got his bucket of chicken out of the Gran Torino and sat in his cruiser with the engine idling, the windows rolled up, and the air conditioner going full blast.

"I'm taking his badge number," Ollie told Jackie. They were leaning against the hood of one of the other cruisers.

Jackie couldn't help it. She had to bring it up.

"You were watching while I was inside on the phone," she said accusingly. "Didn't you see it? A black tow truck pulling my car? How could you miss seeing it?"

"I was watching as close as I could," Ollie snapped. "You were gone a hell of a long time. There was a lot of traffic, you know. Besides, they could have taken it out the other side. How could I have seen it if they did that?"

"You were supposed to be watching," Jackie repeated.

It was another half hour before the cops came out. Ronnie Bondurant locked the office door behind them. He left the strings of lights festooned around the lot burning, and overhead, the slowly twirling pink Caddie's headlights blinked on and off, on and off.

"Sorry for your trouble," Hilley told him. "You change your mind about filing a breaking and entering report?"

"Didn't see anything missing," Bondurant said grudgingly, his eyes boring into Jackie. "Just make it clear to her. She makes any more trouble for me, comes snooping around here or causing any more disturbances, I will file charges. That's my right, am I correct?"

"That's correct," Hilley said.

"You understand that, miss?"

Jackie stood stiffly. Her hands were crusted with blood, her best jeans were in tatters, she was near tears, but she was damned if she'd let the sons of bitches see her cry.

"You're gonna let him get away with murder?" she asked Hilley. "And I'm the one who gets in trouble?"

"I oughta sue," Bondurant snarled. "Get out. But remember. Come Friday, you owe me seventy-seven dollars and ten cents. Miss a payment and I'm gonna be all over you like stink on a dog."

"We'll see about that," Jackie said coldly. "I've still got that can of transmission fluid. That'll prove who stole my car. Let's go, Ollie."

The atmosphere inside the Nova was thick with accusation, denial, and bitterness. Jackie turned the car south on U.S. 19, back toward the Fountain of Youth. She was exhausted and sore.

Ollie craned his neck to see the watch on Jackie's wrist.

"Nearly eleven o'clock," he said, "Truman's gonna be mad."

Jackie shot him a look. "Gonna be even madder when he sees you got duck sauce all over his seats."

Ollie scrubbed at the orange stain on the upholstery, and Jackie drove, plotting her next move.

CHAPTER

ELEVEN

JACKIE SLID THE BASKET OF BISCUITS ONTO THE table and put the car keys right beside it. She made a big show of filling Truman's cup with coffee. So he'd know she'd keep up her end of the bargain.

Truman put down the paperback copy of *To Kill a Mockingbird* that he'd been reading. He and Margaret McCutcheon were supposed to meet for lunch today, and he wanted to be able to impress her with his grasp of the story. This was one Great Book he really was enjoying.

"How did the stakeout go?" he asked. "See any trailer loads of stolen cars being unloaded?"

"He's dead," Jackie said. "They killed Jeff. Now I'll never be able to prove they took my car."

She looked around for Mr. Wiggins again. If he saw her sitting down while there were still customers in the room, he'd have a fit. No sign of him, though. So she told Truman the whole story. How they'd seen the Indian guy leave, and then Ronnie Bondurant. How she'd seen Jeff's body in the red Corvette. And how Bondurant—or somebody—had managed to get rid of the car and the body by the time the cops got there.

Truman ate steadily while she talked, pausing only occasionally to ask questions.

"This Jeff," he said, helping himself to another biscuit. "What's his last name?"

"I couldn't remember. So I looked on my sales contract. He stapled his business card to it. It's Cantrell. Jeff Cantrell."

Truman heaped jelly on the biscuit. He was really going to have to do some extra sit-ups today. Take a walk this evening if it wasn't too blasted hot. Maybe Margaret would join him.

"And Bondurant told the police that Cantrell quit his job and left town?"

"Left the planet is more like it," Jackie said. "Yeah, Bondurant made up some big story about Jeff going over to the east coast."

Truman pushed his plate away. If Jackie hadn't been sitting there, he could have discreetly loosened his belt.

"You think they moved the body?"

She shrugged. "I know they moved the car. Right under Ollie's nose. I could have wrung his neck, TK. The police looked all over the place, for like, half an hour. And there were three of them. You'd think they'd find it if it was there."

Maybe not, Truman thought. Not if they didn't believe she'd seen it in the first place.

Out of the corner of her eye, Jackie saw three youth hostel kids sidling toward the door. Deadbeats. She hustled across the room and met them at the cash register. "Everything okay?" she asked in a loud voice.

The hostel kids, two boys and a girl, wouldn't look her in the eye. "Yeah, great," they mumbled, reaching for their money.

"Four bucks," Jackie said when she got back, out of breath but holding the coffeepot. "They eat like truck drivers for four bucks, and they want to skip out on their checks?"

"Larceny in the soul," Truman observed.

"We've got to do something," Jackie said. "Bondurant says I have to keep paying on the Corvette, even though he stole it. I've got to have a hundred bucks by Friday. This Friday and every Friday for the next two years. You've seen what my tips are like, TK. How am I gonna save up for another car when I'm paying off that bloodsucker for the car he stole?"

"We?" Truman asked.

"I thought maybe you'd help," Jackie said. "Like you did when Mr. Wisnewski was in trouble. You said before that you'd make some phone calls, talk to a friend in the state attorney's office."

"That was when it was just a nasty little scam," Truman said. "Now you're talking about murder."

"You said you'd help," she said plaintively.

"Bondurant Motors." The voice was a man's, high-pitched, with a pronounced Southern drawl.

"Hello," Truman said brightly. "Jeff Cantrell, please."

Long pause. "He don't work here no more."

"He's no longer with you?"

"Who is this?" Wormy Weems demanded.

"This is Mr. Jackson at MCI," Truman said. "I'm

calling about Mr. Cantrell's long distance service. Frankly, I'm distressed to hear he's changed employment. He doesn't answer at home, and on his credit application he gave this number as his place of employment. Do you have a more current number?"

"No."

Dial tone.

Truman hadn't expected much from Bondurant Motors, but it was on his checklist of calls to make, and he was nothing if not methodical. Forty years with the AP would do that for you.

His Nellie had hundreds and hundreds of friends. She'd been dead over a year now, and they still sent Christmas cards and called. Nellie's friend, Nancy Ann, had a daughter, Louise, who worked at the state patrol driver's license office. He hadn't expected Louise to remember him.

"Mr. Kicklighter?" she said. "Of course. Mama misses your Nellie awful bad, you know. We all do. And I saw that big story in the *St. Pete Times* last year. That was really something."

Louise had inherited her mother's tendency to prattle. Truman decided to get right to the point. He did have other calls to make.

"I'm working on another big story now," he confided. "Major stuff. Extremely confidential. Possible organized crime connection."

He'd found over the years that the mere mention of organized crime tended to terrify and motivate.

"How can I help?" Louise said, lowering her voice. "Is it mob?"

"Possibly."

He told her what he needed, an address and a driver's license number for a Jeffrey Cantrell.

"With a 'G' or a 'J'?" Louise asked. He could hear her clacking away on her computer keyboard.

"J—I think," Truman said.

She clacked merrily away. "The mob," she said worriedly. "Right here in Pinellas County?"

"Afraid so," Truman said.

"Here it is," she said.

The address was actually not far from the Fountain of Youth. Allamanda Road, 316-B. Before she'd let him hang up, he had to promise to come to Louise's to dinner, too—any Sunday he liked.

Allamanda Road was a narrow street of close-set wooden houses tucked in back of Sunken Gardens, one of St. Pete's oldest tourist attractions. When Cheryl was little, they'd taken her there on Sundays, let her pose for pictures with a parrot on her head. The gardens were still full of tropical birds—parrots, cockatiels, macaws. There was a flock of wild peacocks, too, whose desperate shrieks still brought calls into police headquarters that somebody was killing a baby somewhere.

Number 316 Allamanda was painted a dull white. Cracked concrete pillars held up a sagging roof, and the grime-encrusted jalousie windows were cranked open. At the end of an abbreviated sand driveway, Truman could see that the tiny, wood-frame garage had been converted to an apartment. The mailbox by the front door had 316-B painted on it. He went to the apartment door and knocked. He was trying the handle when he heard a door open behind him.

The lady of the house was at home. He whirled around to say howdy-do.

"Hey, you."

She stood on the back stoop, a cigarette dangling from her lips. She was only a little taller than Ollie, not quite five feet. Her hair was short and curly and lavender, her eyes large and suspicous behind sparkly cat-lady eyeglasses. She could have been forty or sixty.

"Hello, there," Truman said. "I'm looking for Jeff."

"Gone," the landlady said, flicking some ash into a straggly hibiscus bush by the back door. "You interested in a nice apartment? One-bedroom efficiency. I can let you have it for two hundred dollars a month till the season starts."

"Can I see the inside?" Truman asked.

She took a drag off the cigarette and considered.

"Nope," she said finally. "Hasn't been cleaned. Come back next week, you can have a look."

Truman nodded. "What happened to Jeff? I thought he was pretty well set here."

"He left," the landlady said. "I found an envelope on my front porch with next month's rent, in cash. Note said he had a new job on the East Coast."

"Cash, huh?" Truman asked.

"That's right. Cash spends real good."

The landlady turned to go back inside.

"Wait," Truman said. "Jeff and I had a business deal going. He forgot to tell me he was leaving. I was wondering, uh, you ever see any of his other friends come around?"

She shut the back door and padded over to him. Her feet were bare, the nails painted a metallic purple two shades darker than her hair.

"What's all this to you?" she demanded. "Who

the hell are you, knocking on my door asking a lot of nosy questions?"

"He owed me some money," Truman said. "Lousy punk. I'm surprised he paid you off."

"Me, too," she admitted. "Usually, I couldn't run him down for the rent until the middle of the month. Cute kid, but he lied like a dog."

"That was Jeff," Truman said. "Anybody else beside me come around looking for him? Maybe one of his buddies would know where he went."

She took a long, last drag on the cigarette and tossed it on the ground. Truman had to take a quick sidestep to avoid having it land on his shoe. The sand driveway was littered with dozens of other spent filter tips.

"No buddies," she said. "Just the skinny Jap girl with the big boobs. If those things are real, mister, I'm Mother Teresa."

"She have a name?"

The landlady was patting the pockets of her cotton housedress, looking for more cigarettes.

"None of my business," she said. "Come back next week if you want to see the apartment. I got other people interested."

He had to bang on the back door repeatedly to get her to come back. And then she wouldn't open up. Just talked through the open jalousie window.

"What kind of car was Jeff driving?"

"Which time? He was in the car business. Drove a different one all the time."

"What was he driving the last time you saw him?"

"Saturday night? Some fancy red sports car. Made a big racket."

Red.

"A Corvette?" Truman asked.

"How the hell should I know?"

The security guard at the *St. Petersburg Times* wanted to give him a hard time. The guy was pushing seventy, had a self-important navy-blue blazer and a walkie-talkie strapped to his hip. Retired beat cop, probably.

He tossed Truman's AP press card back across the desk. "This thing expired nearly two years ago."

"They only issue them every few years," Truman lied. "They're making new ones right now."

"Get one then," the guard said. "Can't let you in without an ID." He went back to reading the TV listings.

There was a phone sitting on the security desk. Truman picked it up and dialed the city desk.

Gary DiLisi, the editor he'd been doing some freelancing for, came on the line.

"Gary? Truman Kicklighter. I'm down here in the lobby. This rent-a-cop won't let me up to use the library. Can you come down and sign me in?"

Truman hung up. The guard acted like he hadn't been listening to any of it.

Gary DiLisi looked like he was barely old enough to operate the elevator by himself, he certainly didn't look old enough to be assistant city editor on a paper the size of the *St. Pete Times*. He wore blue jeans, sneakers, and a blue work shirt with a red Mickey Mouse tie knotted around his neck. No socks. He was a baby, but as babies went, he was okay.

"Truman," Gary said, clapping him on the shoulder. "You giving Stanley here grief? He's pretty tough, you know."

Gary laughed. Stanley didn't. Gary signed Truman in on the log book.

"What's the guy gonna do?" Truman asked. "Beat me up with his walkie-talkie?"

In the elevator, Truman told Gary what little he knew about the alleged murder of Jeff Cantrell.

"I've seen that car lot, Bondurant Motors," Gary said. "I always wondered how they got that old Cadillac up there on the roof like that. But if Cantrell was working for this guy, Bondurant, why would he kill him?"

"I don't know," Truman said.

"The used-car scam is kind of interesting," Gary said thoughtfully. "If you go anywhere with that, I might buy a story. Especially if it's got a consumer angle. Christ, everything's gotta be 'News You Can Use' these days."

Most of the time, Truman hated what technology had done to newspapers. But in the paper's morgue, technology was a blessing. No more dusty envelopes full of yellowing clips, no more envelopes missing because some reporter had lost it or spilled coffee all over it.

The *St. Pete Times*'s back files were mostly on computer.

After the librarian signed him onto the system, Truman typed in Bondurant. And Ronnie.

There were forty hits. Most of the references were items about special sales promotions, or golf tournaments Bondurant had played in. Bondurant Motors gave away roses to moms on Mother's Day and pony rides to kids on the Fourth of July. Ronnie was a real citizen.

But two of the items made him seem less so. In

1983 and again, in 1985, Ronnie Bondurant had been arrested along with six or seven other men in what the newspaper described as bar brawls, both times at The Candy Store, a strip joint on U.S. 19. One of the men arrested with Bondurant had a name Truman recognized: Bradley "Junior" Stegall.

Stegall had been a defense witness at a drug trial Truman had covered in the 1980s. He was a very small-time doper who always seemed to wriggle off the hook. Junior Stegall had turned an otherwise boring trial into a lowlife situation comedy with his South Georgia twang and his protestation that the defendant could not have been off-loading a sixty-five-foot shrimp boat full of Colombian gold as the state charged because he was with him, Junior Stegall, at a whorehouse down in Bradenton at the time the incident allegedly took place.

Truman had halfway mourned the news when he heard years later that Stegall had been found knifed to death in a cow pasture in Arcadia. So few small-time hoods were memorable these days.

Truman had logged off the computer and was ready to leave when he spotted the sign by the door saying that the computer files only went back as far as 1980.

He wandered down the aisles of clip envelopes, his nose twitching from the smell of dust and old newsprint. He found Bondurant, Ronnie, wedged between a long row of thick envelopes for Bond, Julian.

Bondurant, Ronnie, had three crumbling clips in his file. In 1973, Bondurant had been picked up in a drug bust at a motorcycle repair shop where he worked as the manager. Two other employees,

William D. Weems and a Keith Peters, had been charged with single counts of possession of marijuana. But they'd found a set of scales and a ten-pound block of marijuana in the trunk of Bondurant's car. He was charged with possession with intent to distribute.

There had been a hue and cry back then, because the cycle shop was across the street from a high school, and parents complained that Bondurant was corrupting young minds.

The two subsequent clips detailed Bondurant's plea bargain. He pleaded guilty, closed the shop, and was sentenced to eight months at the county work farm.

Truman photocopied the clips, thanked the librarian, and left.

He waved to Stanley on his way out of the lobby. "See you later, old-timer."

CHAPTER

TWELVE

As usual, he felt a sharp pang of longing leaving the newspaper building. Separation anxiety, Nellie called it. He missed being a part of daily journalism, the busyness of it all, the smug look on the faces of reporters and editors who knew today about the inner workings of tomorrow's news. No matter how much freelancing he did, he was now an outsider, a dabbler. His press credentials were outdated and so were most of his contacts.

He started to walk back to the Fountain of Youth. The relentless blue of the sky overhead had a gray tinge to it. Were they in for an early morning storm? Fine. Anything to break up the sameness of August.

Boredom was not an emotion he had ever been acquainted with until Nellie died. When she was alive, his life seemed to buzz with activity. His Nellie was a planner, a schemer, a doer. And he'd been a willing accomplice through the years. Now she was gone. The house was sold, and time seemed to be the one commodity he had to spare.

When he got to the hotel, he kept going. He had no particular destination in mind, he just needed to think.

As he walked he thought about Ronnie Bondurant and his unimpressive criminal career. Murder was a big step up from bar brawls and nickel-and-dime drug dealing. And how did car theft fit into the picture? He needed to know more about Bondurant than the *St. Pete Times*'s old clippings. He needed a police source.

But who? His most recent dealings with local cops hadn't been pleasant, especially last year, after he'd revealed the involvement of a St. Pete uniformed officer in a murder scheme.

Clyde Guthrie came to mind. He was retired from the FDLE, the Florida Department of Law Enforcement. Truman hadn't known him well, because Guthrie had been based out of the FDLE's Orlando office, but Guthrie came into the El Cap now and again, and they'd swapped war stories.

Chet's Newsstand was only a block away. There was a slight breeze now, and the clouds were black-tinged and bulging.

"Hi, partner," Ollie said. He was lifting stacks of magazines off a pallet, counting and sorting them. "You on the case?"

"Sort of," Truman said. "Okay if I use your phone?"

"Any time," Ollie said magnanimously. "As long as it's not long distance. You know how management is."

He called Frankie at the El Cap. Frankie knew everything about everybody.

"Guthrie?" Frankie said. "Yeah. I know the guy.

He lives on a boat. Tied up at a slip over on Coffeepot Bayou. Let me think. He told me the name of that boat one time. Kind of a cop joke, I think."

Frankie chuckled. "Now I remember. *Saturday Night Special*. Good one, huh?"

"I get off at three today," Ollie said, eavesdropping on Truman's conversation with Frankie. "This guy's former FDLE, huh? You think he can help us get the goods on this Bondurant?"

"He might know something," Truman said, not wanting to make a big deal out of it. "I'll let you know."

Coffeepot Bayou was too far to walk in this heat. He went back to the hotel and got the Nova. It was still parked where he'd left it. He patted its fender affectionately.

As he pulled up to the dock, he felt a drop of water on the arm he rested on the open window. He glanced upward. Black-tinged thunderheads had rolled in front of the sun. The breeze off the bay ruffled the hair on his arms.

It was early for rain yet. These hot August days when it was ninety-eight degrees by noon, they got rain most days, around six o'clock. But it was just noon now.

He pulled the station wagon into the crushed-shell parking lot. The little muncipal dock was a far cry from the one downtown, at the St. Pete Yacht Club, where rich people parked their water toys. This one consisted of just one long dock sticking out into the bay, with four rows of slips radiating out from it. There was a small dockmaster's shack housing gas pumps, bathrooms, and an office. Maybe two dozen boats were tied up, none of them bigger than thirty feet. One of them should be the *Saturday Night Special*.

The rain started coming down hard, and thunder rumbled overhead. The wind blew the rain sideways, and it streamed in through the open car windows.

Truman rolled the windows up, leaving an inch at the top for ventilation, then he settled back in his seat to wait. The storm would blow through in fifteen or twenty minutes. It always did.

But the air in the Nova was hot and sticky. A mosquito lit on his arm and Truman swatted at it, leaving a red-and-black smear on his forearm.

There was a shelter at the end of the main dock. Nothing more than a couple of benches with a table and a spigot where you could clean fish. Still, it had a roof and it was better than sitting in the car suffocating.

He made a run for it, carrying his shoes in his hands, dashing barefoot through the clamshell parking lot toward the end of the dock.

By the time he made it to the shelter, his clothes were soaked and his wet hair was plastered to his head. He sank gratefully down onto one of the benches, breathing hard from the sudden burst of exercise.

This was good, he realized suddenly. He was outside, on the water, soaked to the skin. Not shut up inside his tiny, sweltering hotel room, idly reading the newspaper, glancing at his watch to see if it was time to eat a meal or wash his clothes or take a walk.

The rain made steady plinking sounds on the surface of the bay. A pelican came flapping up to rest on a half-submerged piling beside the boathouse. Truman wriggled his toes on the warm wooden planks of the dock and resolved to go barefoot more often.

"Hey!"

Truman looked up, startled to realize that someone else was out in the storm.

The voice was coming from the deck of a sailboat tied up at the next slip over.

The speaker had his bald head stuck out from the sailboat's tiny cabin door.

"Don't I know you from the El Cap? Truman something?"

Truman took a good look at the sailboat. It was a sloop, maybe twenty-two feet long. An old wooden number with a fresh-painted dark-green hull. *Saturday Night Special* was the name lettered in gold paint on the stern. "St. Petersburg, Fla." He'd found Clyde Guthrie.

Guthrie came back out on deck, holding up a can of beer.

"Happy hour," he said. "Frankie called, said you'd been asking about me."

The rain had slacked off some, to a light drizzle. Truman pulled on the stern rope of the sailboat to bring it closer to the dock. Then he climbed aboard.

His host was standing in the door of the cabin, waving him inside. He was of medium height, beef gone to fat, with pale blue eyes and a ruddy, sunburned complexion.

The cabin was small but tidy, with two bunks built into one wall and a minuscule galley kitchen built onto the other. At the V of the hull, there was a hatch. Probably leads to the head and storage, Truman thought. Built into the wall near the galley was a drop-down wooden table. Two old wooden chairs were drawn up to the table, which held a bowl of peanuts and two cans of beer.

"Frankie says you still do some reporting," Guthrie said, handing Truman one of the beers. "That's the bad thing about law enforcement. You're either in it or out. And I'm too fat and too old to do that security shit some of the guys get into. Sit down. Tell me something I don't already know."

Truman sat down, conscious of his wet clothes. He took a sip of his beer. It was ice-cold, maybe the coldest beer he'd ever had.

Guthrie took a handful of peanuts and tossed them in his mouth, followed by a long pull on his beer.

Truman took a handful of nuts, too, and munched silently.

"You live downtown somewhere?" Guthrie asked.

"Yeah," Truman said. "I used to live over on the south side. I moved into a residential hotel downtown, right after I lost my wife last year."

Guthrie gave him a quick nod of sympathy.

"Never married myself. I sold the condo in Orlando after I got out. I've been living on board here off and on since January. But I been thinking about getting a bigger rig, so I can do some deepwater sailing."

"You were with the state a long time, weren't you?" Truman asked. "Going back to the beginning, I heard."

"Way back," Guthrie said. "I joined the FDLE back in the sixties, right when Claude Kirk put the agency together."

"Right after that flap with the Wackenhuts?" Truman asked. "Old Claude Kirk. Gave 'em fits up there in Tallahassee, didn't he?"

A lifelong Democrat, Truman had viewed Kirk, Florida's first Republican governor since Reconstruction, with a mixture of alarm, amusement, and disgust. Kirk had been flamboyant, autocratic. He'd decided the state should have its own police force, and hired Wackenhut detectives to man his fledgling Florida Department of Law Enforcement. Kirk had served only one term before Florida's voters had returned to the safe, brown-shoe type of Democrat they were used to.

While the rain beat lightly on the deck of the sailboat, they played who-do-you-know, Truman waiting for the right moment to turn the conversation toward Ronnie Bondurant. Truman knew someone he knew, Guthrie knew some of Truman's former colleagues. They discovered that Guthrie had worked a sensational kidnap-murder case in Sebring in the early seventies—a case Truman had covered.

Guthrie got up and got a second beer and held one up for Truman.

Truman looked out the porthole. The rain had stopped and the sun was back out.

"Better not," he said reluctantly. "If I have another beer in this heat, I won't be good for a durned thing."

"Yeah," Clyde said. "A boat's a hell of a lot of work." He shrugged. "But what else have I got to do with my time. Right? Anyway, you wanted to ask me something. Go ahead."

The sky was a brilliant blue. The rain clouds had blown off to the east somewhere, and Guthrie was getting fidgety.

"I'm interested in a guy named Ronnie Bondurant," Truman said. "He's local talent. I know you mostly worked in Orlando, but I wondered if you ever had any contact with the FDLE guys over here on the east coast, somebody who might know something about him."

Guthrie grinned. "I play poker with the Tampa crew every Tuesday night. The agent in charge over there is an old running buddy of mine."

"Is that so?" Truman said.

"Getting stuffy in here," Guthrie said. "Let's go up on deck. Rain ought to have cooled things off a little."

They pulled some lawn chairs out on the deck and Clyde gave Truman an insulated foam holder for his beer. It was blue with a gold seal. "FDLE."

Truman told Guthrie the whole story, including the part about his visit to Jeff Cantrell's landlady and the old clip files he'd found on Ronnie Bondurant. Guthrie listened without making any comment until Truman was done.

"Bondurant," Guthrie said, sipping his beer. "Now that's a name I know from somewhere."

"It's that big used-car lot up on U.S. 19," Truman said. "It's got a revolving '57 pink Caddie on the roof. Kind of a landmark, you might say."

"I know the place, but I'm thinking of another Bondurant, maybe. I knew about a case with a Bondurant once."

"Here in St. Pete?"

"No, I'm thinking this Bondurant was down around Broward County. Fort Lauderdale, maybe. Seems like it was a fella whose name started with an 'L.' Lawton. Lawson. Something unusual like that."

Guthrie scratched his belly as he contemplated. It was a sizeable appendage, that belly. It lapped over his faded, paint-spattered blue jeans, and made a handy shelf for Guthrie's beer.

"Oh, yeah," he said slowly. "Can't get the name, but the rest is coming back. This other Bondurant, he sold cars, too. Had a little lot down there on Dixie Highway. And he had a little twenty-year-old girl-friend, too, who up and disappeared one day."

"Murdered?" Truman's fingertips were tingling.

Guthrie shrugged. "That's what everybody figured. The Broward sheriff's office brought our folks in. We worked it for a long time, two years, maybe. Never could find that girl. No body, nothing."

"Two Bondurants in the used-car racket, two people who disappear," Truman said. "Kind of funny."

"Unless you're one of the ones who disappeared," Guthrie pointed out. "Wasn't my case. Another fella in our office worked it, but I remember this much because it had him stymied. Frustrated."

Truman took a last swallow of beer. He never drank the last inch or so in a can. He couldn't stomach beer that had gotten the least little bit warm.

"Tell you what, Kicklighter," Guthrie said. "You've got me curious now. I'm gonna call over to Tampa and get one of those computer jockeys over there to do some checking around. Ronnie Bondurant, you said. Right?"

Truman nodded.

"I'll let you know if anything turns up. That sound all right?"

"Sounds fine," Truman said, standing up to go. "You want my phone number?"

"Nah," Guthrie said, holding out his hand to shake on the deal. "You're in the book, right? How many Kicklighters could there be?"

CHAPTER

THIRTEEN

IT HAD BEEN A LONG NIGHT. WORMY HAD DONE what he always did. He had taken care of business.

Ronnie was on the phone when Wormy walked into the private office with his cardboard cup of 7–Eleven coffee.

"Yeah. It's all taken care of," Ronnie said. "I told you, Boone, you're not dealing with amateurs. Yeah. He's right here."

Wormy flipped a bird at the phone.

Ronnie shook his head like he agreed. Hernando Boone was a pain in the ass. But he had to be dealt with.

"Yeah," Ronnie was saying. "Wormy took care of it. He's a pro. I'll let you know. Gotta run."

Ronnie put the phone back in its cradle and kneaded the bridge of his nose with his fingertips, like he could rub away the memory of Hernando Boone.

"Boone wants to partner with us on some deals," he said, looking up at Wormy.

"What do we need him for?" Wormy demanded. "We got a thing of our own, don't we? We're doing good without that asshole."

"Good, but we could be doing better. Boone can give us volume. He's a psycho, but he's a psycho with cash. He works with us, we can run deals in other states. Georgia. Alabama. South Carolina. I'm checking with some people I know in Mississippi. It's wide open. Car titles, all that shit."

"What about Doc?" Wormy wanted to know. He didn't trust this big steroid-addled, ex-jock buddy of Ronnie's. That was the trouble with Ronnie. A Napoleon complex, was that what it was? Like a lot of short guys Wormy had known, Ronnie thought anybody who played sports was a god.

"I thought Doc was gonna help us with all this stuff," Wormy said. "Get us more into personal-injury stuff. That's where the money is, Doc says."

"He says," Ronnie said dryly. "Doc says a lot of stuff. But his ex-wife is squeezing his balls right now. She wants the house, the cars, the boat. Everything. He's distracted. So I'm saying maybe we consider another kind of partnership."

"Consider," Wormy repeated. "But it's not a done deal."

"Not at all," Ronnie said soothingly.

The front door to the office opened then, and a bell pealed softly to let them know they weren't alone. They heard the tap of heels on the tile floor in the outer office.

"Hello?" It was a woman's voice. Soft, tentative. "Jeff?"

Ronnie was halfway out of his chair before she got to the door of his office.

"Yoo-hoo. Anybody home?" she called playfully. The door opened.

Ronnie froze.

The woman in the doorway had a way of doing that. To men, anyway. She entered a room and men stood there, quietly, their eyes dilating, their breathing irregular, like deer caught in a set of headlights.

Her hair was what they noticed first. It was a shining blue-black curtain that fell past her hips.

After the hair, they noticed the body. How could you not? She was tall, narrow through the hips and shoulders, but with the most magnificent set of breasts Ronnie and Wormy had ever had the privilege to stare at. Her legs were nice, a little skinny, but nothing to complain about.

She was dressed in a simple white T-shirt, black denim shorts, and high-heeled white sandals. Her hand kept going up to her hair, to touch it, flick a strand out of her eyes. Her face was pretty, regular features, slightly Asian eyes with thick, fluttery black lashes. A little too much makeup for a nice girl.

"Who are you?" Ronnie was bewitched.

"I'm looking for Jeff Cantrell," the woman said. She looked from Ronnie to Wormy.

"Isn't he working today?" Now she was beginning to sense that something was wrong. She took a step backward, shook her hair back over her shoulders. "Just ask him to call me. LeeAnn. Okay?"

Ronnie cleared his throat and turned on the charm full throttle.

"LeeAnn? Is it about a car? Because if it's about a car, I'm the man you need to see. I'm Ronnie Bondurant. President of Bondurant Motors. Jeff's boss."

"I have a car," she said. "Jeff sold it to me. This is personal."

"We can be personal," Ronnie said, winking.

"Very personal," Wormy agreed.

LeeAnn backed away a little bit toward the door. These guys were making her nervous. Where was Jeff?

"Never mind. I'll catch him at home," she said.

Ronnie followed her as she retreated quickly toward the parking lot.

"Listen, LeeAnn," he said urgently. "I'm surprised Jeff didn't mention this to you. He quit yesterday. Went over to the east coast 'cause he had a job over there. He didn't tell you he was leaving? Some friend, huh?"

"What are you talking about?" she asked, her eyes narrowing. "I talked to Jeff yesterday. He was right here, right on this car lot. He never said anything about another job."

"What a jerk," Ronnie said sympathetically. "Afraid of committment. That was Jeff. Am I right?"

"No," she said. "Jeff wouldn't have left town without telling me. Where did you say he went?"

Ronnie shrugged. "Lauderdale, maybe? He knew I was pissed at him for leaving me in the lurch like that."

LeeAnn's hands were shaking as she got her car keys out of her purse. Had Jeff dumped her?

Ronnie put his hand over hers. "Give me your number, okay? If he calls, I'll tell him you're looking for him."

She hesitated, then took a scrap of paper out of her purse, wrote down her phone number, and handed it over.

Ronnie gave her another wink. "You might be getting lonely, with Jeff out of town. Might want some company."

The hairs on the back of her neck started to prickle. "I have a cat," she said quickly.

Wormy stood in the doorway of the office and watched Ronnie put the moves on Jeff's girlfriend. He had a bad feeling. Cantrell had never said anything about a chick. He'd hit on every woman who walked onto the lot, young, old, fat, ugly. Who knew he had a girlfriend? Especially a knockout like this one.

Ronnie waved the slip of paper at him when he came back in. "I'm gonna get me some of that," he said happily.

"What if she keeps asking questions about where Cantrell went?" Wormy asked.

"Once she gets a dose of Ronnie Bondurant, she ain't gonna be asking for nothing but more," Ronnie said and laughed. "You leave that to me, buddy."

Wormy followed Ronnie back into his office.

"We got an operation to run this morning," Ronnie reminded Wormy. "I got the monkey all lined up. How about you? Where's that Corvette at?"

"What?" Wormy said, his voice rising. "We can't put that car back on the road, Ronnie. What if that black chick sees it? What if she does get the cops to come back here and sniff around some more?"

Ronnie waved away his protests. "Don't worry about that little old colored girl. She ain't gonna see nothing. So let's get to it, huh?"

"No way, man," Wormy said. "We talked about this, Ronnie. I thought Joe was gonna take care of cutting the cars up. You said no more wrecks. Let Joe cut 'em up. We just use the monkeys to file the claims."

"Yeah, that was the plan," Ronnie agreed. "But this thing with Jeff, it changes everything. We're behind schedule. Joe's backed up with work. Besides, it's a matter of economics. If Joe cuts the car up, then solders it back together, I gotta pay him twice. That's a mess of money. Now, if we keep letting the monkeys do the job, hell, it's a lot cheaper. These sons of bitches are so stupid, some of them would do it for free. They just like banging up cars. Hell, maybe we should start charging them to get in on the fun. Whattya think?"

"I think it's fucked," Wormy said loudly.

The front door opened and the bell pealed softly again.

An elderly black man with stooped shoulders tapped lightly at Ronnie's office door, came in, and nodded politely at the two men. He was dressed in white overalls, with a paint can in one hand and a large plastic bucket of supplies in the other.

"How ya' doin', Al?" Ronnie said. "That Bonneville still running good?"

"Nosuh," Al said forlornly. "She got a dead battery."

"Get this mess cleaned up, and then Wormy'll see about it," Ronnie said.

"Awright," Al said. He got out a can of spackle and started applying it to the bullet holes left from Hernando Boone's shooting spree. Al had worked for Ronnie's old man. Now he worked for Ronnie in exchange for Ronnie letting him drive the biggest gas-eater on the lot. There was nothing Ronnie wouldn't talk about in front of Al. It was like the old guy was invisible.

Ronnie pulled a sheaf of papers out of his desk drawer and handed them to Wormy. "Here's the name of the insurance company," he said, all business. "You gonna take care of this or not?"

They both knew Wormy would take care of it.

"Billy's gonna do the job today," Ronnie said. "Just get the car and meet him over at Joe's. Get going. I want that check today."

Wormy shrugged and rolled his eyes to let Ronnie know he was pissed off about having to deal with the monkeys and these bogus car wrecks.

"How'd that thing with Jeff work out?" Ronnie asked casually.

Al was smoothing spackle over the holes in the wall, humming softly to himself, the putty knife making smooth, slurping sounds against the concrete.

"It's taken care of," Wormy said simply.

"He get that back rent paid?" Ronnie asked.

"All set. Cash. Like you said."

"Excellent."

Ronnie picked up the morning paper and started reading a story about the crisis in health care costs. He was always interested in national affairs. As a businessman, he had to keep on top of things.

Wormy started to leave again. He had no time to read the newspaper.

"So," Ronnie called out. "You'd say we won't be hearing from Jeff again? And he's definitely left the premises?"

"You want me to tell you where he is?" Wormy asked nastily, losing patience with the game.

"Absolutely not," Ronnie said hastily. "If you say it's taken care of, then it's taken care of."

"He is," Wormy said. Then he left.

◆　　◆　　◆

The monkey drove the liver-colored Pinto slowly into position behind the red Corvette.

They'd taken the cars out in back of Joe's shop for convenience and privacy. The garage had a six-foot-tall board fence running around it. Kept out the nosy neighbors. Ronnie called the proprietor Joe. But his real name, which was posted in Cambodian on the business license tacked up near the garage door, was Xiang Huang Vu. Everyone who worked for Joe seemed to be a cousin of some sorts. Nobody seemed to speak much English. Communication was effected with pointing, gesturing, and large amounts of cash currency.

Wormy leaned up against the wall and watched while the monkey revved the engine of the Pinto, impatient to get started. As always, he wondered where Ronnie found his endless supply of people whose job skills were this negligible.

"Do it," Wormy said loudly. The monkey stomped on the accelerator, the Pinto's engine raced, and the car shot forward, its tires digging into the crushed-shell pavement. At the last minute, the monkey slammed on the brakes, right before the Pinto slammed into the rear of the Corvette, knocking it forward and then spinning it sideways until the front of the 'Vette was smashed up against Joe's corrugated metal fence, pinning Wormy between the fence and the 'Vette.

It felt as though he'd been cut in half directly above the knees. A knife blade of searing pain jabbed into the base of his spine as he fell forward onto the hood of the 'Vette.

"Goddamn!" Wormy roared. The son of a bitch had done it deliberately. For a moment, he thought he'd pass out, the pain was so bad.

"Get it off me," Wormy screamed. "For Christ's sake get me out of here."

The Pinto's motor abruptly cut off. Now the driver was pulling open the door of the Corvette, trying to start it. The 'Vette's engine coughed and then died. "It won't start," the kid called out. "I'll have to put it in neutral and push it.

"Hold on, Wormy," the kid said, grunting as he pushed against the car. A moment later, the Corvette was off him and Wormy was hunched over on the ground, the pain so bad he thought he'd puke.

"Fuckin' A, Wormy," the kid said, standing over him uneasily. "I didn't mean to hit you, man. It was, like, an accident. You ain't really hurt too bad, are you?"

"Asshole." Wormy had to clench his teeth shut to keep from screaming, that's how bad the pain was. The kid offered him a hand, to help pull him up. Wormy slapped at it, rolled away, grimaced, and managed to stagger to his feet before sinking into the front seat of the ruined 'Vette.

Shit. He felt like he'd been knee-capped. His black slacks were ripped across both thighs and his back hurt like a son of a bitch. He'd have to go see Doc, get some of those pocket rockets. The Demerol was good stuff, but he had to be careful how he took it or he'd puke his guts up. He was messed up bad this time.

"Hey, Wormy," the monkey said, dancing from foot to foot like he had St. Vitus's dance or something. "You're bleeding, man. Won't it make Ronnie mad if you bleed in the 'Vette?"

Yeah, blood in the 'Vette, Wormy thought. Almost as bad as a body with a bullet in the head.

Wormy had to grasp the door frame with both

hands to extricate himself from the 'Vette. His head was throbbing and he felt blood trickling down the bridge of his nose from where he'd bounced off the 'Vette's hood. The nose was probably broken. He was getting too old for this shit.

But he wouldn't say a word about his pain to the monkey. Let 'em see you were hurting, they might think you were vulnerable. A searing pain shot down the front of his right leg. With supreme effort he walked stiffly around to the back of the red Corvette to have a look. He'd already seen the front of the car, at a much closer vantage point than was necessary.

The whole rear of the 'Vette was accordion-folded inward. The ground was littered with tiny plastic rubies and glass diamonds from the shattered tail and brake lights and the Pinto's front bumper had made jagged tears in the 'Vette's red-fiberglass rear panel.

He turned to the monkey. "What's your name?"

The kid's face fell. His eyes were set so far apart they were closer to his ears than his nose. His face was the color of a fish's belly. There was not an iota of intelligence there. Where the hell did Ronnie get these people?

"It's Billy, man. I told you ten times already. Billy Tripp. We done two jobs together, Wormy. Last time I had that old sucky Taurus wagon. Remember?"

"Yeah, I remember," Wormy said. He pulled a handkerchief out of his pocket and dabbed at the cut on his nose. He remembered Billy because the Taurus job was the one that had sent the piece of glass flying that opened up the cut on his nose in the first place. It hadn't even had time to heal.

Wormy limped back to the Corvette. No way it was drivable now. Not with the front like this. The wheel wells were too crumpled. He'd have to get Joe to fix up the front end some before he took it to the drive-through claims window.

"You know what to do, asshole?" he asked the monkey.

"Shit, yeah," the monkey said. "Think I'm stupid?" He reached into the Pinto, pulled out an open beer car, and took a long swig.

Yes, Wormy thought. Yes. I think anyone with a shaved head and a nose ring probably qualifies as stupid. "Tell me what you're supposed to do," Wormy demanded.

The kid took another long swig of beer. The nose ring clinked against the side of the aluminum can.

"I call up the insurance agent." Billy Tripp pulled a filthy scrap of paper from the pocket of his cutoff jeans. "Ed Zuniga. Hartford. Office is out in Gulfport. I tell him I was out on Eighty-sixth Street, where they got all that construction going on. I got confused 'cause of all the signs, ran a stop sign, and rear-ended an old dude in a red Corvette."

"Funny," Wormy said.

Billy grinned. "Fucked the dude's car up bad. But I want to make it right."

"You give him my phone number," Wormy coached. "Tell him I'm pissed off. Threatening to sue. You got the registration papers, the policy numbers, all the stuff Ronnie gave you?"

The monkey nodded rapidly. "I ain't stupid, man. It's all in the glove box."

"Get out of here," Wormy said. "There's a pay phone at a gas station up the road. Call from there."

The monkey nodded again, and got in the Pinto.

"Hey, Wormy," he said, getting out quickly.

"When do I get my money? Ronnie said I could maybe get seven hundred dollars this time. He, like, promised."

"Soon as I get the check and it clears," Wormy said. "I'll let you know."

"Outtasight," Billy Tripp said, waving good-bye.

"See you in hell," Wormy muttered.

CHAPTER

FOURTEEN

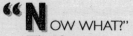OW WHAT?"

The first six months after Nellie died, Truman had felt stupid talking to himself. He'd seen too many slump-shouldered old codgers roaming the streets of St. Petersburg, stomping and muttering to themselves.

Then he got over it. Now he talked to himself whenever he felt like it. Just not on the streets usually.

But these streets were clogged with traffic. Cars were everywhere. People poured out of the cars with baskets and coolers in their arms. The street in front of the Fountain of Youth was a solid line of parked cars. It was nearly six. Downtown should have been deserted by now. Something must be going on in the park.

Truman finally found a place to park the Nova, around the corner from Chet's.

By the time he walked into the hotel lobby, he was in a mood all right. Stomping and muttering like a geezer's grandpa.

"Hey, Grandpa!"

It was Chip. He jumped out of the armchair he'd been sitting in and rushed over and gave his grandfather a hug.

Truman forgot that he was hot and tired and annoyed as hell. The boy was nine now. Pretty soon he'd swear off hugs, fishing with his grandpa, and sneaking off to watch PG-13 movies with an old man.

"We're gonna have a picnic in Williams Park," Chip said. He waved toward the group sitting by the television set. "Ollie and Jackie said they'd come, too. We got fried chicken and Cokes and all kinds of junk."

"How about it, Pop?" Cheryl asked. "It's the Temptations and the Drifters. Oldies. You'll like it, I promise."

Cheryl was wearing a yellow cotton sundress, and she'd pinned her hair up on top of her head. She looked like a teenager. She looked like her mother.

"Too hot for a picnic," Truman groused.

"Don't be such an old crank," Jackie said, coming over to them. "I got some icebox cake I saved back from lunch, and Ollie, he brought a twelve-pack of cold beer. Come on, Mr. K. It'll be fun. Maybe I'll even let you dance with me if you act nice."

"Please, Grandpa." Chip pressed his hands together in front of his face, prayerlike. He was as brown as a berry, new freckles sprinkled across his nose, and his crew cut was sun-bleached a golden white.

In the end, he let himself be talked into it. They set up their picnic under a live oak. Williams Park was a sea of people, dogs, baby strollers, and coolers.

Right at dusk, they switched on the lights in the old bandshell and the huge speakers crackled alive.

A tall, skinny, drink of water in a Hawaiian shirt bounded out onto the stage, and then the first act came on.

To be honest, Truman couldn't tell one band from the other. Aging black men, well, maybe they were in their late fifties, sweated in their splendid sequined tuxes, executing marvelously smooth dance steps. Good, tight harmony, Truman grudgingly admitted.

One of the groups sang a song about meeting a lover under the boardwalk, with the sounds of a carousel and the smell of hot dogs and french fries all around.

Jackie pulled Chip to his feet and tried to show him how to dance.

"White boys," she said, acting exasperated, but laughing and giving it away. She took one of his hands and placed it on the small of her back and held his other in hers. Chip was blushing under his sunburn, but he managed to move his feet to the music after a few bars, and around them, everybody seemed to know the song, singing the lyrics out loud.

Cheryl brought him a beer and sat down beside her father.

"Remember the summer you took us to Myrtle Beach, Pop? I had my first two-piece bathing suit. We had the new car. A Fury, I remember. And we played putt-putt every night and went to a pancake house for dinner."

"You made your mother and me crazy," Truman reminded her. "You were boy crazy."

Cheryl smiled dreamily. "Not really. But I did kiss a boy at Myrtle Beach. His name was Bo and he was from Due West, South Carolina. Bet you didn't know about that, Pop."

"You'd be surprised what I knew back then," Truman told her.

She leaned back on her elbows for a minute, singing along to another song that everybody but Truman seemed to know by heart.

"Hey, Mr. K," Jackie said, rejoining them on the blanket when the band took a break. "There's a lady over there waving at you and calling your name. That your girlfriend?"

"Where?" Truman said, searching the crowd for a familiar face.

"What girlfriend?" Cheryl asked.

Margaret McCutcheon was seated on a folding lawn chair beside some women Truman didn't recognize. When she caught his eye, she waved again.

He got up and walked over to her.

"Hello there," he said, feeling suddenly shy. He could feel the other women staring at him, wondering who he was and whether he was trying to pick up their friend. He didn't know whether to keep standing, or sit down on the grass beside her. "Enjoying the music?"

"It's wonderful," Margaret said. "Is that your family with you?"

"That's Cheryl in the yellow dress, and my grandson, Chip, and that's Ollie, and my friend Jackie."

"Nice." Margaret turned toward her friends, who were indeed watching and listening to her conversation with Truman. "Girls, this is Truman Kicklighter. From my Great Books group. He's a writer himself. And a real lover of literature," she added impishly.

Margaret introduced him to the women, whose names he instantly forgot. The loudspeakers whined, and then a new band ran onto the stage. "You'd better go back to your family," she said, seeing his awkwardness and liking it that he was so vulnerable.

"That's right," he said gratefully. "We're going to have lunch, aren't we?"

"Whenever you say," Margaret said.

He was humming by the time he got back to the blanket. Something about seeing somebody in September. He stopped when he saw that Cheryl and Jackie were watching him and laughing like a couple of loons.

"That was Margaret," he said, ignoring their childishness. "A friend of mine."

"I see that," Cheryl said teasingly. "When do I get to meet her?"

"Sometime," Truman said. "She's a very interesting woman. Sails boats. Likes baseball."

"Where's Chip?" Cheryl asked suddenly. She sprang to her feet. "He was right here a minute ago." She swung around in a circle, calling him. "Chip! Chip!" The teenager was gone, a frantic mother in her place.

Jackie tugged at the hem of Cheryl's skirt. "Ollie took him to get a popsicle from the ice cream man," she said, pointing. "He's right over there. See?"

Cheryl walked a little way aways, searching the crowd until she saw them, a little boy and a little man, standing beside an umbrella-shaded ice cream vendor.

"Oh." She sat back down on the quilt. "It's just that there are so many people here. And it's getting dark. You know how he wanders off."

Jackie and Truman nodded. A year ago, Chip had been kidnapped. It was Truman's fault. He and Jackie had gone after the boy—and nearly gotten them all killed in the process. Cheryl had earned the right to be overprotective.

When they got back from the ice cream man, Cheryl hugged her son for a long time, swaying to the music until Chip managed to squirm out of her grip.

Ollie sat down in a folding beach chair beside Truman.

Jackie came over and flopped down on the grass between them.

"Must be a hundred degrees at least tonight," she said, fanning herself with a paper plate.

She lowered her voice and turned big, sad brown eyes on Truman. "I noticed you missed lunch today. Did you find out anything about that jackleg murdering thief Ronnie Bondurant?"

"I talked to some people," Truman said.

He told them both about the newspaper files, and going over to Jeff Cantrell's apartment, and how the landlady was under the impression that her tenant had moved. Then he told them about meeting Clyde Guthrie, the retired FDLE man.

"I knew it," Jackie said, slapping her thigh. "Now we're getting somewhere. We need to go back over to that car lot, watch them, see if they'll lead us to my car. And the body," she added.

"Run surveillance," Ollie agreed. "That's what private investigators do. We did okay the other night, right?"

"This Bondurant character has a criminal record," Truman said. "And he knows both of you. Especially you, Jackie. You go anywhere near the place and he'll spot you. We know he's violent."

"I'll wear a disguise," Jackie said. "Go in there acting like I want to buy a car off him. Then, Truman, you go sneaking in the back and search the place."

"Forget it," Truman said. He reached into the

cooler, got himself a cold beer, and took a long swig. "I've got an idea."

By the next morning, he'd begun to have doubts.

"Damn fool idea. Probably won't let you near the place. Old fool."

He went on like this through his sit-ups and deep-knee bends and jumping jacks. He should run in place, Truman thought, but it was too durn hot. He was already drenched with sweat, gasping for breath.

After his shower, he put some thought into his wardrobe. Casual, but smart. He reached up on the closet shelf and took down the turquoise knit golf shirt Cheryl had given him for Father's Day. It still had the store's tags hanging from the sleeve. His khaki slacks were fine with it. He added a shiny new pair of Nike tennis shoes, last year's Father's Day gift. He looked pretty good.

When he got downstairs to the lobby, Jackie was standing there, dressed in her waitress uniform, talking to somebody he didn't recognize. She was glancing around, watching to see that Mr. Wiggins, the manager, didn't catch her standing around like that.

"Uh, Mr. K, this gentleman came in a little while ago, looking for you. He was asking in the dining room, and I told him I knew you."

The stranger was slim, with steel-gray hair, a trim mustache, and silver-framed aviator-type sunglasses. Maybe forty-five to fifty. Truman made him for a cop right away.

"Ed Weingarten," the other man said, extending his hand to shake. "Can we go somewhere and talk?"

"Right over here," Truman said, motioning toward the wicker armchairs near the window.

Weingarten sat on the edge of the chair, his back very erect. "I understand you used to be a reporter," he said.

"And I figure you're some kind of cop," Truman replied. "Who do you work for?"

"Florida Department of Law Enforcement, white-collar crime division," Weingarten said. He took out a business card and handed it to Truman. "Clyde Guthrie tells me you were asking around about Ronnie Bondurant and his associates."

"That's right," Truman said. "You know why I'm interested in Bondurant. He ripped off that young lady you just talked to. Sold her a lemon, then stole it back. She went looking for the car and found a body instead. The young salesman who sold her the car. Murdered. I know the FDLE doesn't usually get involved in homicides, so I'm kind of surprised you folks are interested in a nickel-and-dime bum like Ronnie Bondurant."

Weingarten took off his sunglasses, folded them, and put them in his breast pocket.

"This is a white-collar crime matter. We've been watching Ronnie for some time now. Clyde Guthrie said he mentioned the unsolved homicide over in Sebring to you? We believe the old man, Lawson Bondurant, did it, but his son, Ronnie, probably had a hand in it, too. The father seems to be dead. Now Ronnie's running some kind of operation out of that car lot. We've got a man working it. Damn liberal judges over here won't approve a wiretap. But Ronnie's been seen in the company of an individual named Hernando Boone. Maybe you've seen this person, half black, half Miccosukee Indian? What our folks call a badass, if you'll excuse the expression."

"I've heard the expression," Truman said dryly. "The young lady mentioned seeing somebody like that at the car lot, right before she found Jeff Cantrell's body."

"Boone deals in stolen meat, drugs, whatever turns a profit," Weingarten said. "Word is, he killed an Ethiopian who tried to steal from him. We've got no witnesses, of course. If Boone and Bondurant are socializing together, it means they're both planning to move up in the world."

"One of them killed that car salesman. Name's Jeff Cantrell," Truman said.

"Guthrie told me about that and we looked into it. Nobody has reported Jeff Cantrell as missing. We got a tip from the St. Pete cops about that call over to the car lot the other night," Weingarten said. "Officer searched the place, found nothing."

"Jackie and Ollie are the ones who called the cops in the first place," Truman pointed out. "By the time those jokers got there, Bondurant had moved the body."

"I need to talk to your young friend," Weingarten said. "I'll get to her next. We need to get a description of who was on the scene that night."

"Bondurant and one of his people. Older guy who works for him," Truman volunteered.

"Sounds like our friend Wormy."

"Wormy?"

"William D. Weems. He's Bondurant's sidekick. He used to work for Bondurant's old man. Now he's Ronnie's associate. If Bondurant's working an angle, Wormy's the one doing the dirty work," Weingarten said.

"I saw Weems's name in an old story about one of Bondurant's arrests," Truman said. "Didn't know his name was Wormy."

Weingarten frowned. "Those folks know who you are?"

"They don't know me from Adam's housecat," Truman said. "That's my advantage."

Weingarten looked up sharply. "What advantage?"

"I aim to find out what those crooks are up to," Truman said. He told Weingarten what he had in mind.

The FDLE agent looked amused. "Now, you don't want to go and do that," he said. "These folks are into something heavy, Mr. Kicklighter. Hernando Boone is a player. And if you're right—if he did kill this Cantrell—they're into something a lot worse than grand theft auto. You better leave the investigating to us. Of course, if you run across any information on the case, I'd welcome hearing from you."

"I can handle myself," Truman said, getting up stiffly. "I've got a story to research, Mr. Weingarten. So I'll be on my way now, if it's all the same to you."

Weingarten sighed. "You don't back off, do you?"

"No, sir," Truman said. "Never have."

Ronnie Bondurant was sick of hearing excuses. "Listen to me, Tim," he hollered into the phone. "I don't give a flying fuck if you lost your job and your wife is knocked up. You shoulda kept it in your pants. Get another job. Get two jobs. You're three weeks late. If you're not here by six, you and that fat-cow wife of yours are gonna be hoofin' it, because I'm coming to get that T-bird."

Ronnie hung up, and as soon as he did, the phone rang again. It had been ringing all morning. He couldn't get anything done. And now, as he looked out at the lot, he saw a battered white Nova pull in.

"Wormy," he called to the outer office.

"I'm on the other line," Wormy said. "It's Al. The Bonneville died again and he wants us to come pick him up and bring him in to work. He says you wanted him to wash some cars."

"Shit," Ronnie said. It was raining shit today, and not an umbrella in sight. He picked up the phone. "Bondurant Motors. Hold, please."

He put his hand over the receiver. "Tell Al we'll send somebody, and get out onto the lot. There's a prospect out there."

A second later Wormy stuck his head in the door. "What somebody you gonna send to get Al?" he asked sarcastically. "We got rid of Jeff—remember?"

The man with the pockmarked face and a Band-Aid across the bridge of his nose sauntered up to Truman's car as he was getting out.

Weems, Truman decided. Wormy Weems.

Weems walked around the Nova, shaking his head. He kicked one of the tires, stuck his head inside the open window to check out the interior.

"You thinking about a trade-in, mister? Because I gotta tell you, there's not much demand for this model. I could do maybe six, seven hundred. You interested in a nice compact? I got a silver '88 Camry with factory air, just came on the lot."

"Actually," Truman said, "I'm not in the market for a car right now. What I am looking for is a job.

Part-time. I've noticed how busy you folks stay. It occurred to me you could use some help."

Wormy looked at Truman in the same appraising way he'd looked at the Nova.

"We don't need no help," he said. "Maybe you oughta get a hobby. Collecting string, something like that."

"Maybe you ought to mind that smart-ass mouth of yours," Truman replied. "I'm an old friend of your boss's friend. Junior Stegall."

"Junior's dead," Wormy said.

"Did I say he wasn't?" Truman asked. "Are you going to take me to Ronnie, or do I have to go looking for him myself?"

"The boss is in the office," Wormy said.

Ronnie Bondurant was still on the phone, his desk chair leaned way back, feet propped up on the desk, with the receiver cradled under his chin. "Now that's something to think about," Truman heard him say. When he looked up and saw he had company, Bondurant took his feet down and straightened up. "Talk to you later," he said.

Ronnie stood up, held out a hand to shake. He wore some type of college ring on his right ring finger, and a gold signet ring on his left pinkie. "Decide on a car already?" he asked affably.

"Don't need a car," Truman repeated. "I'm looking for a job. My name is Truman Kicklighter. Friend of mine, Junior Stegall, he used to talk about you a lot."

"Old Junior," Ronnie said. "We were running buddies a long time ago, that's true. What's he up to these days?"

Truman stared at Ronnie like he was crazy.

"Junior's dead," he said. "Over in Arcadia. Been two years ago now. I still got a cowboy hat he gave me once when he was drunk. A black Resistol. Nice hat, too. I meant to give it back, but didn't get the chance."

"Junior gave you his cowboy hat?" Ronnie was impressed.

"He was bad drunk," Truman said. He got right to the point. "I can type, file, answer the phone. I've been in sales before, and I can work with any kind of people. But I don't want to work late nights and I'm no good at fixing cars."

Ronnie thought about it. "How did you come to know Junior?"

"Met him in Tampa," Truman said, which was the truth. "I used to work down by the courthouse, and we got to talking that time he had some trouble over there." Also the truth; the AP office wasn't far from the courthouse, and he actually had met Stegall during the trial.

It was enough for Ronnie. He was president of Bondurant Motors, not some secretary or file clerk.

"I haven't been looking to hire," Ronnie said. "But . . ."

He looked over Truman's head, at Wormy, who was frowning and giving the boss the ix-nay sign.

"But then again," Ronnie continued, ignoring Wormy, "we had an opening come up suddenly this weekend, and things are starting to back up."

Wormy was shaking his head furiously. He didn't need any geezers hanging around, especially not this one.

"We don't pay benefits," Ronnie warned.

"Don't need 'em," Truman said. "I need to get paid cash. Off the books. Otherwise I lose my Social Security benefits."

"Five dollars an hour," Ronnie said quickly. "You give me, say, twenty hours a week."

"Sounds fine," Truman said. Five dollars an hour. It was an insult. Kids flipping burgers at McDonald's made more than that. But he wasn't here to make a living.

Ronnie was on his feet again. "Come on out here then. I'll show you how the payment books work. That's what you'll be doing. Taking payments, keeping after people, answering the phone. That way, Wormy and me can concentrate on sales."

He went to the outer office, to a cluttered, old wooden desk, reached in the drawer, and got out a thick ledger book.

"This here's the accounts," Ronnie said, flipping through pages filled with cramped writing and tiny numbers. He ran a finger down the columns. "Here's the names, and the amounts and the date the payment is due." Then he pointed to a metal file box. "Every current customer has a card in there, with all the phone numbers and addresses we got on 'em. You look in that account book, see what their due date is. If they're not here by noon that day, start tracking 'em down. Tell 'em we're expecting to see 'em. And don't take no shit. These people, they got all kinda sob stories. And I don't give a rat's ass about any of 'em. So you gotta be tough. Think you can be tough, Pops?"

"It's Truman," Truman said. "Kicklighter. With a K. And I can be an ornery son of a bitch if I need to be."

CHAPTER

FIFTEEN

THE GOOD THING ABOUT HAVING THE OLD MAN working for them was that Wormy and Ronnie could leave the lot together for lunch. Talk about business.

Ronnie loved spicy tacos and burritos, and the Mexican place down the street had the authentic stuff. You could tell because of the beat-up pickup trucks and station wagons full of Mexican laborers who piled into the place.

Wormy swallowed half a bottle of Di-Gel, and picked at a plate of nacho supremes. His stomach rumbled ominously. He reached in his pocket and brought the insurance check out to show Ronnie.

"Nice," Ronnie said, taking it and putting it in his own pocket. "Good work, Wormy. I thought this deal was gonna be dead after that shit with the black chick and Cantrell and all."

"This Zuniga guy, the claims agent," Wormy said. "I think the guy wants to work with us."

"What makes you think so?"

"He's on the make," Wormy said. "I can spot the

type. He cuts the check, then he makes a big deal about making me take about a dozen of his business cards. Tells me he'll work with me any way he can."

"A claims adjuster?" Ronnie chewed on his taco, took a swig of his Dos Equis. "It's an idea."

"He made a point of telling me he does claims for half a dozen different insurance companies," Wormy said.

"So we could spread the business around to the different companies, but always go through this guy, who's on our side. I like it. But what kind of cut is this weasel going to expect?"

"I didn't talk numbers. Wanted to run it by you first."

"Good," Ronnie said. "Talk to the guy. Offer him five percent. Tell him it's no risk to him. We know what we're doing. Different cars, drivers, insurance companies, everything. All he has to do is what he's already doing, processing the checks. We want everything expedited, of course, since we're paying him."

"I'll call him today," Wormy said, sipping his beer. "I got an appointment to see Doc after lunch. That monkey, Billy, man, he nearly killed me. I'm telling you, Ronnie, he's hopped up on something. He nearly ripped that red 'Vette in half. Opened up my nose again, screwed up my knees and my back. My good pants were ruined."

Ronnie shrugged and took a bite of his beef burrito. "You been hollering about personal injury," he told Wormy. "Let's give it a shot. See what Doc can come up with. Ask him to call the insurance company back, tell him we're holding the check on account of you got some serious injuries. Tell the guy you ain't been able to work since the accident."

"All right," Wormy said. "This is the way to go, Ronnie. I know it is. Back, neck injuries. Physical therapy. Disability. We can milk these guys for maybe fifty thousand more."

"We'll see," Ronnie said. Then he winked at Wormy. "You know that LeeAnn, Cantrell's girlfriend? Guess where it turns out she works?"

Wormy's caution signal went up. "Hey, Ronnie. Don't you think we oughta stay away from her? I mean, if she gets curious about where old Jeff went, she might go looking for him, might ask a lot of questions that could cause us some problems."

"She's a stripper, for Christ's sake," Ronnie said. "I called the number she gave me. She's right across the street, at the Candy Store, shaking those bodacious titties of hers. That's where Jeff must have met her. How come I never noticed her over there before?"

"You said that was a low-class joint," Wormy pointed out.

"Yeah, well, it used to be. She classes it up. Even the name's classy. LeeAnn. Pretty, huh? I never knew a LeeAnn before."

LeeAnn Pilker lifted her hair off her neck, trying to get a little cooler. She'd parked in the shade, across the street from Jeff's garage apartment, but she didn't dare go to the door. Mrs. Borgshultz, Jeff's landlady, was bad to spy on people. She used to spy on LeeAnn and Jeff all the time.

She sniffed a little, feeling sorry for herself, and tugged at her bra. It was hot and itchy. Life had been so much simpler when she was an A cup. But Jeff had insisted. He'd offered to pay, too. Now he was gone, and the plastic surgeon was sending certified letters, threatening to turn her over to a collection agency if she didn't pay up.

LeeAnn had scraped up $2,000 in what Jeff liked to call "up-front" money, for the down payment. She'd been squirreling away tip money to take a trip up north, but Jeff had talked her into using it for the breast enhancement. Her boss had kicked in a $500 loan, saying it would be good for business, and Jeff had come up with another $500. But there was still $6,000 due. Past due.

It was so damn hot in the car. LeeAnn felt her mascara running down her face. She couldn't stay here like this much longer, her implants might start to melt any minute now.

With a little sob, she wiped away the black rivers trailing down her cheeks. She'd try later on in the day, before she went on for the four o'clock show. She started the car and drove slowly down the street. Half a block away, she saw a flash of movement in her rearview mirror. A purple sedan. Old lady Borgshultz.

LeeAnn circled back around the block and parked in the same spot across the street from Jeff's place.

"It's okay, it's okay," she chanted as she darted across the street and past Mrs. Borgshultz's back door.

"It's okay," she told herself, unlocking the door to the garage with the key Jeff had given her.

The air in the tiny apartment was hot and stale. Like a gas oven.

"Jesus," she muttered, but she didn't dare turn on the window air conditioner. It shouldn't take long anyway.

Jeff's bed had been the pull-out sofa. She pulled it

out. The sheets were still on the mattress. Red satin sheets she'd given him. Just like a man.

The galley kitchen was filthy but bare except for the trash basket overflowing with beer cans and fast-food wrappers. LeeAnn wrinkled her nose and went quickly through the trash. Nothing exciting.

The bathroom was hardly big enough to turn around in. She checked the medicine cabinet above the sink. Empty. The last time she'd been in here, she'd teased Jeff about his stash of hair creams, cologne, aftershave, and mousse.

"You've got more cosmetics than any of the girls at the club," she'd told him.

"They're men's products," he'd said, not offended in the least. "Is it a crime for a guy to smell good? I'm in sales, you know. Presentation is everything in sales."

"You just want to smell good when you hit on chicks," LeeAnn had accused him.

He pulled her to him. "It works. Right?"

As she thought about Jeff that last time—how he combed his hair just so, sucked in his belly when he walked around the apartment naked, she was surprised to realize just how much she really did miss him. Aside from the fact that he'd left her in the lurch for a $6,000 pair of D cups.

The shit. She sat down on the lid of the commode and cried for a little bit. When would she learn? Twenty-five years old and she was still falling for the pretty face and the funny lines.

There was a wicker laundry hamper wedged in front of the wall opposite the commode. She gave it a vicious kick. Wait a minute. She could see a bit of red through the hamper's open weave.

She raised the lid of the hamper and peered in. She pulled out a red knit shirt and a pair of Gap blue-jean shorts.

Jeff's lucky shirt and shorts. He claimed he sold a car every time he wore this outfit. Of course he never wore the same clothes for more than six hours at a time. Claimed it wasn't hygenic.

And he'd left this outfit behind?

LeeAnn stuffed the clothes in her purse. She peeked out the front window to make sure old lady Borgshultz hadn't come back.

Then she sprinted for the car. Her shift didn't start till four. Those guys at the car lot were lying. And she was going to find out what was going on.

CHAPTER

SIXTEEN

DR. COSTAS SPERDUTO RAN A PRACTICED HAND down the patient's back.

Wormy jumped at his touch—the cool, calloused flesh on his own. "What's the story, Doc?" he asked.

Sperduto peered over the black-rimmed bifocals perched on the end of his nose. Wormy Weems's back was unexceptional-looking; pale, speckled, a long pink scar on the left-lower side, two smaller punctuation-type scars below that, near the base of the spine. Long, graying hairs were sprinkled lightly over the skin near the shoulders.

"Not good," Doc said. "We'll do a complete workup. But I tell you right now, not good. Ruptured disc at the L4 level. And your neck . . ." He tsk-tsked. "I don't like the feel of this neck at all, possibly a ruptured disk in the neck. Your entire spinal column is out of alignment. Possible tear in the cruciate ligament. I'm amazed you could walk in here, Wormy. These are very serious injuries."

"I knew it," Wormy said, grimacing as Doc's fingers walked to the base of his spine. He groaned and managed to roll over onto his back. He tried to sit up, but flopped back down again. The pain was a sudden, fiery surprise.

"Son of a bitch. I really am hurt."

Sperduto rolled his eyes. "Of course. You're going to require many, many treatments. Months, perhaps years of therapy. I think perhaps you have the permanent disability."

"That's good, right?"

"Not for the insurance company," Doc said drily. As he moved about the examining room his stiffly starched coat made a crackling noise. He picked up Wormy's chart and began writing.

"How much?"

"Full course of treatment, spinal alignments, X rays, consultations with my colleagues, drug therapy, hospitalization if necessary. One of my colleagues is on staff at the Pine Isles Back Institute. They have a new caterer over there. What they do with red snapper, capers, a reduced cream sauce . . ." Sperduto kissed his fingertips and sighed.

"I ain't stayin' in no bullshit hospital," Weems said quickly. "And you can forget about me goin' under the knife. That ain't the idea. Go back to that drug therapy part. You got anything stronger than Demerol? That shit's good, but it makes me puke."

Sperduto made a note of this on the chart. "I've got something new. Very special. The FDA hasn't approved it yet for this country, but a friend of mine brings it in from Malaysia."

"I'll take all you got," Weems said. "Back to how much?"

"Conservative estimate? One hundred thousand easily."

"That's all?" Wormy's right flank felt like somebody had stuck a knife in it. Of course, somebody had, but that had been years ago. This was worse.

"I *said* conservative," Sperduto said, sounding slighted. "If you are forced to leave your automotive career, well, that is many thousands more."

Worrmy rolled over on his side a little and massaged the place where the pain seemed to have its home office.

"Now you're talking. When could I get this on paper? All certified and ready to go? I want to hit the insurance company right away. Get the ball rolling for my settlement."

"Rush the paperwork?" Sperduto's face crumpled like an old paper sack. "This paperwork takes days. My secretary must transcribe the notes. There are forms to be filled out. The company may require a second opinion. I'll have to bring in an associate . . ."

"Ronnie says if this works out good, there'll be more business headed your way. A lot more business. We're getting into personal injury now. We'll need a doctor. And a little bird told Ronnie you're in a cash crunch, Doc. The bird says you're getting you a divorce."

"That bitch," Sperduto said. "My mother, may God rest her soul, was right. This is what happens when a man marries out of his faith. All my hard work, my home, my cars, everything. She will not stop until I am penniless. These blood-sucking lawyers of hers. I tell you, these are the criminal masterminds of our time."

This was Sperduto's third go-round with divorce

lawyers that Wormy knew of. You'd think the guy never heard of a prenup. You'd think, Wormy reflected, he couldn't just pay a hooker to get laid, like the rest of the free world.

"Ronnie says to tell you we'll pay you a thousand bucks. If the claim gets filed right now. Like today. Kind of a show of faith."

"A thousand?" Sperduto was deeply offended. "What kind of fee is that? This is not some car lot. I am a physician. I have patients to care for. People in pain depending on me to heal them."

"You got a empty waiting room, a degree from some dogshit diploma mill, and an upcoming trip down alimony lane," Wormy said, reciting Ronnie's exact same words. "You'll get twenty-five percent of whatever you bill the insurance company. That's on top of the thousand. You show us how good you are at the paperwork, Ronnie said, we'll be running our people through the office every week. Like I said, we're expanding the operation. Taking on another partner. It's a right nice profit center, Doc. And your ex–old lady don't have to know about any of it."

Costas Sperduto was a man of vision. He liked the possibilities at once. "We could set up a new corporate entity," he said. "Let the bitch have Costas Sperduto Neck and Back Clinic. What there is left of it." He ran his fingers through the dark, wavy hair near the single shock of white at the crown of his high, shiny forehead. He would call his accountant immediately.

"It is possible," he pronounced. "If my secretary could work through lunch to type up the charts," he said. "And then, if we fax everything. Does this insurance person have a fax machine?"

"He's got it all," Wormy assured Sperduto. "You call and tell him you'll be sending those papers at once. Don't forget the whole crippled-for-life thing. And make sure he understands who you're talking about. Wormy Weems. This agent, Ed Zuniga. He's all right. There won't be no problem. The claim should go like grease through a goose. Now what about them Malaysian pain pills?"

By three o'clock, Truman was exhausted. The phone never quit ringing. Before he'd left for an extended lunch, Ronnie had dragged a huge cardboard box out from the inner office. Car titles, correspondence, forms from the state, bills from suppliers, all of it thrown willy-nilly together.

"We're kinda behind on the paperwork," Ronnie said. "Just open the file drawers and take a look. You'll figure out the system. Anybody calls, tell 'em to call back. Anybody comes on the lot to look at a car, stall 'em. I ain't got time to give no OJT right now."

"OJT?" Probably some computer thing he hadn't heard about, Truman thought.

"On the job training," Ronnie said. "This is it."

As soon as he saw Bondurant's car pull into traffic, Truman started digging through the file drawers, searching for the paperwork for Jeff Cantrell. There should have been job applications, withholding forms, sales reports. He looked under employees, personnel, Cantrell, every possible heading he could think of.

The drawers were more than half empty. Files had sagged forward into a limp mess, in no logical order that Truman could discern.

He got up from the creaking desk chair and stretched, hearing his own bones and muscles creaking. He walked casually over to the showroom's plate-glass window, looking out to make sure he was alone. It wouldn't do to get caught spying his first day on the job.

The lot was deserted, nothing but some black-birds pecking at french fries that had fallen out of the trash container on the sidewalk in front of the lot.

A bus pulled up at the corner. The doors opened, and two women stepped off. They were dressed alike, sleeveless summer dresses, big straw pocketbooks, white sneakers and socks. In their early fifties, probably. One had short, teased blond hair. The other had black hair in a limp ponytail.

The blonde pointed toward the window. Truman jumped back, thinking he'd been spotted. Now the women were walking straight toward him. Truman stood very still.

They stopped when they got to a powder-blue LTD two rows from the front door. It had "KREME-PUFF!" written in red letters on the windshield. The blonde bent over to look at the price sticker glued to the driver's-side window. Her friend was circling the car, clockwise, then counterclockwise.

Now the blonde opened the front door and poked her head in, exclaiming about something.

Truman was about to go out and stall them, like he'd been told, when Ronnie's car turned into the lot.

Ronnie spied the women with that radar of his. In a moment, he had the car parked in the special slot marked R. BONDURANT, CEO. Another moment later and he pushed open the office door, which made the doorbell peal automatically.

"Hey, Pops," Ronnie called. "Customers on the lot. Didn't Wormy get back yet?"

"Not yet," Truman said, flustered. "You didn't say how long you'd be. I was just going outside . . ."

Ronnie waved at him to shut up. "C'mon, Pops," he said. "Out here. You said you done some sales work before? Watch this."

Ronnie stopped abruptly just outside the showroom door. He gazed at his reflection in the window, then combed his fingers through his hair, adjusted his slacks on his hips just slightly, then snapped his head to the left, then to the right. Truman had seen an Elvis impersonator go through these exact same contortions once, years ago, at a motel lounge up in Tallahassee. When was that: '68 or '69? Maybe it was Tifton, not Tallahassee.

Now Ronnie was moving in on the prey. Wormy drove onto the lot in a white Mustang Truman hadn't seen before. He parked, got out slowly, reached in, and pulled out a large metal cane.

Ronnie nodded at him, but kept going toward the women.

"Afternoon, ladies," Ronnie was saying, caressing the word "ladies."

He reached out a hand and grasped both the blond woman's hands in his. "I'm Ronnie Bondurant. Now who might you two charming ladies be?"

The brunette giggled and nudged her friend. "I'm Polly Womack," she said. "Donna's the one doing the shopping. I'm just the one riding shotgun."

Ronnie raised an eyebrow. "Donna? Donna what, if I'm not getting too personal."

Wormy limped over to Truman, leaning heavily on the cane. "You listening to this?" he asked. Truman nodded.

"Sparks," the blonde said, crossing her arms over her chest. She flicked the hood of the LTD with one fingernail. "Kind of high-priced for an '88, isn't this? Any bargaining room on this car, Mr. Bondurant?"

"It's an '88, not a '78," Ronnie said, acting hurt to hear his inventory being bad-mouthed.

Donna Sparks was looking inside the car again.

"Well, hey," Ronnie said suddenly. "We got a lot of money tied up in this here LTD." He put his hand on the blonde's elbow, and gently, effortlessly, steered her away from the LTD and toward a burgundy New Yorker parked two rows over.

"Look at this pretty play toy," Ronnie said. "Four thousand on the dot. And it rides so smooth, you won't even know you're not sitting right on your living-room sofa."

"I like the blue car, except for the price," Donna protested.

"Let's take a look," Ronnie urged, opening the driver's door.

Wormy chuckled. "If he unloads that dog, it'll be party city tonight. That rust bucket's been on the lot so long it's probably got kudzu growing up through them rotted-out floorboards."

Truman didn't get it. "The other car was more money. Wouldn't he rather sell it?"

"To them two? They ain't got the scratch. Besides, Ronnie's Rule Number One: 'Don't let the sucker buy a car—you sell 'em the one you want.' That blue LTD's only been on the lot a couple days. It'll be killing bugs before the weekend, I guarantee."

"Killing bugs?" Truman was still in the dark.

"You know," Wormy said. "Burning gas."

Truman shrugged, unenlightened.

"Sold," Wormy said.

The two women got into the front seat of the New Yorker. Ronnie reached in his pocket, took out a jumble of keys, selected one and handed it to Donna Sparks.

After two or three halting tries, the New Yorker's engine started. It inched toward the street and finally lumbered out into traffic.

Ronnie mopped at his red, sweating face with a handkerchief, then walked quickly over to Truman and Wormy.

He looked at the cane, but said nothing.

"Nice work, Ronnie," Wormy said.

"Look," Truman said, pointing to a trail of dark, glistening spots that led out of the lot. "That New Yorker's leaking oil. There's probably a quart right there."

Ronnie wiped the back of his gleaming neck, wadded the handkerchief up, put it in his back pocket. "Cars on this lot don't leak, old-timer," he said, giving Truman a sharp look. "And we don't ever point out that kind of thing. If anybody ever asks, you tell them the problem is probably just a little old gasket."

"Yeah," Wormy said. "A valve cover gasket. Very cheap to replace. Two, three bucks."

He walked away, leaning heavily on the cane. When he came back out of the showroom, he carried a child's plastic bucket. He sprinkled white sand on the oil trail, then went over to the puddle of liquid that had pooled in the space where the New Yorker had been parked. He kicked the sand around with his toe, letting it absorb the oil until it was the same color as the pavement.

"How'd it go at Doc's?" Ronnie asked, staring out

past the traffic, across the street, toward the half-empty parking lot at The Candy Store. He still hadn't mentioned the cane.

"Two words," Wormy said. "Permanent disability."

CHAPTER

SEVENTEEN

THE SHOWROOM DOOR SWUNG OPEN, THE doorbell pealing to announce the return of Donna Sparks and her friend Polly. Truman stood to help them, but just then Ronnie stuck his head out of the office, smiling broadly when he saw the two women.

"I'll take care of these fine ladies, Pops. You just answer the phone."

"Didn't I tell you, Donna?" he asked, coming toward the women, arms outstretched. "That New Yorker is a one-owner car. Preacher's wife. Preacher cried when he sold it to me, but he said it reminded him too much of his late wife. He had to make the sacrifice."

"You'd think a preacher's wife would have an FM radio," Donna complained. "Or tilt steering."

Ronnie gave an elaborate shrug. "I can't add options to these cars, Miss Donna. That's why they're called used cars, no offense."

"That air conditioner's broke," Polly said, fanning her face with both hands. "Lord, I never been so hot."

"Broke?" Ronnie looked astonished. "It was fine yesterday. Blowing ice cubes. That's factory air, you know."

"It needs to go back to the factory," Donna said. "I need me a car with air-conditioning, Mr. Bondurant."

Wormy came out of the inner office. He was leaning on the cane, a dreamy expression on his face. The Malaysian muscle relaxants had kicked in, and his legs felt squiggly, like one of those Slinky toys.

"Ronnie?" he said quietly.

The boss and the two women turned to look at him.

"That air conditioner. I had a chance to check it out for a customer of mine who's interested in it." Wormy looked up at the clock on the showroom wall, and it seemed to him that he could see an extra hand there. "I didn't want to say anything before, but Mr. Howard, he's due back here at four with his money. He's a cash customer, Mr. Howard is. And he had his mechanic look at it. That air conditioner, it just needs charging. A can of Freon is all."

Ronnie slapped his forehead, like he'd forgotten all about a cash customer. "Mr. Howard! I forgot all about him. He was looking at the New Yorker for his mother-in-law. Was that it?"

"She's moving down here from Michigan," Wormy agreed. "And Mr. Howard wants her to have something nice and safe."

Donna and Polly exchanged a look. "Will you excuse us a moment?"

The two women stepped out into the parking lot. They stood close, their heads bent together, bobbing back and forth as the debate raged. At one point, they stopped talking, walked onto the lot and circled the

New Yorker again, kicking at the tires, peering into the interior one more time.

Ronnie watched them with only casual interest. "What's that make for me this week?" he asked Wormy.

"Let's see. The white Capri, the white Camry, that black El-Dog . . ."

"Two El-Dogs," Ronnie corrected him. "The school janitor and his wife."

"This'll make five on the street," Wormy said. "Who gets credit for the red Corvette?"

For a fleeting moment, Ronnie looked like he might throttle Wormy. Truman tried hard not to stare. It took Ronnie only a moment to compose himself. "That'd be Jeff's sale," he said smoothly. "Only right he gets credit. Of course, he did go off and leave us in the lurch. So I'd say we'll make that a house account."

"Remember that week you did ten cars?" Wormy asked.

"February of 1994," Ronnie said. "Three of 'em to Canadians. It's only Wednesday now, you know."

The doorbell chimed and Donna Sparks walked back in with her pocketbook thrust in front of her like a prize-winning pie at the state fair. "I'll take it," she said.

Ronnie took Ms. Sparks into the inner office to do the paperwork while her friend Polly sat in the showroom and leafed through old issues of *Newsweek*. Fifteen minutes later, Ronnie escorted Donna out. He opened a closet door in the showroom, reached in, and came back with an armload of goodies.

"Ice scraper," he said, handing one to Polly. "Key

chains for both of you. Yardsticks. Penlights. And," he said, with a grand flourish toward the door, "right now, Mr. Weems is loading a case of complimentary soft drinks in the trunk of your new vehicle. It's our way of saying thank you for joining the Bondurant Motors family of satisfied customers."

Donna Sparks turned the ice scraper over in her hand, like she was seeing one for the first time. Maybe she was, Truman realized. You didn't get much call for ice scrapers in this part of Florida.

"Well, thank you," Donna said. "For everything."

Wormy pulled the New Yorker up to the canopy outside the office, got out, and opened the doors for the women. They chugged off with Polly waving gaily out the open window.

"What's the story on that AC?" Ronnie asked, watching them go.

"Aw, hell," Wormy said. "That compressor's blown."

A dilapidated pickup truck bristling with ladders, metal scaffolding, five-gallon buckets, and long-handled brushes came coasting onto the lot. Three men were squeezed cheek to jowl onto the front seat.

"Busy day," Truman said to Ronnie and Wormy. "These folks look like they need a car." He'd already made a note to himself to get Donna Sparks's phone number out of the files, maybe leave an anonymous message that she'd just bought herself a big fat lemon. Might have to wait, though, at least until he got the goods on these weasels. He didn't want to blow his cover.

Ronnie took a look. A thin, paint-spattered man

unfolded himself out of the right side of the truck, took a last deep puff off a cigarette, then tossed the butt onto the asphalt.

"Son of a bitch Wesley Coombs," Ronnie said, disgusted. "I hate a goddamn litterbug."

Wormy slouched down into a chair, his eyes half closed. "Wes Coombs. King of the Bogs," he said, pronouncing the word to rhyme with "rogue."

"Heeyy," Ronnie said, his face brightening. He was still looking out the showroom window. "What have we here now? My next best girfriend, looks like to me."

LeeAnn Pilcher's gold lamé hot pants were so short and so tight, the matching gold leather boots so high-heeled, that she had to take quick, mincing half steps, dodging in and out of the traffic on U.S. 19. Each step sent the overflowing halter top bouncing, the curtain of ebony hair streaming down her back. Cars came to a halt, horns blared, there were whistles and shouts of approval.

"Wormy, you deal with Wes Coombs," Ronnie said as he stepped out onto the lot to give LeeAnn an appropriate greeting.

"Nah, man," Wormy said, "I gotta get some rest." His speech was slurred, his jaw hanging open, his eyes closed all the way.

"What'd Doc give you?" Ronnie asked, looking down at Wormy, whose jaw had dropped completely down onto his chest. Wormy snored softly in reply.

The showroom door opened, the doorbell pealed, and Wes Coombs stood aside, holding the door, not necessarily a gesture of gallantry, more likely that he was completely frozen by the vision of LeeAnn Pilker and her surgically enhanced chest.

"Have you heard from Jeff yet?" LeeAnn asked, skipping the hellos. "He owes me some money."

"Uh, no, but I do have some things I'd like to discuss with you in my office," Ronnie said. He nodded curtly at Wesley Coombs, who stood stock-still in the doorway. "Coombs. Mr. Kicklighter here is helping us out now. He'll take your payment."

Ronnie put an arm around Truman's shoulder and his lips close to Truman's ear. "This son of a bitch is the original hard-luck story. He's three weeks in arrears on an '86 Monte Carlo we sold him six weeks ago. Like Wormy said, he's a bog. You know, bogus, always got a story. I need to have a word with this young lady here, but you stay out here, shake that money out of him."

Before Truman could protest, Ronnie was leading the girl into his office. "I go on in five minutes," LeeAnn was saying, trying to shake his hand off of her hip.

The door closed softly behind them. Truman became aware of a sour smell that emanated from Wesley Coombs. It was sweat, very old sweat that had dried and reactivated again. Truman went through the file and found Coombs's payment card and tried to breathe through his mouth.

"I can't pay nothin' today," Coombs said flatly. "That's what I come to tell y'all."

"Seventy-three dollars, and you're three weeks behind," Truman said. He did the math. "Two hundred nineteen dollars you owe."

Coombs blinked. Even his eyelashes were coated with flakes of paint. "My dog's been sick, man," Coombs said. His voice was high, toneless. "Hadda pay two hundred dollars to the vet. Pizza man ran over the dog in the driveway. Dog was bad hurt. Next week, I got some money coming in. I'll pay then."

Truman got up and looked out the window at the truck Coombs had arrived in. The truck was still running, and the men in the front seat were downing what looked like quarts of malt liquor.

"Mr. Coombs, why don't you ask your boss out there for an advance?" Truman said, trying to be polite. "Because Mr. Bondurant, he told me to make sure you pay up today. No excuses."

Coombs shook his head and a fine mist of white paint flakes filled the sour air around him. "That's my buddies, not my boss," he said. "Bossman don't give no advances."

As if on cue, the painter behind the wheel gave three long blasts of the car horn.

"I gotta go," Coombs said, edging toward the door.

"Hey, asshole." Wormy was still slumped down in the chair and his words came out slowly, slurred but recognizable. Coombs stopped, stared at Weems.

Truman relaxed a little. Maybe Wormy could make this deadbeat see reason. He'd had little training in his time as a shakedown artist.

"What's this shit about a sick dog?" Wormy was sitting forward now, his eyes hardened slits. The slackness in his face was gone.

"It's true," Coombs said uneasily. "That pizza guy took off when he seen what he done. And the vet wouldn't let me have the dog back unless I paid first. Cash."

"Fuck the dog," Weems said. "You owe two hundred and nineteen dollars for that Monte Carlo."

"That's my kids' dog," Coombs whined. "He was

hurting bad, howling, bleeding all over the place. The kids were screaming. What was I supposed to do?"

"Shoulda ordered another pizza, finished him off," Wormy said. "Come on, Coombs, you know the drill here. Gimme fifty dollars now, come back here Monday with the rest."

"I'm tellin' you, I'm stone-cold broke," Coombs said. Two thin rivulets of sweat beaded down his flat, paint-streaked face. The truck honked its horn again. Coombs bolted for the door. The truck was already moving as he jumped into the front seat.

"Now what?" Truman asked.

Weems slumped back into the chair. "Now you tell Ronnie you couldn't get jackshit out of a scumbag like Wesley Coombs. He ain't gonna like that. You work here, old-timer, you gotta pull your weight. You gotta know the customers. You gotta realize, we're dealing with the bottom of the food chain here."

Truman scanned Coombs's index card. It didn't look like he'd ever gone more than two weeks without being in arrears on his payments. There was a home phone number, an address, and a work phone on the card. "I could call his boss," Truman suggested. "Tell him his employee has a bad debt he needs to settle up with us."

"Forget it," Wormy said. "He works for his brother-in-law."

"Call his wife, ask if she could come in and make a payment?"

"It's his girlfriend, and that number was disconnected last month," Wormy said. He sighed. "Nut-cutting time. Call Eddie."

The office door opened then, and LeeAnn Pilker and Ronnie emerged. LeeAnn's face was pale, her smile forced. Ronnie had an arm draped around her shoulder, fingers resting lightly but possessively on her left breast. "I really gotta go," LeeAnn said. "The manager docks my pay if the show starts late because of me."

Ronnie gave her a wink, and squeezed her breast hard. She winced, but this time didn't try to shake him off.

"You just tell that manager he better start treating you right, or he'll be looking for a new star attraction," Ronnie said. "Tell him Ronnie Bondurant knows people around this town. And Ronnie likes his friends to be treated right. You tell him that, okay, hon?"

"Okay," she said, moving fast for the door.

"I'll see you tonight, after the show," he called to her. "Get us some dinner."

When she was gone, Ronnie gave a loud war whoop. "How about that, friends and neighbors?" he said, perching on the edge of the desk where Truman was seated. "Is that a fine piece of grade-A pussy or what? And it's mine, my friends. All mine."

"I don't like it," Wormy said flatly. He cut his eyes over at Truman, reminding Ronnie that they weren't alone.

"You don't have to like it," Ronnie said. "I'm still running this operation, last time I checked. And speaking of which, Pops, how'd you do with old Wesley? You didn't take a check off him, I hope. That card should make it clear we don't take none of Wesley Coombs's bad paper."

"Coombs gave him a load of bullshit, then ran off," Wormy said. "Pops here didn't get a dime off him."

"That right?"

"Yes," Truman said. He was steeling himself for the firing. It had been a good try, but maybe he wasn't still the investigative reporter he thought he was. Maybe he'd lost his edge. At least he'd found out something about Jeff Cantrell's girlfriend. Now he knew what she looked like, where she worked. It was a lead. It was better than nothing.

Ronnie was in an unusually good mood. Nothing, not even Wesley Coombs, was going to change that. He turned the dial of the Rolodex, plucked out a card, flipped it across the desk at Truman. "We're done dicking around with that lowlife. That's Eddie's number. Does our repos. Call him. Tell him to come by and pick up the key to the Monte Carlo. Tell him Ronnie wants the car back on the lot tomorrow."

"Better tell him about Wesley's neighbors," Wormy added. "That's a snake nest over there, with all his brothers and half-brothers and cousins living there. Hell, even the girlfriend packs a shotgun, way Wesley tells it."

"Eddie can take care of himself," Ronnie said confidently. "Make the call, Pops."

CHAPTER

EIGHTEEN

THE BACK BUMPER OF THE CREAM-COLORED Mercedes made a scraping sound as it came onto the Bondurant Motors lot. Its right rear looked like it had been attacked with a baseball bat, the brake and tail-lights shattered, the bumper hanging and actually dragging on the ground.

"Shit," Ronnie said, watching as the driver parked and got out. "What now?"

The driver looked huge to Truman, with a braid hanging down his back. Part Indian, part black. He matched the description Ed Weingarten had given for this Hernando Boone character.

The doorbell jangled as Boone pushed his way into the showroom. Wormy gave a loopy smirk. "How," he said, holding up the palm of his hand.

"Shut up, Weems," Boone snarled. He clapped Ronnie on the shoulder. "My man. Had a little dustup. Need to talk to you in private."

"Go on in," Ronnie said. "We'll be with you in a minute."

When the office door closed behind Boone, Ronnie's smooth facade faded. "Damnit, Wormy," he whispered. "Shut your stupid mouth. Boone's crazy. He'd just as soon kill you as look at you, anyhow. Eddie should be here any minute. Get that paperwork together on Coombs's Monte Carlo. And straighten up your act before you go in there. Or I'll kill you myself."

He took a thick clip of folded-up bills from his pocket and counted out ten twenties, which he stuck in an envelope and handed to Truman. "Eddie likes to deal in cash," he said.

Wormy yanked open the file cabinet drawer, tossing the files Truman had just straightened onto the floor. When he found the file for Wesley Coombs, he slammed the top drawer shut and opened the next one, creating the same kind of chaos until he found another folder with a stack of blank forms. He took one of the forms and began filling it out.

"What's that?" Truman asked.

"Repossession papers, pick-up order, that kind of bullshit," Wormy said, not looking up from his furious scribbling.

He finished the paperwork and opened a recessed cabinet in the wall, revealing a pegboard hung with dozens and dozens of sets of keys. When he'd found the one he wanted, he tossed it on top of the other papers. "Tell Eddie it's all there," he said. Then he went into Ronnie's private office.

Truman decided to seize the moment.

He opened the filing cabinet drawer, conveniently next to the closed door of Ronnie's office. If anybody came out, he could say he was straightening up the files. They sure as hell needed it now.

The voices inside the office were only barely audible. Truman edged closer to the door. Hernando Boone's deep voice was unmistakable. "Son-of-a-bitch crackheads. While I was upstairs doing business, one of 'em took a tire iron to my Mercedes. Good thing it wasn't my Gator truck. Nobody messes with that. Time I got down there, they'd scattered. Didn't even get a shot off. You seen what they did. The Mercedes is ruined. So I was thinking, Ronnie, my man, you being the collision specialist, we could have us an accident, me and you and one of your monkeys."

Truman strained, but he couldn't hear Ronnie's answer. Monkeys? Accidents? Was this the scam Weingarten was investigating? He didn't dare hang around the door any longer to find out.

He was hungry, and no wonder. It was after six and he'd skipped lunch. He remembered having seen a candy machine in the garage during one brief foray out there while Wormy and Ronnie were gone.

Truman opened the door leading out to the garage, being careful to pull it closed behind him. It was dark and stupefyingly hot. He felt around among the stacks of tires and tools until he came to the vending machine he'd remembered. Most of the slots were empty, but there were some bags of peanuts, two kinds of candy bars, and some ancient-looking snack cakes. He fed in three quarters—for a Baby Ruth, which had been a nickel not so long ago—and put his hand under the delivery slot so the candy wouldn't make a noise when it fell out.

The candy bar disappeared in three bites.

Truman looked around the garage, saw the partially open back door and a flash of red paint.

He crept back into the showroom, satisfied himself that everything was still quiet, and walked quickly around to the back of the sales lot. The garage bay was surrounded with a high chain-link fence, and half a dozen cars were parked inside. One was a red Corvette.

Jackie's red Corvette? Hard to tell from this distance. After all, he'd only seen her car once. He moved over to the fence, felt his heartbeat jump up like a startled rabbit. A jolt of sugar from the Baby Ruth? Or was it the old adrenaline rush he'd always felt on the trail of a juicy story?

He felt in his pocket for the pack of HavaTampas. Took one out and lit it, inhaling deeply. Cheap cigars, he reflected, were one luxury he'd never give up.

This Corvette looked a lot like the one Jackie had bought. But this one had heavy damage to the front and the rear. Hers had been a lemon, but the body had looked pretty good, he recalled. Damn his eyes and damn old age. He couldn't see much from here. Have to go back inside and come out through the garage door. It was risky, going into the showroom again and past Ronnie's office, but the cigar seemed to have calmed his nerves.

As he glided noiselessly through the showroom he was thankful he'd thought to wear sneakers this morning. Out into the garage, then through the back door, into the fenced-in area. Act casual, he told himself, inching toward the Corvette. You work here. Nothing wrong with familiarizing yourself with the inventory.

If Jackleen had seen a body in the back of the

Corvette, if it had been Jeff Cantrell, there might still be traces of blood. He bent down and peered into the back window of the red 'Vette. Some kind of black plastic sheeting was stretched out over the hatch area. He couldn't see anything unless he moved that plastic aside.

Wait. He could hear voices from inside the showroom. Quickly, he walked over to the garage door, leaned wearily against the doorjamb, and took a long pull on the HavaTampa. Even that wasn't enough to chase the jitters. His hands were shaking.

"Hey!" Wormy's voice echoed loudly from inside the garage. "What the hell are you doing out here, Pops? Snooping around?"

Truman willed himself to be calm. It's the dope, he told himself. He took the cigar and flicked the ashes on the ground.

"Just taking a smoke break, that's all," he said. "I didn't think Ronnie would want me to smoke inside, so I came out here. That's all right, isn't it? I can hear if anybody pulls into the lot. I got great hearing for a man my age."

"This here area is off-limits," Wormy said, giving Truman a shove.

Truman stood where he was. "I said I was sorry," he said. He had no intention of letting anybody lay hands on him, drugs or no drugs. He gave Wormy a long, level stare. Wormy's eyes were glassy.

"Back in the office," Wormy said.

Truman walked slowly and deliberately through the garage with Wormy at his heels. Ronnie's office door was still closed.

Outside, a horn honked. A black pickup truck pulled onto the lot. "That's Eddie," Wormy said.

Eddie turned out to be young and black, probably not even twenty years old, Truman thought. He was big, over six feet, and built like an overgrown baby. Baggy black shorts hung down to his pudgy knees and the black T-shirt wasn't quite long enough to meet the waistband of his pants, exposing a roll of flabby belly flesh. His hair was shaved close to his scalp, a gold hoop earring hung from his right earlobe, and wraparound mirrored sunglasses hid his eyes. He wore black leather gloves with the fingers cut out, and when he swaggered into the office of Bondurant Motors, he acknowledged Wormy with one word.

"Yo."

"This is Pops," Wormy said curtly. "He'll fix you up with everything." He turned and went back into Ronnie's office.

"Dickhead," Eddie said. He gave Truman a sheepish look. "Uh, sorry, man."

"Not at all," Truman said. He began gathering up the paperwork, car keys, and money. "I was thinking the same thing myself. He is a dickhead."

"That's the truth," Eddie said. He took off the sunglasses and wiped them on the hem of his T-shirt. "Hey, man, where's Jeff?"

Truman looked up. "You know Jeff?"

"Sure. Me and him hang together some. He likes to go with me on pick ups sometimes. The nastier the better. So where's he at? Partying with the ladies?"

Truman glanced at the office door, then lowered his voice. "According to Ronnie, Jeff quit. Ronnie says Jeff took a job over in Ft. Lauderdale."

"No way," Eddie said. "We were supposed to get together Friday night. Me and him and his girlfriend. She was gonna fix me up with some girl from that club over there." He jerked his head in the direction of the Candy Store.

"His girlfriend. Is that LeeAnn?"

Eddie grinned. "You seen her, huh? Check out those hooters?"

"She came in a little while ago," Truman said. "Trying to find out if Ronnie knew anything about where Jeff went. I guess Jeff didn't tell her he was leaving town."

"Shit," Eddie said. He picked up the keys and read over the pick-up order for Wesley Coombs's Monte Carlo.

"This Coombs. Is he a white dude?"

"Yes," Truman said. "Skinny little S.O.B."

Eddie got down to the Coombs address and frowned. "I know the street this guy lives on. Full of crackers and rednecks. I ain't going in there in the daytime. Last time I made a run over there, these people had a ten-foot logging chain wrapped around the bumper of the car. The other end was wrapped around a brick column holding up the carport. Pissed me off."

"What'd you do?" Truman asked.

"Bolt cutters," Eddie said. "But the guy's old lady heard me. She come outta the house, chased me with a knife."

He pulled up the sleeve of his T-shirt. A two-inch puffy pink scar made a stripe on the smooth brown shoulder. "See that? That place over there is worse than the projects."

"You probably see a lot of crazy stuff, the line of work you're in," Truman observed.

"All kinds," Eddie said. "Say, what's your real name? That dickhead Wormy, he's got no manners."

"Don't call me Pops. I'm Truman Kicklighter," Truman said, offering his hand.

Eddie grasped Truman's wrist in both his hands and gave it a quick up-and-down motion.

"Eddie Nevins. You wanna see my rig, Truman? State of the art, man."

"Okay," Truman said. He could still hear the men talking inside Ronnie's office. It was past his quitting time. And if that snot Wormy gave him any lip, Truman decided, he would let him have it.

The truck's black paint gleamed in the late afternoon sun. It was a heavy-duty Chevrolet pickup, but that's where its resemblance to a tow truck ended. Where the bed would be on an ordinary truck, Eddie's truck was built up, with a menacing looking twin-pronged set of H-shaped jaws extending off an arm that folded up and down. There were two sets of what looked like wheeled dollies strapped on either side of the tow bar. A decal on the back of the truck cab summed up Eddie's approach to his life and work. "No Fear," it said.

"Impressive," Truman said.

"Get in and I'll give you a demo," Eddie offered. "Where's Wormy's car? We'll tow his ass outta here in a New York minute."

Behind them, they heard the showroom's door-bell pealing.

Ronnie and Hernando Boone were still talking rapidly as they walked toward the Mercedes. Wormy trailed a few steps behind.

Bondurant slowed only a little and nodded quickly at the repo man. "Hiya, Eddie," he said. Then he joined Boone beside the Mercedes.

Eddie was staring at Boone. "I know that brother from somewhere," he muttered. "Not a real brother. Part Indian or something."

"Miccosukee," Truman put in. He was straining to catch part of the men's conversation, which had turned aggressive.

"I don't like it," Ronnie was saying.

"Don't have to like it. Just be there," Boone shot back. "Weedon Island. They're putting in a new road to the visitors' center. Midnight."

"Eddie!" Wormy had snuck up behind them. "Don't you got a job to be doing? We ain't paying you to stand around here and jerk off with this old man all night."

Eddie's cheerful round features tightened into a wooden mask of hatred. "I do the snatch on my timetable," he said, "not yours. And I ain't going in that snakepit down there till late tonight. You don't like it, get the car yourself."

Wormy rocked back and forth on his heels and made a sucking sound with his tongue against his front teeth.

"Think I can't, boy?"

Eddie clenched his fists and took a step closer, glaring down at the top of Wormy's head. Truman half hoped Wormy would start something so that Eddie would finish it. He wasn't a violent man, but it was beginning to look like violence was the only thing somebody like Wormy Weems could understand.

Eddie's mouth didn't move as he spoke. "You notify the cops about the pick up?"

It was not what Truman expected to hear.

"It's taken care of," Wormy said. He turned and stalked back inside the office. Eddie let out a long sigh.

"I thought you were going to haul off and flatten him," Truman said.

"Would have, if he'd called me a nigger," Eddie said. He laughed ruefully. "And if the brother in the Mercedes wasn't still here. Three against one, that's bad odds where I come from."

Truman touched Eddie's elbow. "Two against one." He liked the way the kid handled himself. Like a man.

"Right," Eddie said.

He got in the tow truck and started the engine. It was surprisingly quiet for such a big vehicle. He pulled up beside Truman.

"You done for the night?"

"I'm done," Truman said decisively.

"What about going over there, to the Candy Store, getting a cold brew?" Eddie asked. "I'm thinking Jeff's girlfriend might be working tonight. Maybe she'd still fix me up with her friend."

"Or tell us whether she thinks Jeff really left town," Truman said. "She told Ronnie she was working tonight. In fact, he's supposed to take her out to dinner after she gets off. Yeah, sure, I could stand a cold beer. Been a long day."

Truman hadn't been in a strip joint since he was in the marines.

Not that he was a prude, or that Nellie wouldn't have allowed it. Paying to watch naked women wasn't his style. Anyway, Nellie always did claim he liked his thrills homegrown.

The bouncer was a woman, short, built like a fire hydrant. She had a peroxided-blond crew cut and a bright orange tank top to better display a powerful set of trapezoids and biceps.

"Ten bucks cover charge. Happy-hour beer is five bucks a pitcher. Free buffet. You coming in or what?"

"Senior citizen discount?" Truman asked, reaching for his AARP card.

"You're kidding, right?" the woman asked. "You ask me, we should charge extra for dirty old men like you. In case you need oxygen or your pacemaker gives out."

"Watch it," Eddie warned. "Have some respect, here, huh?" He reached for his own wallet, which was attached to his belt by a thick, chrome-plated chain. His stubby fingers extracted a twenty. He pushed the money through the window at the blonde.

"No, no," Truman protested. "I pay my own way. I was just surprised it was so much. It's been a long time since I've been to a place like this."

"No shit," the blonde drawled.

"Come on, Truman," Eddie said. "I'll let you buy the first pitcher."

It had been over forty years since Truman had been in a strip bar, but one thing hadn't changed: the smells. A thick blue cloud of cigarette smoke hung over the low-ceilinged room. It smelled like sour beer and aftershave, sweat and rancid grease.

There was a horseshoe-shaped bar at one end of the room, a long, neon-lit stage with a runway that projected out into the room, and in between, a sea of tables and chairs. The bar was lined with customers, the tables half full.

Onstage, colored lightbulbs flashed on and off, and a milky-white spotlight lit up three girls who wore wisps of cheesy see-through lingerie and bored expressions while they writhed around to a background of rap music. At least that's what Truman thought it was. The music had a dull, thudding bassline with multiple female voices dully reciting an invitation to "Do the Dirty Thang."

Eddie led the way to a table near the stage. As soon as they were seated, a waitress appeared. She was wearing a black leather bikini with a metal-studded dog collar around her neck.

"You gentlemen like some champagne?" she asked, fluttering her eyelashes.

Something else that hadn't changed.

"No thanks," Truman said quickly. "A pitcher of beer. It's five bucks, right?"

"Miller or Bud? Imports are extra."

Truman looked questioningly at Eddie.

"Bud," Eddie said. He was bouncing his head up and down to the music, his eyes fixed on the girls onstage.

"I thought you said LeeAnn was working tonight," Eddie shouted over the din.

"I saw her go in here, right before four," Truman shouted back.

The waitress came back with their beer. It had a three-inch-thick head of foam.

"That's five dollars," she told them. "Either of you guys like a table dance? Fifty bucks. Lap dances are a hundred. Cash. MasterCard or Visa. No personal checks."

"Not for me," Truman said.

"Nah," Eddie said, clearly disappointed at the fee schedule. "Is LeeAnn working tonight?"

"She's here," the girl said.

"Can you do us a favor?" Truman asked. "Tell her Jeff's friends would like to say hello."

"Yeah," Eddie said. "Ask her to come out to our table."

The girl put one hand on her hip. She was so thin her pelvic bone protruded from the waistband of the thong bottom. "This is a business," she said. "Favors aren't free. Personal messages are ten bucks. And LeeAnn's not supposed to fraternize with the customers. Not for free, anyway."

Reluctantly, Truman reached for his wallet. Ronnie hadn't mentioned payday yet. He had a twenty, a five, and some ones. He gave the girl the twenty and the five.

"Five for the beer, ten for you, ten for LeeAnn," he said.

"Whoopee," she said, flouncing off.

CHAPTER

NINETEEN

TRUMAN WAS FEELING QUEASY. THE CANDY STORE'S free buffet consisted of Buffalo chicken wings, cold tacos, and cocktail wienies floating in some gelatinous red sauce. He'd tossed the food down quickly, along with two big mugs of beer. It was free, wasn't it? He leaned against the Dumpster in back of the Candy Store and wished for antacid tablets.

"You think she'll come?" Eddie asked.

"She'd better," Truman said, swallowing hard to quelch a rising bubble of gas. "I've got twenty dollars invested in her already."

"Why are you so interested in Jeff? I mean, it ain't like you knew him or nothing."

Truman gave Eddie the condensed version of the whole story, leaving out the part about the FDLE's involvement. "We're pretty sure your friend Jeff is dead. And one of those guys across the street killed him. If I can find out what's going on, we'll nail these clowns. And I'll have myself a story. Front-page byline. Exclusive to the *St. Petersburg Times*. By Truman Kicklighter."

"Jeff's really dead?" Eddie asked, kicking at the edge of a pothole in the parking lot. "Man, it don't seem real."

A heavy steel fire door opened slowly and noisily.

LeeAnn Pilker stepped down into the parking lot. She was wearing an oversized Tampa Bay Bucs football jersey and a pair of rubber flip-flops. Backlit that way, Truman could tell she hadn't bothered with undergarments. She flipped her hair back over her shoulders, the way she'd done when she came into the showroom.

"Hi, Eddie."

She looked Truman up and down. "I know you. From across the street. At Ronnie's place. The note said you were Jeff's friend. What's that supposed to mean?"

"This is Truman," Eddie said quickly. "He's a buddy of mine, actually. What's this bullshit about Jeff leaving town, LeeAnn? He didn't say nothing to me about getting a new job."

She shrugged. "Guess it was sudden."

"Real sudden," Truman said. "I overheard you asking Ronnie if he'd heard from Jeff. Don't you know where he is?"

"I'm not his wife or anything," LeeAnn said. "We went out a couple times, that's all."

"Not what Jeff told me," Eddie said. "What he told me—he paid for those hooters you're in there shaking for the money."

"*Loaned* me some money," LeeAnn corrected him. "They're not paid for yet. That's why I was looking for your sorry-ass friend. It was his idea, not that it's any of your business."

"What idea?" Truman asked.

"These," she said, thrusting her chest forward. "The implants. That surgery hurt like hell, too. Those lying doctors. And I had bruises for weeks. The customers all thought I was into bondage or something."

She glanced backward, toward the door. "Look. I gotta go. I got a date, and I don't want the boss to see me out here. We're not supposed to hang around outside. It gives the vice cops the wrong idea."

"You're going out with Ronnie Bondurant," Truman said. "How would Jeff feel about your dating his boss?"

She toyed with a strand of hair, shifted from one foot to the other. "Jeff's gone," she said finally. "I got bills to pay. I gotta look out for myself."

Jackie and Ollie were in the Fountain of Youth lobby watching an old black-and-white movie, arguing about the identity of the actor playing the French foreign legion officer.

"Dirk Bogarde," Ollie said.

Jackie looked up as Truman pushed through the front door. "Mr. K," she called. "Tell Ollie that that's Humphrey Bogart on the TV."

Truman sank down into the sofa beside Jackie. "You're both wrong. It's Yves Montand."

"Who?" Jackie asked.

"You're too young," Truman said wearily, rubbing at his eyes. "You still got any coffee left in the kitchen?"

"Coffee?" Jackie said suspiciously. "Why are you drinking coffee this late? You're going somewhere, aren't you? It's about my car, isn't it?"

"Maybe. Hernando Boone—the big guy you saw that night you went back to Bondurant's—he came in to see Ronnie today, right at closing time. I think they're mixed up in some kind of insurance scam. I overheard them talking about meeting at midnight, out at Weedon Island, by the old Florida Power plant."

Jackie leaned over and started lacing up her sneakers. "Gimme just a minute and I'll be ready. I've got a flashlight in my room."

"Absolutely not," Truman said. "These people are hopped up on some kind of drugs. They're dangerous. I just came home to put on some dark clothes and get some Rolaids. My stomach is in flames. Anyway, I've got a flashlight in my car."

Jackie jumped up from the sofa. "Two flashlights are better. And I know all about how bad these dudes are. I saw Jeff's body, remember?"

Truman changed into a threadbare pair of dark trousers and a navy-blue sportshirt, got a box of Rolaids from his room, then brought the station wagon around to the front of the hotel. Jackie was waiting at the curb, a black gym bag slung over her shoulder.

A light drizzle had started to fall, so quiet and fine it was more of a mist, really, and clouds of steam rose up from the hot pavement. Tampa Bay was only half a mile away, and sometimes, at night like this, a breeze off the bay would waft across and set the palm trees planted down Fourth Street a-rustle, making the summer nights almost tolerable. Tonight was not such a night.

Jackie got in the Nova. It still bothered him, her insisting on going along. What if there was shooting? None of the parties involved in this deal tonight were playing with a full deck, as far as Truman was concerned. Anything could happen. "This isn't right, your going along like this."

She leaned her elbow on the open windowsill, then reached over and switched on the radio to avoid arguing with him. The station was Truman's favorite big-band station. Woody Herman and his band were playing "Laura." This was Woody's earlier band, The Woodchoppers. He liked them better than The Thundering Herd, which was too jazzy for his taste.

"What would your mother say about all this? Running around at night, getting mixed up with criminals?" he demanded.

Jackie didn't talk much about her family. He knew she called her mother every day and went over to her house to visit at least once a week. Jackie was the youngest of four girls. One was in the army, stationed at Fort Benning, one was married, with kids, and lived somewhere in Ohio, and Charleen, the one closest in age to Jackie, was unmarried, with two babies and another on the way. He'd met Nita, the mother, only once—in May, when Jackie brought her to the Ponce de Leon Room for Mother's Day lunch.

Nita was an older, heavier version of her youngest daughter, with the same smooth, light-brown skin, big, long-lashed eyes, even the same tiny gap between the top front teeth, a gap that showed a lot because they both tended to smile frequently.

"What my mama don't know won't hurt her," Jackie said tartly. "Besides, if you knew what my sisters put her through, you'd say I was an angel on earth, compared to those three. Besides, Mama's not afraid of nothin'. It was my daddy who worried every-thing to death. 'Lock the doors!' 'Be home at ten!' 'Take a quarter for the pay phone.'"

"He died while you were in high school?"

"My senior year," Jackie said softly, looking out the window. "He had a heart attack at work. First week of May. He didn't even get to see me in my cap and gown."

"Too bad," Truman said. "You turned out fine. I bet he'd be proud."

"Maybe," Jackie said. She was a young woman with strong ideas. The Glenn Miller Orchestra came on the radio, and the song was "Little Brown Jug." Jackie made fun of the words, but he noticed she sang along after the second chorus.

"This is a long way away," she said, looking out the window at the unfamiliar scenery after the song was over. "I've never been out here. This is Gandy Boulevard, right?"

"Those lights up ahead are the dog track," Truman said. "You remember that, don't you?"

"Oh, yeah," Jackie said.

"If I remember right, there's a good road in back of the track. Nobody ever used to come out this way. Hell, I haven't been out here in years myself," Truman admitted. "We used to come out here by boat with a buddy of mine, years ago. Good fishing, or at least it used to be."

"What exactly are we going to do?" Jackie asked. "Hide in the car?"

"Not the car," Truman said. "Ronnie and Wormy know what I drive. I'll know better when we get there. We're looking for a lot of construction equipment," he told her. "Probably after we cross over Riviera Bay up ahead."

"Kind of a spooky place," Jackie said, rubbing the goosebumps on her arms.

Truman slowed down. A yellow sign loomed out of the darkness. CAUTION: CONSTRUCTION AHEAD. Five hundred yards down the road there was another sign. HEAVY EQUIPMENT ENTERING TRAFFIC.

The traffic part was a joke. The road was two lanes, and not another soul was in sight. After another quarter mile, neon rubber pylons marked the way as the road narrowed down to one lane, with the right side of the roadway blocked off by wooden barricades. The skeleton of an overpass was in progress: huge T-shaped concrete columns, steel beams and girders, a mountain of crushed rock, and the requisite construction equipment—cement mixers, motor graders, forklifts, dump trucks, even a construction trailer.

"This is the place," Truman said.

"Why are they building something like this way out here?" Jackie wondered.

"Progress," Truman said, slowing to a stop.

Jackie hopped out of the car and swung two wooden barriers inward, like opening a gate. Truman pulled the station wagon through, and she swung them back in place.

"There's a kind of road back into the woods," Jackie said, pointing in the direction of the construction trailer. "Maybe you can hide the car there."

Truman inched the Nova toward and around the trailer. The road was more of a sand footpath really, with walls of thick green scrub oaks, palmetto clumps, and spindly young pines.

"I don't know," Truman said dubiously. "Looks like a pretty tight fit."

"Mr. K, this car is older than I am," Jackie said. "A couple of scratches on this old paint can't hurt anything."

"Original paint job," Truman grumbled. But he headed into the thicket, flinching each time a tree branch slapped at the windshield or scraped on the sides.

When he was about 100 yards down the trail, he stopped.

"Guess what I brought?" Jackie reached into her gym bag and brought out two brightly colored plastic figureheads, with antennae sticking out from between their ears.

"Batman and the Joker?"

"Walkie-talkies," Jackie said. "My sister's kids left them at my place when they were down in June. See," she said, pushing a switch on the Joker's ear. The crackle of static filled the car. "New batteries and everything."

"What are we supposed to do with these?" Truman asked, looking distastefully at Batman.

"We can split up and hide," Jackie said, opening her car door. "So we make sure we can both hear and see what they're doing."

"Might work," Truman said.

The rain was still misting, but it hadn't dropped the temperature below ninety. Mosquitoes swarmed in the thicket, lighting on their exposed arms, necks, and faces. Their feet sank into the soft, sandy path and saw-edged palmetto fronds slapped at them as they trudged along. The tiny beam of the flashlight wavered in the cloaklike darkness.

"Ow," Jackie said, swatting her arm. "Should have brought bug spray. I'm getting eaten alive."

Truman slapped at a mosquito on his neck. "Keep moving," he advised.

There was a sliver of moon and it seemed to flit in and out of gray-tinged silver rain clouds. "Not much moonlight tonight," Truman said. They were at the edge of the woods, in back of the construction trailer.

"There's a dump truck right up close to the road-side," Jackie said, flashing her beam on it. "Maybe one of us could hide in the back."

The truck's cab doors were locked, as Truman expected. He watched admiringly while Jackie climbed nimbly over the side of the truck, pausing to unfasten a heavy black tarp that had been pulled tight over the cargo area.

A few seconds later, he saw the tarp rumple. She popped her head out near the truck's tailgate. "This thing is really big," she said. "But it's half full of gravel, so I can see out a little bit. Hotter than seven devils under this tarp."

"Can you hear under that thing?" Truman called. She disappeared. "Can you hear?" he repeated.

"Yeah," came a muffled voice. "I can hear, but I can't see unless I peek out like I was just doing."

"Stay down then, and just listen," Truman instructed. "I'll find a place nearby where I can see what's going on."

Jackie's head popped up. "What's my code name?" she asked, holding aloft her purple-and-green walkie-talkie.

"Just talk when you need me," Truman said.

There was more light up close to the road, from an

overhead streetlight and the flashing flares mounted on the barricades.

He pulled himself up into the cab of a motor grader and looked around. There was a good view of the road, but it was too open, he concluded. The only way he could see here was to be seen. He'd be a sitting duck.

The other pieces of equipment scattered around were just as visible. He needed to find a vantage point, and quickly. It was nearly eleven-thirty. He swung around in a slow circle. The bright-blue Porta Potti caught his eye. It was in front of the dump truck, maybe five yards away from the shoulder of the road, to the right of the second set of barricades.

He stepped up into the pillbox, leaving the door ajar. The booth was tiny, maybe four feet square, with a white one-piece toilet and a minuscule metal sink. The stench was incredible. Like a chicken house in July. He tried to breathe through his mouth.

The only fresh air coming into the Porta Potti was from a set of louvered vents, up high, near the ceiling. Dim rays of light from the streetlamp shone through in narrow strips.

"Something to stand on," Truman said aloud.

He darted outside, saw a trash pile, and ran over to it. There were plenty of plywood scraps, but they all looked too big. He kicked at the pile, bent down, and clawed through the debris until he found some rough scraps of two-by-fours. He pulled two of the boards out and dragged them over to the Porta Potti. Wedged side by side across the commode bowl, they made a narrow platform. Gripping the edge of the sink for balance, he pulled himself to a standing position.

The view was disappointing. The flimsy plastic louvers were too narrow. He climbed back down and tried to think. Tools. Maybe one of the construction workers had left some in one of the trucks. Or in the trailer. He glanced down at his watch. Ten of. Too late, he couldn't risk leaving his post now.

Truman planted both feet apart, so they rested on a single plank, each on the edge of the commode bowl. Slowly, he leaned down and picked up the second board. Once, he felt the two-by-four teetering, and he edged his feet apart, slightly wider.

He used the end of the board as a battering ram, gripping it with both hands and jabbing hard at the plastic vents. After the third strike, he heard the plastic cracking. He jabbed some more, on either end of the vent, trying not to lose his balance, throwing only his upper body into the effort.

More of the plastic cracked. He felt it with his fingertips. The material had gotten brittle and weakened from exposure to the sun. He tore at the louvers, ripping out two and shattering another with his fists.

Better. He'd broken out the bottom half of the vents and now he stood at eye level, looking directly out at the barricaded section of the road closest to the overpass pilings.

The walkie-talkie crackled. He'd set it down in the sink and to get it he had to do a careful deep-knee bend.

"Breaker one-nine, breaker one-nine," a tinny voice said. "Joker to Batman. Do you read me, Batman? Over."

"I read you," Truman said.

"Where are you, Batman? Over."

Truman sighed. If he told her he was hiding in a

Porta Potti, Jackleen would never let him hear the end of it.

"I'm about twenty yards north of you," he said. "I can see the road from here."

"What's going on out there, Batman? Talk to me. It must be a hundred and twenty degrees under here."

Truman saw a set of headlights outside. The car slowed, the lights were cut, and then it veered sharply to the right, stopping in front of the first set of barriers. It was a cream-colored Mercedes.

"Gotta go," Truman said softly. "We've got company."

"I copy," Jackie said. "Joker, over and out."

CHAPTER

TWENTY

HERNANDO BOONE WAS FIVE MINUTES EARLY by Truman's watch. He finally got out of the Mercedes, pushed the wooden barricades aside, and drove through, running over and crushing one of them. Truman heard the wood splintering as the tires rolled over it.

Good. He could see and hear, unless they decided to take up whispering.

Boone snugged the Mercedes up against one of the concrete overpass pilings. He strolled around to the back of the car, reached in the trunk, and brought out a large, clear-glass bottle. He hopped on the closed trunk, fiddled in his pocket, and brought out a stout, hand-rolled cigarette, which he lit with a disposable lighter.

"Spliffs," the Jamaicans called them. Big as a Havana cigar, only instead of tobacco, this little number was grade-A ganga. Boone opened the quart of Stoli and let it trickle down the back of his throat, savoring the cool burn. He took a long hit off the spliff, then settled back to wait for Ronnie and his crew.

Bondurant wasn't used to not running the show, but neither was Hernando Boone. He'd had a high school coach once, shitty coach, didn't know jack about running a passing offense, but old Coach Jackson told him one thing that stuck with him.

"Starting out," Coach told Hernando, "you gonna work for the man. That's all right. You listen to the man, take his money, learn how things work, make your mistakes on the man's time. Then, when it's time, you do your own thing. And the man comes to work for you."

Boone trickled some more Stoli down his throat. The bottle had been in the freezer at the meat locker all day, now the frosty wetness felt good in the blanketlike heat.

Bondurant was the man. He was the classic small-time hustler on the make to get in on the big score. Maybe he would, maybe he wouldn't. The home-delivery meat business was a gold mine, but Boone was bored with ghetto enterprises. Insurance. Now that was white collar. Upscale. Florida was the perfect environment for it, but other states were wide open. Texas, for sure. Mississippi, too. With his organizational skills, and for the time being, Ronnie's knowledge of the racket, he could pull down some heavy change. Get him some computers, hook up to some databases, do it right.

Hernando had already decided that he would take on only one partner. Weems would have to go. It was only a matter of timing. Might piss off Ronnie, but that was okay. Let him know who he was dealing with, in case he got any ideas.

There were lights coming this way. Two sets, close together. As they got closer he saw that one was the big gray Lincoln, the other some kind of yellow Plymouth with a muffler that sounded like one of the old bomber jets.

The Lincoln glided past the splintered barricades, pulling over on the shoulder near a bright-blue Porta Potti. Seconds later the Plymouth came through, running smack over the barricades, sending chunks of wood flying. The driver screeched to a halt maybe two feet from the back of the Mercedes.

"Jesus," Ronnie yelled, jumping out of the Lincoln. He ran over to the car, an old Fury, and grabbed the young driver by the collar of his T-shirt, hauling him out through the open window. "Who told you to pull a stupid stunt like that? Huh? A piece of that barricade hit the hood of my car, you asshole. You dinged my Lincoln."

Wormy pushed open the driver's-side door and eased out of the seat. His back was killing him. He'd taken two of Doc's Malaysian mind benders, and they hadn't kicked in yet.

He walked, stiff-gaited, toward the Plymouth, where Ronnie had the monkey by the scruff of his neck, shaking him like a dirty dishrag.

It was the same kid, the monkey who'd hit Wormy and made him fuck up his back like this. Billy something.

Wormy pulled his pistol out of his waistband and put the gun's barrel in the kid's ear. "Tell me your name again?" Wormy demanded. "I like to know a guy's name before I blow his brains all over the place."

"It's Billy. Billy Tripp," the kid said in a small, strangled voice. "I'm sorry, Ronnie. I was kidding around. Okay? You said . . . you said we were gonna total the Mercedes. So I just, you know . . ."

Ronnie released his hold on Billy, but Wormy stood his ground, the pistol drilled into Billy's ear.

Boone, watching, was tired of Weems's theatrics. The dude was a definite liability. He slid off the trunk of the Mercedes, took a long hit off the spliff, and threw it to the ground.

"Yo, Ronnie," he said. "Thought we had some business to do here."

He offered Ronnie the vodka bottle.

Ronnie hesitated. He was particular about who he drank after. But now Boone was waiting, the bottle in his outstretched hand. It was a test. What the hell, Ronnie decided. It was vodka, same thing as rubbing alcohol with some rotted potatoes thrown in for flavoring.

Ronnie closed his eyes and took a long drink, then handed the bottle back to Boone.

"Come on, Wormy," Ronnie ordered. "You're scaring Billy. He's learned his lesson, haven't you, Billy?"

The monkey's face was pale and still. "Yeah. I'm sorry. I wasn't thinking."

"Wormy?"

Wormy put the gun away reluctantly. "I'll catch up with you later, pissant."

Billy scuttled out of Wormy's line of vision.

"Let's do it," Ronnie decided.

"Boone, I'd fasten that seat belt if I were you. Put it in neutral and wait. Billy, back up some so you'll have some momentum. Not too fast, now. That Fury's a big hunk of steel. Hit him too hard and our friend Hernando will be having a concrete sandwich for a midnight snack."

Weems's brays of laughter echoed in the deserted construction site. It was a nice thought—Boone with a couple tons of concrete shoved down his throat.

Hernando buckled himself into the Mercedes. His mind was made up. Wormy's disposal would be a priority item on his schedule.

The monkey backed the yellow Fury up past the first set of barricades. He stuck his head out the window. "Ready?"

"Stomp it," Ronnie shouted.

The Fury's motor roared to life as it accelerated across the asphalt, hurtling straight toward the rear of the Mercedes. Billy Tripp's face was a blur as he shot by.

"Get him," Wormy said under his breath. "Flatten the nigger."

The kid hit the brakes moments before impact, and the Fury skidded fast and hard. The sound of squealing rubber, metal on metal, metal on concrete, concrete on glass, was deafening.

"Too hard," Ronnie said, shaking his head. "The kid's got a lead foot." They stood, gazing at the Fury with its whole front end embedded in the back of the crumpled-up Mercedes.

"Shit. I think he busted a fuel line," Ronnie said, alarmed.

The smell of gasoline filled the air. There was a boom then, and flames shot out of the hood of the Plymouth.

"Shit," Ronnie screamed, running toward the Fury. "Billy! Get out."

Hernando Boone threw open the door of the Mercedes and stumbled out. His face was cut and bleeding. He stumbled, fell, got up, then stood there, dazed, watching the flames leap up in the air.

Ronnie Bondurant wrenched the door of the Fury open. Billy Tripp half fell, half jumped out.

"Help me get him up," Ronnie called. "Come on. The car is gonna blow."

Boone hesitated, then stepped forward, grabbing Billy under one arm, while Ronnie grabbed the other. Haltingly, they dragged the unconscious monkey across the pavement, off the shoulder, toward the construction trailer.

When the explosion came, Boone and Bondurant dropped to the ground, covering their heads with their arms. The life they had saved was suddenly irrelevant. Billy Tripp was forgotten.

Greasy, black smoke poured out of the gutted Fury, and the hood and front doors blew out, sailing off into the no longer quiet night.

Crouched under cover of the gray Lincoln, Wormy Weems could see nothing. But he heard chunks of the car raining down around him. "Two birds with one stone," he mused with satisfaction.

Something big hit the side of the Porta Potti. It rocked crazily for a moment, knocking Truman off the commode and into the sink. He felt the Porta Potti wobbling, felt it toppling over. He tried to brace himself against the impact. In his panic, he forgot to breathe through his mouth, and nearly swooned from the stench.

When the Porta Potti hit the dirt, Truman's head banged against the steel sink pipe so hard he thought he heard his skull bones splintering. Tears sprang to his eyes, and he bit his lip to keep from crying out from the pain.

He listened to his own breathing for a while, then wiggled his fingers and toes to make sure that he could. His ears were still ringing. Gingerly, he felt his head. A lump was already rising on the back of his head, and he could feel a small cut oozing blood.

Get your bearings, he told himself sternly. Sit still and wait for equilibrium to return. Finally, on his hands and knees, he inched out from under the sink, crawling forward until he bumped his head on what had been the roof of the Porta Potti. With his hands, he felt the air vents. His hiding place had pitched over backward, landing the vents against the ground, and its inhabitant in total darkness. At least it hadn't landed on the door. For this, Truman silently thanked his maker.

There were voices close by.

"Wormy!" It was Ronnie's voice.

"Back here, behind your car," Wormy called back. "You okay, Ronnie?"

"We're both okay, asshole," Boone shouted. "Thanks for asking. Your driver's breathing, but I think he broke something. You need to help us get him to the car."

Ronnie's voice was closer still. "Come on, Wormy," he said. "Somebody will have heard that explosion. We've got to get out of here before the cops show up. Help us get Billy to the car."

"Fuck him," Wormy said, standing up. "Leave him where he is. Let the cops deal with it."

"What about my Mercedes, man?" Boone cried. "We can't just leave it here like this. What am I gonna tell the insurance man?"

"Tell him your car was stolen earlier tonight," Ronnie said. "The thieves must have wrecked it out here, then run off. Come on," he urged. "You wanted it totaled, it's totaled."

Truman heard footsteps again, then the sound of four car doors being opened, then closed. The Lincoln's engine purred to life, and he heard tires on gravel.

From somewhere at the other end of the Porta Potti, Truman heard a familiar crackling noise.

"Joker to Batman. Come in, Batman. What the hell was that noise?"

CHAPTER

TWENTY-ONE

JACKIE YANKED OPEN THE DOOR OF THE PORTA Potti, and gave Truman a hand so he could crawl out.

He sat on the ground, dazed and shaken, feeling every inch his age. Mosquitoes swarmed around him in a buzzing cloud. He was too tired to slap them away.

"You're bleeding," Jackie said, gently touching the back of his head. "And, excuse me, but you smell like a shithouse. Phee-eeww!"

"I've got to get to a shower," Truman said, struggling to his feet.

"I saw a sign on the way in here tonight, for a Boy Scout camp," Jackie said. "I'll bet they got showers. We could drive over there. I never knew Weedon Island had anything out here but the Florida Power Plant."

Tired as he was, Truman wouldn't hear of trying to drive to the camp in the Nova. "The way I smell? We'd never get rid of the stink. Besides, I saw that road, too. There's a big metal cattle gate pulled across it. The only way we're getting in there is on foot."

The walk seemed endless in the heat and the damp. Truman trudged along in the dark while Jackie stayed a few yards ahead—and upwind—keeping the flashlight trained on the crushed oyster-shell path.

Jackie was thin enough to be able to squeeze through the bars of the cattle gate. Truman sighed and put one leg up on the middle rung, somehow summoning the energy to haul himself up and over the top bar.

A wooden sign nailed to the trunk of a pine tree notified them that it was .6 of a mile to the Boy Scout camp. Truman groaned, despite his resolve not to let on how bad he felt. His head wound was throbbing and his knees were cut and swollen from the pounding they'd taken when the Porta Potti toppled over.

"You okay?" Jackie asked, turning around to check on him. They'd been through a lot together, and it wasn't like Mr. K to complain.

"I'll be better when I get this muck washed off," he told her.

Somewhere along the way, Jackie started whistling softly to herself.

"Where'd you learn that?" Truman asked, stopping in his tracks.

"Ollie and I watched *The Bridge Over the River Kwai* a few weeks ago. I'd heard the song before, but I never knew where it came from."

"You know the real name of that song?" It was the kind of trivia Truman loved.

"Nope."

"'The Colonel Bogey March,'" Truman informed her.

They passed a clearing in the woods that revealed a patch of water thickly ringed with mangroves. As they got closer to the path, the mangrove branches rustled loudly and they heard the furious flapping of wings and startled calls. Jackie shined the flashlight up into the treetops. "Lookit," she said, awed. "Flamingoes. This must be where they nest. I never saw so many flamingoes except on TV."

"You still haven't," Truman told her, watching a bird flap off to a nearby treetop. "Those are roseate spoonbills. Same color as flamingoes, but the bill is different, like a flattened spoon."

"Here's some kind of building," Jackie said after they'd walked another five minutes. She played the flashlight over the building. Large cedar poles had been sunk into the ground around a raised concrete platform, and more cedar logs formed a high-pitched roof. There were concrete picnic tables and benches and a large, open-stacked rock fire pit.

"This is it?" Jackie asked. "This is their idea of a camp? What about bathrooms, cabins, all that kind of thing? What's with the Boy Scouts?"

"Boy Scouts are supposed to rough it," Truman said. "They sleep in tents. Dig latrines. This must be their dining hall. Come on, let's look and see if there's at least a spigot."

At the back of the fire pit they found a wall-mounted shower head with a rusty stream of water dribbling from it.

"Take a walk," Truman told Jackie, "unless you want to see another rare bird. The white-tailed stink-pot."

"Hurry up," she said, slapping at her arms, "these skeeters are eating me alive."

Truman turned the nozzle on full force and got a half-hearted spray of sulphur-scented water. He stood under the spray and stepped out of his excrement-spattered clothes. When he'd soaked every part of himself and the smell of sulphur finally overpowered the latrine smell, he picked the clothes up, held them under the water for a long time, and then wrung each piece out separately.

He pulled the light-blue boxer shorts on. They were waterlogged and hung loosely on his hips, but he was decent. He buttoned the navy-blue sport shirt, but the stink clung to his pants like a sandspur on a dog. He could not bear to put them on again. He rolled them up and dropped them in a wire trash bin at the edge of the encampment.

"Aren't you forgetting something?" Jackie asked as he met her on the path back to the main road.

"Boxers. They're all the rage now," he explained. "Chip even wears them to school."

"Look like men's underwear to me," Jackie said. "Droopy underwear."

Truman's waterlogged sneakers made a squishing noise with each step he took. But the wet clothes and the shower had cooled him off, and he had more energy than he knew he still possessed.

"Did you hear what they were saying to each other before the crash?" Truman asked her. "I couldn't quite make it out."

"The black guy was asking how they were going to be able to file for the insurance without a witness or a police report. And then Wormy, the mean one? He just laughed and said they didn't need the cops. Said that's what made Florida great. Insurance companies don't require a police report or witnesses—just one party who admits the accident was his fault."

"That tells us for certain what the racket is,"

Truman said. "Fake car wrecks. But why Corvettes? And why steal back yours?"

"They didn't talk about that," Jackie said. "But Ronnie told the black guy, Boone, that getting the insurance company to total out a Mercedes was going to be a pain in the ass. Over ten thousand dollars, he said, you can't go to no drive-through claims window."

"Why Corvettes?" Truman wondered again.

They were coming out of the path now, and into the area of the construction site. The air was filled with the acrid smell of burning rubber, and flashing red-and-blue lights throbbed on and off near the wrecked cars. A fireman stood at the edge of the clearing, aiming a hose at the now steaming cars. There was a uniformed police officer, too, shining a large black flashlight at the rubber skid marks that led up to the crash. Another man, not in uniform, sat in the police cruiser, and they could hear the low chatter of radio traffic.

"Shouldn't we talk to them?" Jackie asked. "Let them know what we saw and heard? That young guy they called Billy, when I peeked out, I saw them dragging him to the Lincoln. He was hurt bad, Mr. K, maybe even dead."

"They'd never believe us," Truman said, gesturing down at the waterlogged undershorts that threatened to fall off unless he kept them hitched up with one hand. "They'd probably arrest me for indecent exposure. Or worse, try to pin that wreck on us. No, let's go get in the car and wait them out. The fire's died down, there can't be too much to see in the dark. I'll call that FDLE agent in the morning. Let him know what went on."

◆　　◆　　◆

Ollie slid into the chair across from Truman, who was watching the butter pat melt in his bowl of grits.

"Where you been?" Ollie asked breathlessly. "It's third seating already. I was getting ready to go up to your room to see if there was any sign of life. Finally, Jackie stopped long enough to tell me about what all happened last night. Wish I'd have been there."

"No you don't," Truman said. "You know women. They dramatize things." He tasted his grits, then added a fine layer of salt and pepper and tried again. Much better. He finished them off while Ollie waited expectantly to hear more details of the previous night's escapade.

There was a stir across the room. "Very funny," Jackie said angrily. Ollie and Truman turned around to see what the commotion was about.

Jackie was standing over two of the youth hostel kids, both boys of maybe eighteen, with long, unkempt hair. They sniggered wildly as Jackie dumped the contents of a hunter-green knapsack out on the table. Foil-wrapped packages came tumbling out in a heap. She tore one open.

"See!" she exclaimed. "Bacon. Sausage. Fried ham. I knew it. What else have you two been squirreling away?" The foil from another package fell to the floor. Half a dozen biscuits and as many jelly packets were added to the heap of breakfast meats. Now she had her hand in the bag, digging around to see what else she'd find. A set of silverware clattered onto the table, followed by two of the restaurant's small service plates, salt and pepper shakers, and a jumbo-sized McDonald's drink cup. Orange juice slopped over the side as Jackie held it triumphantly in the air.

"There's enough food in this bag to feed six people," she said accusingly. "I told Mr. Wiggins somebody was stealing food. Y'all ought to be ashamed of yourselves."

The young men looked anything but ashamed. "Lighten up, babe," one of them said, snatching the backpack out of her hands. "It's not like we broke into Fort Knox or something. Just a little snack for the guys back in the room."

Both of them got up from the table, threw a handful of pennies on top of the mess, than swaggered out of the restaurant.

Jackie stood for a moment, speechless. Then she scooped up the change and followed the boys out into the hotel lobby, where they were unlocking their bikes from the wrought-iron planter they had chained them to the night before. "Here!" she shouted, flinging the pennies in their faces. "Buy some bubblegum for the dudes back in the room. And get those bikes out of this lobby before one of our regular guests trips over them."

The boys glared at her and mumbled something under their breaths, but they wheeled the bikes quickly out of the lobby, while Jackie stood there, hands on her hips, daring them to give her any more lip.

"Good for her," Truman said. He scraped up the last bit of scrambled eggs with the crust of his toast, then pushed away from the table.

"Time to get busy. I've got a lot of research to get done before I go in to work," Truman said.

"Yeah," Ollie said reluctantly. "Me, too. You got

anything you need me to research? I got all those magazines at the newsstand, you know."

"Not today," Truman said. "Let me get my feet wet at Bondurant Motors. Then maybe I'll have a better idea of how you can help. Things are starting to heat up though, I can tell you that."

"Gonna be a big story," Ollie said. "Blow this town apart."

Jackie stomped back into the dining room and began cleaning up the mess the hostel kids had made at their table. Truman watched in sympathy. "I'd be satisfied just to help her get her car or her money back," he said.

"And solve a murder," Ollie added.

Truman didn't correct him.

Ed Weingarten, the FDLE agent, was visiting a sick friend, his secretary said. Truman left a message telling him it was urgent that they talk.

Then he called Clarice Umbach, his insurance agent. Actually, Clarice was his old agent's daughter-in-law. When Jack retired, Clarice took over all his clients. She'd been helpful and sympathetic during Nellie's hospitalization, and later . . . And over the years, he'd referred a lot of business to Jack and Clarice.

She greeted him enthusiastically. "My favorite client! Want to hear about our new annuity program for that grandson of yours?"

He felt a pang of guilt. Someday, he'd put some more money in that college fund he'd started for Chipper. Someday.

"Actually, Clarice, I need information for a big

story I'm working on for the *St. Pete Times*. A car insurance scam."

Clarice groaned. "That's all we need around here. A new way to cheat insurance companies. Pretty soon there won't be an insurer in the country willing to write a policy down here. So tell me how this one works."

"They stage car accidents," Truman started.

"Nothing new in that," Clarice said.

"This guy owns a used-car lot. From what I've gathered, they buy a collision policy on a junky car, put it in the name of one of their flunkies, then stage an accident with a much more expensive car. Corvettes, usually, for some reason I can't figure out. And they said something about wanting to be able to make the claim at a drive-through."

"I can help you with that," Clarice said. "A Corvette's body is made almost entirely of fiberglass. No metal on it. You hit a Corvette and it crumples like a paper doll. That's why their rates are so high, higher even than your average sportscar. On the upside though, a good body man—one who knows fiberglass—can put one back together pretty quickly. Unless the frame is bent. If that happens, not all the king's horses and all the king's men can make it right."

Truman was taking notes almost as fast as Clarice was talking.

"Could you take the same car, take it apart, and put it back together again and again? Without most people being able to tell?"

She paused. "I don't know. You need to talk to a body shop about that. Want me to see who's on our approved list?"

"Yeah," Truman said. "But what about the insurance

claims? Wouldn't somebody notice the same guy getting hit over and over again?"

Clarice laughed. "Theoretically, yes. There are two or three huge companies, Globalfax is the biggie, that keep computer databases on every policy bought, every claim filed, everything. They sell that data to insurance companies so they can check up on people before they write a policy. See if they're a good risk."

Truman was appalled. "They can do that?"

"And more," Clarice said. "But if you're worried about somebody checking up on you, Truman, you can relax. I happen to know that your insurer, Gulfshores, isn't a subscriber."

"I should have known," Truman said. "They don't even send out a calendar at Christmas."

"Don't knock it. Their rates are the cheapest in town," Clarice reminded him.

"I'd sure like to think of a way to find out whether these crooks have a history of this thing," Truman said.

"I've got a friend at Allstate," Clarice said thoughtfully. "They do subscribe to Globalfax. We trade favors sometimes. Do you have the names of these scam artists?"

"Just three," Truman said. "Ronnie Bondurant. Wormy, uh, William D. Weems. Hernando Boone. Oh, yeah, and there's a fourth. Billy Tripp. Two 'P's, I think."

He could hear her pencil scribbling away. "Got it," she said finally. "What kind of currency can I use for the trade?"

He had to think. In the old days, at the wire, he had access to all kinds of riches: passes to the latest concerts, movies, the circus, Broadway plays, free records, books, booze, hotel rooms, fancy restaurant meals. Everybody wanted to show off their wares to the Associated Press. Later, the bosses had started to frown on freebies. Backlash from Watergate. So you took the freebies under the table.

Now he was retired. He had a Nova station wagon with a busted window, a half share in an aluminum boat with no motor, and an AARP discount card.

What about Ollie though? He griped all the time about all the magazines and paperback books he had to destroy so Chet could get credit for unsold merchandise. Truman had access to every cheesy paperback novel and magazine he could ever want.

"Does your friend like to read?" he asked Clarice.

"She likes to eat," Clarice said. "I bet she weighs three hundred pounds. It's a cinch she's not spending her spare time working out at the gym. Let me give it a try. Anything else while I'm at it?"

"No, but thanks," Truman said. "Wait. Yes. One more name. Just in case. Jeff Cantrell."

When Ed Weingarten called back, he was not in a chatty mood.

"You're not still sniffing around Ronnie Bondurant and his bunch, are you?"

"Hell, yeah," Truman said, getting defensive. "In fact, that's why I'm calling. Last night we saw them in action. Bondurant, Weems, Boone, and a kid named Tripp. Out on Weedon Island, where all the construction is going on. We saw them total Boone's Mercedes. On purpose. This kid named Tripp was nearly killed. And I know about the Corvettes, too—why they use them, probably even why they killed Jeff Cantrell."

"We already know most of that stuff," Weingarten snapped. "Mr. Kicklighter, I asked you not to get involved in this matter. You're endangering yourself as well as our agents."

"I can take care of myself," Truman said. "In the meantime, you people can't tell me a single thing about this young man they killed, can you? While I've tracked down his girlfriend, staked out his apartment, what have you people been doing? Tell me that, Mr. FDLE."

It had been years since he'd told off a cop like that. Felt good, too.

"It's against agency policy for me to tell you this, Mr. Kicklighter. But I'm going to do it anyway, just to get you off my back. We have reason to believe that Jeff Cantrell is not dead. We think he's very much alive. Probably still mixed up with Bondurant."

"No," Truman said. "Jackie saw him. With a bullet in the side of his head. You can't fake that. And nobody's seen or heard from him since that day."

"Just a moment."

Weingarten's voice was muffled. He was talking to someone else.

"I'm looking at a printout of the activity on his Visa card and his checking account," Weingarten said grimly. "He's been using his ATM card, as recently as last night. There are long distance calls to his girlfriend's apartment from Ft. Lauderdale."

"It's a trick," Truman insisted. "I know it is."

"Dead men don't call collect, Mr. Kicklighter. Do yourself a favor. Find a nice hobby. Shuffleboard, maybe."

CHAPTER

TWENTY-TWO

LEEANN PILKER SLIPPED OUT OF THE KING-SIZED bed, pulling the sheet up over Ronnie's shoulder so he wouldn't notice she was gone. She stood there, looking down at him, feeling something like tenderness.

There was something about men in their sleep. They looked so helpless and vulnerable. Even Ronnie Bondurant. With his hair mussed you could see a little quarter-sized bald spot on the back of his head. And with one cheek flattened against his pillow, his dark features were soft, almost sweet. She stopped herself there, though. Sweet? Ronnie? No, she wouldn't go that far.

Her suitcase was on a chair, near the door. She rummaged around and found the black tank bathing suit. She'd just barely had time to throw a few things together on Tuesday, after Ronnie called her apartment a rathole and insisted she move in with him. Right then.

Well, why not? It was a nice place. A sprawling white-brick ranch house, smack dab on Tampa Bay, on Pinellas Point. There was a dock out back, and hanging high in the air on a set of davits, a gleaming new turquoise-and-white Hydrasport. A practiced look told her those were twin 200-horsepower Evinrude outboards. There was a time, when she was a teenager, when she knew the make and model of every boat on the bay. Especially the cool ones. Ronnie's house had a pool, too, on the screened-in porch that led off the kitchen. Everything was very neat, if just a bit shabby. There were tiny rips in the leather sofas in the Florida room that looked out over the pool and the bay, and two or three panels of the screening on the porch were torn. The lawn was in bad shape, half the grass dead or dying, and the bushes scraggly and unkempt. Ronnie didn't spend a lot of time at home, she'd learned.

She made a pot of coffee, found a towel, and headed for the pool. She plunged in, dove all the way to the bottom, hovered there for a minute or two, then let herself bob to the surface.

This, LeeAnn thought, was heaven. With long, even strokes she swam to the shallow end, touched the tile coping with her fingertips, and executed a respectable flip turn. She swam two more laps, then paused at the deep end, holding on to the wall, inhaling that sharp, distinct smell. Chlorine. It really was her favorite scent. Absolutely clean and clear. She'd always loved swimming. And it was great exercise because it kept your legs toned and your chest muscles strong. She couldn't swim too much, though, or she'd end up with a set of shoulders like Arnold Schwarzenegger. The management at the club frowned on big shoulders. Except on bouncers like Margie.

What the hell? LeeAnn did another lap. Who needed the Candy Store? Ronnie was already making noises about her moving in here permanently. And he kept talking about plans, big plans.

That first night he came into the club while she was dancing, a dozen Pasco County shitkickers, dressed up in cowboy hats and boots, the whole rig, were whooping it up at the front table.

Ronnie walked right up, with that creepy friend of his, Wormy, threw five hundred-dollar bills down on the table. "Round-up time, boys," he announced. Wormy pulled a chair out from beneath one of the scrawnier guys, then pulled his jacket aside so the guy could see something shoved into his belt. A gun, probably. The cowboys cleared out in a hurry, taking the money with them. And Ronnie and Wormy sat through both shows. All the girls got $50 tips that night, except for LeeAnn. Ronnie was waiting by his big gray Lincoln when she got off work at three A.M.

She went with him. He was generous, for sure. When they'd gotten back to this house on the water, he'd given her $500. Cash. "Go shopping," Ronnie said. "Buy yourself some sharp clothes. And high heels. I like high heels. The kind with ankle straps."

That old guy, the one who showed up at the club with Jeff's friend Eddie. He'd tried to make her feel bad about two-timing Jeff. Hinted that maybe something bad had happened to Jeff. LeeAnn was a realist. Jeff had dumped her. The plastic surgeon had turned her account over to a collection agency. They called constantly, day and night. Once the bastards even showed up at her apartment. That was another reason to move in with Ronnie. No hassles. And he loved her implants.

"The bigger the better, sugar," he told her.

She was back at the shallow end, going into the kick turn when she felt a hand on her head.

Her heart almost stopped. She opened her mouth, took in a lungful of the chlorinated water, and surfaced, sputtering for air.

Ronnie sat by the side of the pool. He was dressed in white cotton slacks, a white golf shirt, Docksiders, no socks. Like he was headed for a day of yachting.

"Morning, sugar," he said brightly.

She shook the long, dark hair out of her eyes, spraying him with droplets of water.

"You scared me."

Ronnie ran his index finger down the side of her face.

"I been sitting here watching you swim. No prettier fish in the sea. But I can't figure out why a beautiful body like yours is all bundled up in an ugly old bathing suit? Huh?"

He took the strap of her suit and gently slid it off one shoulder, then the other.

LeeAnn felt goosebumps on the back of her neck. It was just the cold, she reasoned.

"I need the support when I'm swimming, Ronnie," she explained. "You know, when you're a D cup, they tend to get in the way."

He threw his head back and laughed and laughed at that one.

"In whose way?"

So she left the suit at the edge of the shallow end, near the handrail, and she did what Ronnie requested. Swam to the deep end. Got out and stood there. And dove in again. Swam to the shallow end, got out and walked, bare-ass naked, back to the deep end, to repeat the performance all over again. It bugged her. Made her feel what? Nasty?

Dancing naked at the club never bothered her. She'd started there as a waitress, quickly seen that the big tips were for the dancers, and within a month, she'd gotten rid of her inhibitions, and most of her clothes.

She was padding dutifully back to the deep end when he called her over to him.

Ronnie was sitting on a wrought-iron chair, part of a patio set. She reached for the towel she'd left on the glass-topped table, but he pulled it away. So she sat there, with the wrought-iron chairs making little flower and vine marks on her butt.

"Those," he said, reaching out and touching her nipple, "are the most perfect titties I've ever seen. That doctor of yours was an artist."

"I guess so," she said and shrugged. She really did not see what the big deal was about large breasts. It probably went back to caveman times, she decided. Besides, she'd always remember those bruises, how sore she was after the surgery.

"What'd you say that doctor's name was, sugar?"

She made a face. "Dr. Newcomb. It's hard to forget when they call you over and over again to remind you what you owe them."

"He's supposed to be good?"

"I guess," she said. "A lot of girls at the clubs in town use him. He gives some kind of courtesy discount. Supposedly. It's still expensive as shit."

"But worth it," Ronnie said. "I believe I'll call this Dr. Newcomb. See if we can't get that bill of yours paid off. Maybe we'll do a little dickering."

LeeAnn frowned. "Dickering? He's a doctor, Ronnie. He has set prices. You don't dicker with a plastic surgeon."

He threw the towel back to her. "You just leave that to me. I got a red Corvette, got plastic surgeon written all over it. There ain't a doctor alive who can resist the call of a Corvette, sugar."

They were drinking coffee in the kitchen when the doorbell rang. Ronnie didn't bother to look up from the sports page. "Get that, will you?"

It was Wormy. She didn't know why he made her feel so creepy. It wasn't like he looked at her the way men did all the time. It was more like he looked right through her.

He followed her into the kitchen without saying a word. Poured himself a cup of coffee and sat down at the table with Ronnie.

Ronnie put his cup down. "LeeAnn, honey," he said. "How about you go outside and give that grass a good watering? I just noticed it's looking a little brown. Think you could do that?"

"Sure," LeeAnn said. She'd been looking for an excuse to get out of the kitchen. Anywhere would do. Maybe later, she'd get Ronnie to let her take the Hydrasport out for a ride on the bay.

She found the hose coiled up on the side of the house, turned the water on, and walked out to the worst part of the lawn, close to where the seawall was. The water came out in a blast, kicking up dead grass and pea gravel from a sick-looking bed of hibiscus. What she needed was a spray attachment. She walked around the yard, looking for a toolshed or something.

There was a door to the garage back by the spigot. Maybe Ronnie kept his yard tools in there. She'd find some clippers too, give the hibiscus a trim.

There was a set of metal shelves near the door to the kitchen, with clippers and tools and bits and pieces of nails and other crap scattered all over, not neat like Ronnie usually was. She was standing there, surveying the mess, when she heard Ronnie's voice.

"No more real accidents. I mean it. That monkey last night, Billy, he bled all over my car. Remind me to get some of that carpet cleaner from the shop later on."

"The kid called the lot and left a message on the machine," Wormy said. "They're supposed to let him out of Bayfront this afternoon, maybe. And guess what? He's already running his mouth about who pays the bill."

"Unbelievable," Ronnie said. "Who the fuck told him to hit that Mercedes going forty miles an hour? It's his own goddamn fault he got hurt."

"He tell you he wanted seven hundred dollars to do Boone's car?" Wormy asked.

"Yeah, like I'm Santa Claus," Ronnie said. "Tell him to tell it to Boone. Billy gets two hundred, I get the rest. Make sure he understands that."

"He'll understand."

"You see," Ronnie continued, "that's why I'm thinking, what do we need with all these monkeys and cars? They're a pain in the ass."

"How else do we do it?" Wormy asked.

"This is the beauty part," Ronnie said. "We go to a parking lot somewhere. Office building, shopping center, whatever. We look in the windshield, write down the VIN number off the metal plate on the dashboard, then take down the tag number. Then we call up an insurance agent, tell him we want a collision policy on the car."

"Whose car?" Wormy asked, confused now.

"The car in the parking lot."

"But it ain't ours."

"You ever had an agent ask you for the title when you buy a policy?" Ronnie asked. "No. They want your money. They get the VIN and your tag number, and away we go."

"How we gonna stage a wreck with no car?" Wormy asked. Just when he thought he had stuff figured out, Ronnie threw him a new curve. That's why it was good working for Ronnie, 'cause with a mind like that, you never knew what was coming.

"We don't need a car, we don't need a wreck," Ronnie said. "Just a Corvette, and Joe and his air knife."

"But you said it was too expensive to keep having Joe do 'em," Wormy complained.

"That was when we were having to wreck our own cars," Ronnie said patiently. "This way, we do away with the monkeys, the cars, everything. Put an ad in the paper and sell off the Corvettes after five or six jobs. We got our original investment back, plus fifty or sixty thousand in gravy."

"What about Boone?"

"We'll see," Ronnie said. "This new setup gives us greater profit potential. Could be we don't need him."

"We never did need him, you ask me," Wormy said. "Him or Billy Tripp. Billy's done too many jobs for us, Ron. He knows all the angles. And now he knows Boone, too. It's kinda bugging me. What if

Tripp gets pissed off about this Mercedes deal? What if he decides to go to the cops or something, or worse, goes to work for Boone?"

LeeAnn had forgotten about the lawn and the clippers and everything. She sat on the concrete floor of the garage, fascinated. What all was Ronnie into? And Boone? He must be the big mixed-breed dude with the braid. Why were Ronnie and Wormy so worried about him?

"Quit worrying so much," Ronnie said. "We'll watch Tripp. He gives us any reason, he'll end up the same place as Cantrell. Billy Tripp takes a trip, huh?"

At the mention of Jeff's name, LeeAnn gasped involuntarily. She had to clamp her hand over her mouth to keep from crying out. What did they mean? The same place as Cantrell?

"Which reminds me," Wormy said. "We're gonna need to move old Jeff in the near future."

"I don't want to know," Ronnie said firmly. "You take care of it. That's your job."

"Yeah, Ron, but don't you forget to take care of your end of business, too," Wormy said slyly. "That chick of yours, LeeAnn. Why you want to mess with Cantrell's girlfriend? Thousands of chicks in this town waiting in line for a guy like you. Why get mixed up with her? How do you know she's not using you to try to figure out what happened to her boy-friend?"

Ronnie slapped his newspaper on the kitchen table. "Her? Using me? That's a good one. Let me tell you something. LeeAnn's not much on personality. She's got shit for brains. And half the time she dresses like a friggin' nun. But her body, her face. Wormy, she's got the potential. Big-time potential."

"For what?" Wormy asked, astonished. "Slut of the month? Stripper of the year?"

"Perfection," Ronnie repeated, as matter-of-factly as if he were discussing the paint job on a new Lexus.

"You kidding?"

In the garage, LeeAnn thought she might gag. Money or no money, she'd found herself a real sick ticket this time.

"I been looking, watching," Ronnie went on. "The fat to body weight ratio is excellent. All that dancing, her legs are perfect, arms slender, with well-defined musculature. The tits? Well, they're the work of a pro. Perfect Ds, both of them. I checked."

"So?"

"I'm not saying there's not some problem areas," Ronnie said. "Her ass is just the tiniest bit saggy. And she's got a bump on her nose. But they can do liposuction. Rhinoplasty on the nose. I'm gonna get the same guy who did the tits."

"I don't like them Jap-looking eyes of hers," Wormy put in. "Like she thinks she's smarter than Americans like us. All them Japs think that."

LeeAnn put her hand to her eyes. Her grandmother had been Korean. LeeAnn had only a faint memory of her, but she'd always loved her almond-shaped eyes. They were unlike anybody else's.

"Some people find the Eurasian look mysterious and exotic," Ronnie said, "but you could be right. I'll have the eyes straightened out while they're fixing up the other stuff."

"Cost a shitpot of money," Wormy pointed out.

"Perfection doesn't come cheap," Ronnie said. "Anyway, I'm thinking big. Playmate of the year. Why not? Cash, endorsements, movie contracts, appearances on *Howard Stern* and *Jay Leno*. I'll have special tops made for her that say "Bondurant Motors" right across the tits, like those NASCAR chicks."

LeeAnn did not hear the part about her exciting show-business prospects. There were not enough clothes or money or good times in the world to make up for how Ronnie Bondurant proposed to cut her up and put her back together again. Like one of his Corvettes. All plastic. She walked quietly around to the front of the house, crept up to the bedroom, grabbed her purse and the shopping bag of new clothes, stuffing in just a few of her old things. As she passed the dresser, she saw Ronnie's gold money clip lying there with a heap of change and a penknife. She helped herself. And she left behind the four pairs of ankle-strap high heels. Ronnie Bondurant could shove those shoes right up his ass.

Her gold Honda Civic—the hatchback model Jeff had sold her, telling her the hatch made it better for resale—stalled twice before she got it started.

She was around the semicircular driveway and half a block down the street by the time Ronnie and Wormy came running out into the driveway. They jumped into the Lincoln, luckily. She hadn't had time to take the distributor cap off Wormy's pickup, too.

"Truman? Mary Anne says to tell you she likes Barbara Taylor Bradford, Anne Rivers Siddons, and FBI books."

"FBI books?"

"She reads them all," Clarice said. "I think she's got a J. Edgar Hoover fetish."

"I'll see what I can do," Truman said. "Did she find anything?"

"Yes. Although nothing on Hernando Boone. Let me just get my notes. All right. Ronald Bondurant has had three different insurers in the past five years. And three different auto collisions. All rear end. None of them his fault."

"What kind of cars?" Truman asked.

"Um. An '89 Lincoln, a '91 Corvette, and a '92 Corvette. All claims paid by the other driver's insurer. And here's something interesting. There's a code on the report for the claims adjuster who approved the claim. The number is the same on both the Corvette claims. I'll have to call Mary Anne back to see what name goes with the approval code."

"I thought you said it was three different insurers," Truman said.

"I did," she said patiently. "But lots of companies use freelance claims adjusters. The same guy could work for twelve to fourteen different companies, especially if he's set up with a drive-through arrangement. A one-person outfit can handle a lot more volume in one of those, because there's less paperwork."

"And how does the claims payout work?" Truman asked.

"Different ways for different companies. But if you've got the right documentation, and the damages aren't too high, some of these places have authorization to issue checks right away. If the damage is less than ten thousand dollars."

"And it always is," Truman said. "What about the others? Did she find anything on them?"

"Remember, if the insurance companies aren't reporting members to Globalfax, the claim might not be on their database," Clarice said. "I found one for William D. Weems. He was at fault in a collision in '92, involving, hey! a '91 Lincoln owned by Ronald Bondurant."

"Before they figured out it wasn't a good idea to file cross-claims," Truman guessed. "What else?"

"Weems was the victim of a rear-end collision last week. He was driving a Corvette."

"Who was the driver at fault?"

"William Tripp," Clarice said. "Poor guy. He's driving a '74 Pinto. His insurer paid Weems eight thousand nine hundred."

"What about the claims adjuster's code on that one?"

She laughed. "I get it. Yeah, it's the same code as the others. 0012381."

"So it's likely they've got a claims adjuster working with them," Truman said.

"He's the one I'd like to nail," Clarice said. "Don't worry. I'll get you this guy's name. We don't need this kind of scum in the business."

"Any other claims for Tripp?" Truman asked. "I think he's one of Ronnie Bondurant's gofers. Monkeys, he calls them."

"That was all I found," Clarice said. "You better pony up with a lot of paperback books for this."

"A box load," he promised. "What about the last name I gave you? Jeff Cantrell?"

"Funny you should mention," Clarice said. "Mary Anne couldn't find any auto claims at all. But she likes to be thorough. I think it's another fetish. So she checked everything. Home, life, personal, the works. Your Mr. Cantrell had a burglary at his home just last month."

"An apartment on Allamanda Road?"

"Mmm-hmm. Cantrell had some pretty valuable stuff taken. Two fur coats, some gold jewelry, a four-thousand-dollar gold Rolex, and a lot of expensive electronics. Laser disc movie system, CD player, a PowerBook laptop, altogether, twenty-eight thousand dollars worth of goodies."

"All that? The guy was single. He lived in a converted garage and sold used cars for a living. Where does a twenty-six-year-old get the money to buy all that?"

"He's actually twenty-four," Clarice corrected him.

"A single twenty-four-year-old with two fur coats? In Florida?"

"State Farm paid the claim," Clarice said. "Talk to them, not me."

"Any chance there are other claims we don't know about?" There were only a handful of claims. Not enough to really establish what you could call a crime ring. And not enough money involved in what he had uncovered to suggest a motive for killing Jeff Cantrell.

He had a start, but the *St. Pete Times* wasn't going to run a big story on some penny-ante racket run by a small-time used-car king. There had to be more. Truman knew there was more.

"According to Mary Anne, the database is supposed to be up-to-date within seven days," Clarice was telling him. "But it's the same old story. Somebody has to type the stuff into a computer. Not everybody's reliable about doing that. They'll save the claims up for a month or six weeks or longer. You know how it is. More paper-work."

They cruised the streets around the neighborhood for forty minutes, but there was no sign of the gold Honda hatchback.

"I can't believe it," Ronnie was saying. He was hurt. "We had a good thing going. I had plans. Everybody knows, Ronnie Bondurant treats the ladies right. Why'd she want to rip me off and run away like that?"

"How much cash did she get?"

Ronnie winced. "Seven thousand. I was going to put it in the safe at the lot. This morning."

"She must have heard us talking," Wormy said. "About everything. Including Cantrell."

"Conniving little bitch," Ronnie said. "Now we've got to stop what we're doing and go after her. Make sure she keeps her mouth shut."

"Let Boone do it," Wormy suggested. "It's right up his alley."

"Boone's not going to know about this. Any of it," Ronnie said. "We'll take care of it ourselves. Like before. Right?"

"If you say so." Wormy was getting moody. "Like I don't have enough to do. Shit. It's nearly noon now. What about the lot? We got people due in with their payments today."

"I'll call the old man," Ronnie said. "Tell him where the keys are. He can open up, take care of business for a few hours. People don't start really coming in till later anyway."

Wormy scowled. His back was starting up, and his pain pills were in his desk. At the lot.

"I don't trust that old guy. I caught him snooping

around out back the other day. Right near the red 'Vette."

"Chill out," Ronnie said. "He's a harmless old buzzard. What's he gonna do? Find a skeleton in a closet?"

CHAPTER

TWENTY-THREE

TRUMAN FOUND THE SPARE KEYS TO THE LOT right where Ronnie had said they'd be, under the floor mat of a dusty gray Crown Victoria at the very back of the lot. After he unlocked the front door, set out the signboards that said INSTANT CREDIT! EVERYBODY RIDES!, and moved the barricades that kept the lot lizards off the property after dark, Truman took a good long look at the keys in his hand. There were five of them, all of the same general make and color.

Moving as quickly and calmly as he could, Truman tried the keys on each lock he could find. One opened Ronnie's inner office door. Another opened the middle drawer of his desk. There were some bank deposit slips, odds and ends of pencils and pens, a few business cards, nothing else of interest. He swiveled around in Ronnie's chair, looked down, and noticed where the carpet had been cut. With his toe, he moved the carpet. The safe.

No time to fool with it now.

Another key fit the door to the garage, where

he'd been once before. And out back, in the storage area, a padlock kept that gate locked. His last key was for the padlock. But no red Corvette.

Disappointed, he went back into the showroom. Someone called to say they couldn't make it in today, "'Cause I gotta work double shifts."

"He'll be expecting you tomorrow," Truman said severely. "With the full amount of payment."

While he was at Wormy's desk, Truman slid open the top drawer. It was much more interesting than Ronnie's desk. For one thing, there was a large clear-plastic medicine bottle containing probably fifty light-orange oval-shaped tablets. There was no label, no name on the bottle. He'd seen Wormy popping these pills at different times during the day. Truman took one of the pills and stashed it in his shirt pocket. There were more bank deposit slips in Wormy's drawer. Truman took one from what looked like three different accounts. He rifled through a small black-bound appointment book, found notations for "Doc Sperduto" and "Call Joe" as well as a scribbled phone number with a local exchange. He jotted down the names and the phone number. At the back of the desk, he found a key attached to a blank paper tag. It was unlike the other keys on Ronnie's desk.

He got up and roamed the room, looking for other locks the key might fit. Not the file drawers, not the bathroom, not the supply cabinet. He was still roaming around with the key in his hand when Eddie's black pickup roared up.

"Sonofabitch Weems," Eddie shouted, throwing open the showroom door. "Where is the sonofa-bitch?"

"Not here yet," Truman said. "What's the problem?"

"You know that snatch I made the other night? I was opening the door with my Slim Jim, you know, to release the parking brake, when all of a sudden two cop cars pull up. Now, you know they don't believe a black dude is supposed to repo a car from a white man, even if the white man is the biggest lowlife cracker in the city of St. Pete. I tried to explain, but they said they didn't have no papers from Bondurant Motors. Cops wanted to impound my truck. My forty-thousand-dollar truck! I got hot and we got into it, and they locked me up overnight for resisting arrest. That sonofabitch Wormy did it on purpose. I ask you, Truman, did he or did he not say he'd taken care of the paperwork?"

"He said he had," Truman said.

"I'm gonna kick his sorry white butt all over town when he gets in here," Eddie stormed. "And that's the last time I do business with Ronnie Bondurant. Man, I never did like them two. Some of these cars I grab for them? Shit. People be driving cars they had no business trying to buy. Some of them owed twice what the cars be worth. Ronnie Bondurant is a maggot, sucking the guts out of the sisters and brothers."

Truman had seen the way Ronnie did business, and he had to agree with Eddie. Maybe now was the time to do some gentle interrogation.

"Do you know anything about an insurance scam they're working? Corvettes usually, sometimes Mercedes or BMWs?"

"I'm not supposed to be a wrecker service," Eddie said, looking uncomfortable. "But yeah. They had me pick up cars two or three times that had been in bad wrecks."

"Where do you take them?" Truman asked.

"There's this guy named Joe. That's what they call him, he's Cambodian so nobody really knows his real name. He's got a body shop out in Kenneth City. I think I pulled all the cars out there to him. Ronnie paid me an extra fifty dollars for the wrecker service."

"Did you tow a red Corvette over there lately?"

"Nah," Eddie says. "Last time was a white one, maybe a month or so ago."

Truman went to the showroom window to be sure there was no sign of Ronnie and Wormy.

"Eddie, I'm pretty sure Ronnie and Wormy, and maybe Hernando Boone, killed Jeff Cantrell. He was apparently mixed up in this insurance scam they've been running. I saw them stage a wreck last night. One of their drivers almost got killed."

"Where was this?" Eddie asked.

"Out on Weedon Island. They're building some kind of overpass or something out there. Right at the entrance to the wildlife refuge. There's a barricade, all kinds of heavy equipment, and no traffic at night, because the park closes at sundown."

"I know the place," Eddie said. "One of those 'Vettes I pulled, I picked up out there. It had been smashed into the concrete. Messed up bad."

"That's how they work it," Truman said. "Look, Eddie, I hate to get you mixed up in this mess. I know you're just an honest businessman trying to make an honest buck."

"Usually," Eddie said, dropping a broad wink.

"But I need to see this body shop, Joe's. And I don't want these people to tell Ronnie I've been snooping around out there."

"You go out there with me," Eddie said immediately. "None of them boys speaks English too good.

I'll just tell them you're thinking of buying a new lot and you want to see how good their body work is. Nobody's gonna pay no attention to you if you're with me. They all think I'm some kind of freak anyway."

"It's a deal," Truman said.

"Where them two maggots at now?" Eddie asked.

"I think they're up to something," Truman said. "Ronnie called me at home and asked me to open up for him. I've been looking around, trying to find some evidence, something on paper. But Ronnie's smart. The books and important files must be locked up somewhere. Probably in that safe in his office."

Eddie nodded. "He's always got plenty of cash on hand. I always figured he had a safe. But what about Jeff? If they killed him, where's the body?"

"It can't be too far away," Truman reckoned. "The night he was killed, Jackie and Ollie were watching the place. They swear it was only maybe twenty minutes between the time Jackie found the body in the red 'Vette until the cops arrived and searched the place."

"Cops," Eddie said disgustedly. "Don't talk to me about cops. Is that 'Vette still here?"

"No," Truman said. "It was out back Tuesday before I left. Now it's gone."

"Twenty minutes," Eddie said. "And they didn't see anybody leaving the place?"

"Jackie didn't. Ollie could have been distracted. He was watching the comings and goings at the Candy Store. Hoping to see some skin, probably. He's had kind of a sheltered life," Truman said apologetically.

"So the body could still be here," Eddie said, glancing around the showroom.

"Or they could have moved it later," Truman said. "Where the heck could you hide a body on a used-car lot? With the police swarming all over the place? And I've been here all week. In this heat, it's hard to keep a corpse secret."

Eddie made a gagging sound. "Shit. Man, I hope we can figure out where Jeff is at. I just don't want to be the first one to find the body. You know?"

"I know," Truman said.

"You looked all over?" Eddie asked, opening the supply closet and peering in.

"All over in here," Truman said. "I've been wanting to take a good look in that garage. Wormy made it real clear when he caught me out there the other day that the garage and the fenced-in lot were strictly off-limits."

"Off-limits?" Eddie said. "That's the magic word."

They moved Eddie's truck around to the side of the lot, to make it less conspicuous.

"If they show up," Truman cautioned, "don't pick a fight with Wormy. Just tell him, uh, . . ."

"I'm gonna tell them if they want Wesley Coombs's Monte Carlo, they gonna have to pay me to go back over there," Eddie said. "Cops wouldn't let me take it without the paperwork."

In the daylight, with the overhead work lights on, the garage didn't look nearly as foreboding.

They divided the area into quadrants. "Like they do on search-and-rescue missions on TV," Eddie suggested.

The garage had a dusty, disused smell, like it hadn't seen a lube job or a brake adjustment in a long time.

"As Is" was Ronnie's motto. There was a grease rack in the center of the garage, and the lift was in the up position. Truman stood away from it to get a good look. Crude wooden boards had been laid across the platform, and now the lift was being used as storage. From where he stood, Truman could see a rusty Pepsi vending machine, odds and ends of lumber, some chrome fenders and hubcaps, faded wooden sign-boards for Bondurant Motors, even an old toilet.

"Eddie," he called.

"Whassup?" Eddie asked. He was kneeling down on the floor examining a seventy-five-gallon steel drum marked "Solvents."

Truman pointed up. "That grease rack would be as good a place as any to put a body."

Eddie went over to the workbench and picked up a rusty screwdriver. "Yeah. We can get to that. What about this drum, though? It's real heavy, and the lid's on there really tight. If it was me, I'd bend the body in half, stick it in there. Put some acid or shit like that in there, presto. No body." He shuddered at the grisly possibility his own imagination had conjured up.

While Eddie worked at one side of the drum's lid, Truman fetched a tire iron and started prying on the other side. The lid made a metallic clank, and then the sucking sound of a vacuum being broken. A viscous bile-green syrup floated within an inch of the drum's surface. The foam at the edge of the liquid had an oily sheen and a sharp, chemical odor, like the smell of nail polish remover or dry-cleaning solution. They took a half step backward.

"Shit," Eddie whispered. "That's nasty."

From the door leading out of the garage to the

office came the soft dinging of the doorbell in the showroom.

Wordlessly, Eddie picked up the lid and put it back on the drum, pounding it back into place with a single thump from his fist. Truman took the tools and dropped them on the workbench. He reached in his pocket for a handful of coins.

He dropped the money in the slot of the snack machine, jabbed a button at random. He dropped in two more coins and made another selection.

The corn chips he tossed to Eddie, keeping the beef jerky stick for himself.

He gave Eddie the nod. They strolled together into the showroom.

"Where the hell were you?" Wormy snarled.

CHAPTER

TWENTY-FOUR

JACKIE COUNTED OUT HER TIP MONEY AT THE table nearest the dining-room door. Lunch had been as slow as breakfast. She had a discouragingly small pile of bills, all singles, and a hill of silver: quarters, dimes, nickles, and pennies. Way too many pennies. She needed $77.10 to make the car payment tomorrow. And she had exactly $56.50 in tips saved. Tomorrow was payday. She'd get around $220 after taxes, but her room rent and phone bill were due, and she tried to give her mama $20 every week, when she could.

The red Corvette blazed seductively in her imagination. Not broken, ruined, worthless, as good sense told her it was, but the car that had beckoned her in the beginning: speedy and shiny and sinful.

Jackie swept the money into the pocket of her apron. Twenty bucks, she thought. Twenty bucks and she could make her payment to that bloodsucker Bondurant and keep her claim to the 'Vette alive. Maybe she could get Milton to do the work, if she swapped him baby-sitting for car repairs. But tonight was tuna casserole night. Not even the youth hostel kids would show up to eat that mess. No customers meant no tips.

She was recounting, out loud this time, when Ollie pulled up a chair and invited himself to sit down. "Any lunch left?" he asked.

"You made me lose count. Not that it matters," she added. She was about to give up, call it quits. But a glint of an idea worked itself around in her head. "Might be I can make you a ham sandwich."

"Good," Ollie said, rubbing his hands together. "I'm starved."

Out in the kitchen, Jackie piled two inches of thick-sliced ham onto the bread, then added a finish coat of mayonnaise, then mustard. She added a mound of potato chips to the plate, and a fan of dill pickle slices. When she was putting the food back into the walk-in refrigerator, she spied a lonely-looking bowl of banana pudding way in the back. After removing the plastic, she topped the pudding with a healthy spoonful of whipped cream and a maraschino cherry.

"Wow," Ollie said when she put the dishes on the table with a little flourish. "Thanks!"

"That'll be twenty dollars," Jackie said. "Cash."

Ollie nearly fell off the chair. "What?" he yelped. "Since when does a ham sandwich cost that much?"

"Since I came up twenty dollars short for my car payment," Jackie said. She whipped the plates back onto her tray. "If you don't want this, I'll just take it back in the kitchen. Lunch is over, you know."

"There's a name for this," Ollie told her. "It's called extortion. What if Mr. Wiggins finds out you extort money from the guests?"

"You let me worry about Mr. Wiggins," Jackie

said. She hoisted the trayful of food to her shoulder. "Well?"

He reached for his hip pocket. "All you had to do was ask. I would have loaned you the money since you need it that bad."

"Right," Jackie said sarcastically. She knew, as did all of his friends, that Ollie was a hoarder. It wasn't that he was selfish, or even miserly, it was just that he had been tucking away bits of money for years, "in case of a rainy day."

Ollie took out his moth-eaten black change purse and turned away so that Jackie would not see his stash. He counted out twenty ones, then turned back around and put the faded bills into her outstretched hand.

"I thought you weren't going to pay those crooks any more money," he said, just a hint of maliciousness in his voice. After all, they had left him out of all the fun the night before. "Thought you were going to get Truman to prove they stole your car and make them give it back. What happened to that idea?"

She put the money in the pocket of the apron with the rest of her savings and gave it a pat to reassure herself. "We're still working on it," she said. "But I need to make that payment. Just in case."

Ronnie and Wormy were world-class pissed off. Two hours they'd spent trying to find LeeAnn Pilker. Her apartment was empty, and nobody was around to say whether or not they'd seen her lately. Her boss at the club, a guy named Ike, claimed he hadn't seen her, even after Ronnie flicked a $100 bill his way.

"Anywhere else she'd go?" Wormy asked. "Like, if she was hiding?"

"Why would she be hiding?" Ike asked coolly. He pushed the $100 bill back at Ronnie. He remembered these two from earlier in the week. Big spenders, but they'd scared away half his regular clientele. And he knew LeeAnn had gone home with the guy in the golf shirt. Bondurant—who ran the car lot across the street.

"Like, if she stole some money or something," Wormy said, heavy-lidded.

"Let me talk to your other girls," Ronnie said, cutting Wormy short. "All these girls tell stuff to each other. One of them probably knows something. I'll pay for their time," he added.

"No dice," Ike said. "The girls work for me, not you. And they mind their own business. If LeeAnn shows up, I'll tell her you're looking for her."

Ronnie cussed him out good, until the hulking blond dyke from the front door heard him shouting and showed up at the manager's door brandishing a bad-looking length of iron pipe wrapped in black tape.

"Anything wrong, Ike?" she asked.

"Naw," Ike said. "You wanna show these guys the back door? They got a business appointment to get to."

Ronnie cussed all the way across the street. "Fucking pimp," he fumed as they dodged between cars. "He's probably got the bitch hidden somewhere right inside that club."

His mood didn't lighten any when they walked in the front door of the showroom. Nobody was there. The place was deserted, the front door unlocked so that any asshole could just walk in off the street and rip them off.

"Where's the old man?" Ronnie asked, looking

around the showroom. "I told that old bastard to mind the store. Where the hell is he?"

"I told you this was a bad idea," Wormy said.

"Shut the fuck up and find him," Ronnie said.

Just then, the door from the garage opened, and Truman strolled inside, still working on the cellphane wrapper of a beef jerky stick. Right behind him was Eddie Nevins, both of them chatting away like long-lost chums.

"You're supposed to be out here answering the phones," Ronnie said. His voice was almost a whisper. A dull pink flush was creeping up his neck. All day long, he'd been getting no respect, now even the hired help was treating him like he was nothing.

"What if somebody came in here, wanting to make their payment?" Ronnie demanded. "What if somebody walked on the lot, wanted to talk to a salesman about a car? You just put out a sign, 'Gone Fishin'? Screw that, Kicklighter! You're here working for me, you better be working, not wandering around feeding your face, snooping someplace you got no business."

Truman felt his face burn. He counted silently. "I've been here since noon, Ronnie," he said, sounding cooler than he felt. "No lunch. Nothing. I just went in back to get a snack. Eddie was here, too, waiting to talk to you. We were gone maybe two minutes. I could hear the phone ring from the garage, and the doorbell, too. You want to fire me, go ahead. I'm not a young man, you know. I've got to keep my blood sugar up."

"Who called you?" Ronnie asked, looking at Eddie.

"I called me," Eddie said, crossing his arms across

his chest to show off the rippling biceps below the cutoff sweatshirt sleeves. "You want to know where Wesley Coombs's Monte Carlo is at?"

"It'd better be right here," Ronnie said. "You been paid. I want that car."

"Ask Wormy here what happened when I went to get the Monte Carlo," Eddie suggested. "Ask him if he deliberately set me up to get hauled off to jail. Ask him if he notified the cops about the pick up."

Wormy's expression did not change. "Tough luck, Nevins. I forgot. Guess I must have been busy with something . . . important."

Eddie cracked his knuckles, one at a time. "I had to pay five hundred dollars to get out of jail and get my truck out of the impound lot. And as far as I know, Wesley Coombs is laughing his ass off, 'cause he's still driving that Monte Carlo and he ain't paid a dime on it for three months."

"Goddamn," Ronnie said, slamming his fist down on the desk. "Can't I trust anybody around here? I'm surrounded by morons and incompetents."

"Hey!" Wormy protested. "It slipped my mind. Honest."

Ronnie stomped off to his office and slammed the door behind him. He opened the safe, reached past the pistols, and retrieved a stack of bills. Peeling off the needed amount, he closed the safe and twirled the lock around.

After this whole mess was over with, with LeeAnn, Boone, everybody, Ronnie promised himself, he was gonna have to rethink his personnel situation. Even Wormy. Especially Wormy. His daddy had warned him time and time again about putting trust in others. Lawton Bondurant had always been a friendless type, suspicious of everybody, including his own flesh and blood.

Not Ronnie. He believed in getting along and going along. He liked to party, liked to wheel and deal. A people person, that was Ronnie Bondurant. Him and Wormy, they'd been a team for a lot of years. Going way back to Dixie Highway Motors when Wormy came in to buy a '68 Cougar and stayed to work for Ronnie's old man.

Wormy had his quirks. His moods. His hang-ups. He hated blacks, Cubans, Mexicans, women, and fags. But up until now, he'd been invaluable. Lately though, Wormy had let him down. Those pills he was popping kept him blitzed out of his mind. And the thing with Cantrell. Wormy had fired first, Ronnie was sure. He'd screwed up the red Corvette grab, too. He couldn't get along with people. Take LeeAnn. She was afraid of him. Wormy had said or done something to make her suspicious of him. And now she was gone, his one shot at perfection.

Now Eddie. The best repo man around. Cheapest, too. If only Wormy didn't know so much about the business, Ronnie thought. Too late now. Wormy knew, literally, where all the bodies were buried. Old Dad was right again.

He took the money out into the showroom. Wormy sat, Buddhalike, in his chair, staring straight ahead at the wall, like there was something fascinating on that wall he looked at all day, every day. Eddie held his hand out. Ronnie counted out eleven twenties and a ten and ignored Wormy's pout.

"That's half," Ronnie said. "When you grab the Monte Carlo and bring it back here, I'll pay the rest."

Storm clouds gathered on Eddie's face. Truman

gave him the slightest signal: appeasement, at any cost.

"That sucks," Eddie said. "And I ain't goin' back down there to Crackertown till I hear you, Ronnie, call the cops and give them the info."

"Wormy can call," Ronnie said.

"No way," Eddie said. "We do this my way, or I call my lawyer and get him after y'all for wrongful imprisonment. I already talked to him when he got me outta jail."

"Lawyer," Wormy said and laughed.

"Shut up," Ronnie said. He picked up the phone and got through to the warrants division and gave them the title number and pick-up authorization for the Monte Carlo to be repossessed from Wesley Coombs.

Ronnie put the receiver down. "Everybody happy? Now get the hell off my lot."

Truman straightened the papers on his desktop and walked out of the showroom and over to his station wagon.

Eddie pulled alongside him in the truck. "Jeff's in there, man," he said, his face ashen. "In that drum. Just like I told you. How we gonna prove it?"

"I don't know," Truman admitted. He could see Wormy and Ronnie inside, watching their curbside conference. "Meet me down the block, at that Texaco station," Truman said. "We'd better talk."

By the time Truman got down the block, Eddie had already gone inside the station and gotten them two cold bottles of beer, brown paper bags twisted expertly around their necks.

Eddie handed Truman a beer as he climbed into the truck.

"We don't know for sure Jeff is in that drum. Or

even on the car lot," Truman said. "But Ronnie's gotten mighty paranoid all of a sudden. Did you hear the way he talked to Wormy?"

"Maybe the love bug's bitin' at Ronnie," Eddie said. "I forgot to tell you, I dropped by the Candy Store. One of the girls was saying LeeAnn moved in with Ronnie. Big house on the south side. Right on the bay."

"She'll never talk to us now," Truman said. "Even if she does know what happened to Cantrell. You know," he said, taking a sip of the beer, "I talked to the FDLE agent who's working this big investigation of Bondurant and Hernando Boone. He says Cantrell might not be dead at all. Weingarten says they've traced phone calls to LeeAnn's phone that they think were from Jeff, and that somebody's been using his credit card and ATM card."

"How could that be?" Eddie asked.

"Two possibilities," Truman theorized. "Jeff Cantrell is alive, and he's hiding out for some reason, maybe because he crossed Bondurant. Which means he maybe faked his own death. Maybe Jackie didn't see what she thought she saw that night. Or, we were right in the first place. Ronnie or somebody killed Jeff. The body's hidden someplace close by. And the phone calls and credit card transactions are part of Ronnie's plot to keep anybody from wondering whatever happened to Jeff Cantrell."

Eddie drummed his fingers on the steering wheel of the truck.

"We've gotta get back in that garage. And we gotta get LeeAnn to level with us."

"Maybe we need some help," Truman suggested.

❖   ❖   ❖

Ollie was adamant. "I'm not setting foot on that car lot again. Those guys know us. They've got alarms and everything. They caught us last time. And it's not just me. I don't think it's right to drag a girl into this."

Jackie threw a pizza crust at Ollie. "I'm not afraid of going in there again. Only way I'm ever going to get this Corvette thing settled is to prove that those guys stole my car. And that Jeff Cantrell got killed, maybe because of it. And he was, too, dead. I know dead when I see dead."

Eddie sat back on the small chair they had dragged into Truman's room at the Fountain of Youth Hotel for this meeting. He'd greeted everybody after Truman made the introductions, and now he intended to let the others do the talking. Besides, he liked watching this Jackie Canaday. She wasn't about to let two old birds get away with treating her like a sissy girl.

"We need both of you," Truman said. "With the four of us working this thing, it should go smoothly. No car alarms or unexpected police this time."

CHAPTER

TWENTY-FIVE

HERNANDO BOONE'S NECK HURT LIKE A SONOFA-bitch. He couldn't move it to the right but maybe two inches, couldn't move it to the left at all. No time to do anything about it now.

His brother had called earlier in the day. A whole eighteen-wheeler full of beef baby-back ribs was on its way from Lakeland to St. Pete.

"Grade A," Orlando had babbled. "And you know what's coming up—right?"

"A migraine," Hernando had said. "I've got spots in front of my eyes. I need to lay down."

"No, bro," Orlando had said. "Labor Day weekend. Everybody barbecues on Labor Day weekend. You should see the meat on these ribs. I saved back a case for myself. They're marked three ninety-nine a pound. Blue Light Special—right?"

Hernando had squeezed the bridge of his nose between his thumb and forefinger. He'd looked at the calendar on his desk and had felt the vein throbbing in his forehead.

"Labor Day is two weeks away. What am I gonna do with an eighteen-wheeler full of meat until then?"

"Shit. Throw it in the walk-in cooler like always," his brother had said carelessly. "Ribs freeze good."

"I got no more room," Hernando had shouted. "I still got twenty cases of the boneless breaded chicken breasts you sent me for Fourth of July. You know what those tasted like, bro? Breaded chickenshit! My ladies can't repeat sell to the sisters after they gone and bought chickenshit for a Fourth of July cookout."

"How I'm supposed to know they're bogus?" Orlando had asked. "I just steal the shit. I don't run no taste tests."

"Never mind," Hernando had said. "Even if the walk-in was empty—even if I gave away all that chicken—I couldn't store that much ribs. And the girls ain't never sold a whole tractor-trailerful before."

"Warehouse sale," Orlando had prompted him. "Have the ladies call up and tell folks it's a tractor-trailer sale. Three dollars a pound. Tell them they gotta show up at a certain time and place. Bring their own coolers. Park the trailer someplace nice and quiet. We sell 'em right off the back, like we used to do with the Guccis and the Ray-Bans."

"Might work," Hernando had said reluctantly. "When did you say the truck will be here?"

"Better get your ladies jamming on those phones," Orlando had said and chuckled. "I mapped out a back way since I had to borrow the truck to get the meat. Say nine o'clock. My driver's calling me in a little bit and he'll need an address. Where you want to set up?"

Nine o'clock. Hernando would have to work fast. And find the right place. That was crucial. His neck had throbbed. A reminder. "You know a place called Weedon Island?"

He called his cousin Alma, who ran the phone room. "Truckload of beef baby-back ribs coming in tonight," he told her. "Tell the ladies, whoever sells the most is gonna win a prize. Let's see. How about a—"

"Diamond tennis bracelet," Alma suggested. "We got two left from that last shipment of stuff Orlando sent over."

"All right," he agreed. He told her the details. "Tell everybody the sale only lasts for an hour. Nine till ten. We gotta be out of there before anybody notices the traffic. And tell the girls we're doing ten-pound minimums. For every twenty-pound order we throw in a case of breaded chicken breasts."

"Huh," Alma said. "Ought to throw that chicken in the trash. I'll tell 'em. That meat better be right this time."

"Weedon Island. Ronnie ain't gonna like that," Billy Tripp said. The gauze around his jaw muffled the words and Boone had to listen hard to make out what he was saying. Billy Tripp wasn't a treat for sore eyes today. The small patches of his face that weren't swathed in bandages were red and shiny, like fresh-ground chuck. He had a high cervical collar that kept his neck immobile, and his left wrist was in a cast. Where he wasn't burned, he was bruised, and one of his ferretlike front teeth had been knocked out, giving him an unfortunate cartoon-character appearance.

"I ain't running no opinion polls," Boone told Billy. "Anyway, after this load, I'm clearing out inventory. Getting out of home-delivery meat sales."

"Hot meat, you mean," Billy wheezed, his chest heaving a little, his blistered lips too swollen to smile.

"Never mind that," Boone said. "What's this deal you talkin' about?"

"Bondurant fucked me over," Billy said. "Wouldn't pay my hospital bill. I had to sneak out of there when the nurses weren't looking. Now Ronnie's trying to stiff me on account of what happened to your Mercedes. And he's the one who told me to punch it. Know what I think? I think he hoped we'd both get killed."

"You totaled my Mercedes," Boone said. "Who's gonna pay for that?"

"I'm telling you, Ronnie's going to fuck you over, too," Tripp said. "I heard him tell Wormy. After they dropped you at that phone booth. They thought I was unconscious. Near dead. I thought so, too. And Ronnie said he'd put in the claim for the insurance, collect, and then tell you the insurance wouldn't pay the whole amount. Keep all the money himself."

Tripp swallowed hard. Talking was painful. "Wormy said they should get rid of you. Like they did Jeff Cantrell. The guy who used to work at the lot. Ronnie told everybody Jeff left town. I think he killed him."

"Well, he's dead," Boone said carelessly. "That part's the truth. I was there. So they think they can cut me out, huh?"

"That's why I came over here," Billy said. "I know how they run things. I can help you. Could use me a job. And a place to crash."

Boone's lips stretched into a wide smile, his high

cheekbones revealing his Indian blood. "Crash. You like to crash, don't you?"

LeeAnn Pilker squeezed her eyes shut and took a deep breath. "Just do it. And fast, before I change my mind."

Danielle picked up a hank of the long, shimmering hair and sawed away at it with the big shears. LeeAnn felt it fall on her back. She allowed herself one tear. One tiny tear. "Keep going," she told Danielle.

She breathed again. Ever since she'd left Ronnie's house this morning, LeeAnn had to remind herself to breathe. She was wound as tight as a three-dollar wristwatch. She had to keep moving.

Her first stop had been at Jeff's apartment. She'd parked two blocks away and jogged to the apartment. Mrs. Borgshultz's car was there, but LeeAnn was desperate. She used her key and slipped into the apartment.

The phone was still hooked up. Ronnie must have forgotten to have it cut off. Or Wormy, most likely.

She called Danielle, her old roomate. There was nobody else.

"What do you want?" Danielle had asked, not bothering to hide her annoyance. Danielle was married, had two little kids. Her husband didn't know anything about his wife's old life and Danielle intended to keep it like that.

"I need help," LeeAnn said. "I need to disappear for a while."

Danielle didn't bother to ask why. The old life was gone, but not forgotten. And LeeAnn always had terrible taste in men. "I can't give you any money," she said "Dave's been laid off."

"I've got money. Some," LeeAnn said. "But I can't go to a motel. He'll find me. And the police will probably be looking for me too. It's his money."

The trade wasn't great, as trades went. Danielle's Isuzu was eleven years old, needed new tires, and the clutch was nearly shot. To get in the front seat you had to get in on the passenger side, because one of the kids had shoved a popsicle stick in the door lock. The Coleman camper was hitched onto the back.

They took the license plate off LeeAnn's Honda, and Danielle replaced it with one from her grandma's Plymouth. "She's in a nursing home. She'll never know the difference," Danielle said.

LeeAnn had to promise to bring the Isuzu and the Coleman camper and the other stuff back within a week. "Dave thinks I rented it to some friends," Danielle explained, counting the twenties LeeAnn gave her, then tucking them in the pocket of her shorts.

After Danielle helped crank up the tent part and showed LeeAnn how to use the little butane stove and the lantern, she glanced anxiously around the Fort DeSoto Park campsite. The crickets were starting up, and the baby was stirring in her car seat. Dave would be expecting dinner on the table real soon.

LeeAnn shook the hair off her shoulders one last time, and tried not to look at the ground. Her neck felt naked.

"How do I look?" she asked anxiously.

Danielle gave her a critical going-over. "Well, it's kind of raggedy, but actually, with your bone structure, people will probably think it's the latest style."

LeeAnn looked stunning, but there was still some lingering jealousy over a man Danielle had brought home one time, and LeeAnn had taken over. They'd sworn all that was behind them, but maybe it wasn't.

"How are you gonna hide those?" Danielle asked, nodding at LeeAnn's chest.

"Did you bring a couple of Dave's shirts?"

Danielle handed over two of Dave's biggest, baggiest short-sleeved blue work shirts, and LeeAnn buttoned them over the tight T-shirt she'd been wearing.

"You look like shit," Danielle said encouragingly. "I gotta go now. But by Sunday night, you can probably move to a better spot. Ft. DeSoto's usually full on weekends. You were lucky somebody canceled out at the last minute. Think you can take the camper down and move it by yourself?"

"I don't plan to still be here on Monday," LeeAnn told her. "Soon as I find out what I need to know, get enough money to get clear of here, I'm going as far away as I can get. Some place where they have leaves that fall in the autumn, and no bugs. And no men."

"Antarctica?" Danielle asked.

"Maybe," LeeAnn shot back. "I'll call you Monday. Tell you where to pick up your car. Somewhere at the airport."

When Danielle was gone, LeeAnne went inside the camper and sat on the foam pad that was supposed to be a bed. She looked at Ronnie's big gold Rolex, double-wrapped around her wrist. She could hear bugs outside, thudding softly against the sides of the canvas tent. The tent top smelled of pee, and hot dogs and baked beans.

Right about now, she thought, Ronnie would be tearing up the town, looking for her. And his money.

And his watch. And wondering how much she knew about Jeff Cantrell. And everything else.

She took the bottle of bug spray Danielle had left and sprayed it all over her arms and legs and neck. Then she set out in the direction of the ranger's station, where there was supposed to be a pay phone.

Wormy was getting ready to lock the front door when he saw Billy Tripp get out of a yellow cab.

"Sonofabitch," he yelled to Ronnie, who was in the office, getting some cash to replace what LeeAnn had stolen. Ronnie believed in carrying at least a few thousand in walking-around money at all times. "Look what the cat just dragged in."

Tripp was limping badly. "Heya, Wormy," he said uneasily, looking around the darkened showroom. "Is Ronnie around?"

"Come on back here," Ronnie said, recognizing the voice.

Billy followed Wormy into the private office, and Wormy closed it behind them.

"Thought you disappeared," Ronnie said. "Wormy here says you been calling up, making all kind of demands. My employees don't make demands, Billy. Not if they want to stay alive."

"I'm sorry about that, Ronnie," Billy said. "A misunderstanding. Don't you wanna know why I'm here now?"

Wormy crossed his legs and leaned carefully back in his chair. He had to do everything carefully now, even with the pain pills. The back reminded him of who'd caused his pain, and he thought longingly of the safe, where Ronnie made him lock up his pistol.

"Boone wants me to help him set you up," Billy said. "He came to the hospital, paid my bill, took me over to his office. You know, in that old store over there in colored town?"

"I know where Boone's at," Ronnie said. "What makes him think he can set me up, with or without your help?"

"Boone knows you keep a lot of cash around here, especially on Fridays, when people come in and make their payments. He's got one of those gangs, robbing crews he calls them, he just wants me to give him the inside story. You know, where you keep the money and all."

"Let him try it," Wormy put in.

"I ain't working for Boone," Billy said, shaking his head vigorously. "He's a crazy man. But what I wanted to tell you was, while I was at his place a while ago, I heard him setting up a deal. For tonight. Back out on Weedon Island. He's got a load of meat coming in. Ribs. I thought maybe we rip him off before he gets you."

"Meat?" Wormy hooted. "Do we look like Oscar Meyer to you?"

Ronnie sat back in his chair and gave Billy Tripp an indulgent smile. "Wormy's right. I'm in the used-car business here, Billy. What would I do with a load of ribs? Buy a car, get a rack of ribs?"

"It ain't the meat you want," Billy said. "Boone only sells cash and carry. The ribs are two ninety-nine a pound. Ten-pound minimum. That's thirty dollars a person, at least. And it's a whole tractor-trailer. You know how those people love their ribs."

"Wonder what one of those rigs carries?" Ronnie mused.

"No, Ronnie," Wormy protested. "Don't even start. You said we were done with Boone. We take his insurance money and get rid of him, first chance we get."

"A holdup," Ronnie said. "Like we used to do back in the good old days when my daddy was getting started. Stick 'em up. Hand over the loot. Oops. Bang. Adios, amigo."

"I heard Boone talking on the phone," Billy continued. "He figures that truck can carry five hundred cases of ribs. Thirty pounds of ribs in a case. That's fifteen thousand pounds."

"Forty-five thousand dollars," Ronnie said. "I'm liking this more and more." He got up and sat on the edge of the desk, inches from where Billy Tripp perched like a wounded bird.

"Why would Boone cut you in on something like this, Billy? He's got his own crew he works with, he told you himself."

Billy's right eye flickered in an attempt at a wink. "I told him you double-crossed me. And you were gonna double-cross him, too. I think he had that part figured already. So I said we should work together. Get you before you get him."

Ronnie put his hand on Billy's shoulder. The kid flinched. "I did double-cross you, Billy. So why come to me? Why not go to work for Boone?"

Tripp looked down at his dust-covered tennis shoes. You could still see some blood drops on the laces and the toes. "You know."

"What?" Ronnie said.

"He talks about being an Indian," Tripp said. "Mostly he's a nigger. My mama wouldn't stand for me taking orders from no nigger. That's not how I was raised."

Wormy shrugged. It made sense. "Let's do it," he said.

Jackie put the phone down and looked at the others in the room.

"LeeAnn's not at the Candy Store. Her boss said she didn't show up for work today. And two other guys already came looking for her, in a really bad mood. The boss said that if I was a friend of LeeAnn's, I should tell her this guy was talking about calling the cops. Because she stole a lot of money from him."

Truman was puttering around his room, cleaning up the empty soda cans and paper plates and pizza crusts. His place was so small, that if you left any messes at all, it became unbearable. "She's on the run from Bondurant," he said. "If we could find her, maybe she'd help us."

"If we don't find her, and Ronnie does, she won't be helping anybody," Eddie said. "He'll kill her, too."

All this talk of people killing each other was becoming increasingly alarming to Ollie. "Not to be a killjoy or anything," he started, stopping to chew on a piece of pizza crust he managed to snatch up before Truman disposed of the box, "but I thought all we were supposed to be doing was finding Jackie's car. Now we're chasing runaway strippers and dealing with murderers and everything."

He hadn't forgotten about Jackie's holding him up for twenty dollars. "How are we going to find a stripper on the run? She probably took the first bus out of town if she knows what's good for her."

Jackie gave Ollie a withering look.

Ollie didn't care. "Am I the only one in this room

with any common sense? Truman, you talk to her. I mean, we don't even have a plan."

But Truman and Eddie were quietly conferring at the desk, with Eddie drawing diagrams on a paper napkin, and Truman's finger hovering over a city map.

"Truman?" Ollie repeated.

"Oh. A plan," Truman said. "Eddie has some suggestions, and some rather handy expertise. And he insists that he wants to help out."

Three sets of eyes turned toward Eddie. He felt surprisingly bashful.

"See, we need to get Wormy and Ronnie out of the way for a while, so you guys can look for Jeff's body. On the car lot anyway. Me and Truman figure that's where the body's hidden. So I'll go do what I'm supposed to do. Pick up Wesley Coombs's Monte Carlo. Then, once I snatch the car, I call Bondurant and Weems and tell them they gotta meet me halfway to pick up the car. 'Cause I gotta go out right away on another pickup. Or else I leave the Monte Carlo right where it's at."

"How do you know Ronnie will bring Wormy with him?" Jackie wanted to know.

"Because somebody has to drive the Monte Carlo back to the lot, and somebody has to drive their car," Eddie explained.

"And why wouldn't they just pick up the car and go right back to the lot? Or hire one of those drivers of theirs to go pick up the Monte Carlo?" Ollie said, wanting to pick holes in Eddie's plan.

"Their favorite driver, Billy, is in the hospital," Truman said. "We're just going to assume it'll be Ronnie and Wormy. But Eddie's got a phone in his truck. If anything goes wrong, he'll call the lot to warn us. Give the signal. Three rings and a hang-up. That'll give us time to get out."

"And how are you going to keep Ronnie and Wormy occupied long enough to give us time to search the car lot?" Jackie asked. "It's a big place. I've been there, remember?"

"I'm gonna snatch that car of theirs," Eddie said. "With them in it. That'll give y'all plenty of time."

CHAPTER

TWENTY-SIX

THE RANGER'S STATION WAS CLOSED, AND THE campground was quiet. Anybody who would voluntarily camp in August in Florida, LeeAnn had decided, was probably already institutionalized. On the clamshell road in front of the station, four kids rode their bikes around in dazed circles.

A middle-aged man was standing right in front of the only pay phone she'd seen in the whole place. His face and neck and arms were burnt lobster red and his pale blue eyes stared intently at the camp bulletin board.

LeeAnn stood beside him, pretending to be just as engrossed in all the institutional postings. There were fishing regulations: "No speckled trout to be taken under twelve inches long, no redfish to be taken due to a statewide fishing ban, no snook to be taken with any method except hook and line, only one snook per person per day to be kept, no snook under twenty-four inches to be kept, and no gill-netting, trotlines, or spearguns of any kind to be used in a Pinellas County Park."

Also prohibited were firearms, explosives, loud radios or televisions, unleashed animals, and alcoholic beverages or controlled substances of any kind.

The rules baffled LeeAnn, whose family considered all those forbidden commodities as essential to any worthwhile outdoor activity.

"What's a snook?" The sunburnt man's broad, blistered forehead was wrinkled in puzzlement. "I never heard of a snook. We don't have them up home," he said apologetically. The accent was flat, midwestern.

Up home must be Illinois, she decided. They got a lot of guys from Illinois in the club. Apparently they got their rocks off looking at skin that wasn't the same hue as milk.

"It's a fish," LeeAnn said. Growing up, her brothers would point a lantern down into the bay, and when a snook came swirling up out of the depths to take a friendly peek at the light, they'd blast it with their BB guns. Big sportsmen, her brothers.

"I think they only have them in Florida," she added. "And it's illegal to sell them. They're like, holy or something."

"Interesting," he said. He picked up his little toy tacklebox and Zebco fishing reel and wandered away.

She dialed the number at Bondurant Motors and turned around, so she could keep an eye out for more bulletin board readers.

LeeAnn glanced idly down at herself and was pleased with what she saw. She was wearing a pair of muddy construction boots she'd found in the trunk of Danielle's Isuzu, along with a moldy pack of cigarettes, which she'd stuck in her shirt pocket. She'd chewed off the acrylic nails, stuffed all her jewelry in the pocket of the baggy, oversized jeans, and had also appropriated Dave's baseball cap, which she wore backward over her new haircut.

The phone rang a long time. "Pick up," she muttered. She hadn't stopped to think about getting Ronnie's home number.

"Bondurant Motors." It was him.

She almost lost her nerve. And then she thought again of his intentions to have her cut apart and glued back together like some Frankenstein Barbie doll.

"LeeAnn?" he said softly. "Is that you, baby?"

"It's me all right," she said.

"Why, LeeAnn?" he crooned. "Why'd you leave, baby? If you wanted money, you know I'd give you anything in the world."

Especially if it involved rhinoplasty or liposuction. "Cut the crap, Ronnie," she said. "I know Jeff's dead. You guys killed him. Wormy hid the body, only he's got to move it pretty soon, before buzzards start circling Bondurant Motors. And let's not forget this whole scam you're working on Hernando Boone. Pretty scary guy to mess with, Ronnie."

"No, baby," Ronnie said. "You got it all wrong. See, your mama was right. People shouldn't eavesdrop. Because they get things misconstrued. Come on back to the house, LeeAnn, and I'll explain everything."

"Like hell." Her voice had taken on a new coarseness, a bravado that she'd never heard before. Yeah, bravado. You cut your hair and dress butch, and you could say anything to anybody. It was like you'd suddenly grown balls.

"I want twenty thousand dollars, Ronnie, or I go to the cops. Or Hernando Boone. Both, maybe. Yeah, I like that idea. Boone will pay me for tipping him off, and if he doesn't kill you first, I'll go to the cops, maybe collect one of those big rewards they're always giving away for crime tips." LeeAnn laughed from a new place, down in her gut. "Although, to tell the truth, I will turn you in for free if it comes to that."

Ronnie waved for Wormy to pick up the extension in the outer office.

"I don't have twenty thousand, baby," he said. "I'm in the used-car business, remember? Besides, the bank is closed."

Wormy put his hand over the receiver and held up ten fingers. "Offer her ten," he mimed.

LeeAnn had heard the click of the extension, knew Wormy Weems was listening in.

"There's a safe in your office," she said. "Jeff showed it to me. I'm not playing now, Ronnie. I want the cash. Tonight."

She heard the crunch of shells and saw a white sedan with a blue bubble on top cruise slowly past. The park ranger gave her a fingertip wave before cruising off to apprehend some heavily armed beer-drinking, dog-owning snook-catchers.

"Right after sundown," LeeAnn said, telling him where the drop was to be and how it was to go. "And leave that scuzzy friend Wormy at home, or the deal's off." She hung up the phone and allowed herself a little victory dance.

"Scuzzy?" Wormy said. He popped open a beer and washed down a couple of the Malaysian mind benders. "Scuzzy?"

Ronnie was still fiddling with the safe combination when the phone rang again, not five minutes later.

He snatched up the receiver. "What now?"

"Yo, Ronnie, my man," Eddie said. "Got a slight problem on my end, dude. I'm on the way to get your Monte Carlo, but soon as I pick it up, I gotta drop it off, 'cause I got a call on my beeper. From the bank. I gotta pick up a Jaguar and a Viper down in Sarasota. Now. Before the folks get back from the airport. Can't come all the way north to you."

Ronnie felt a sheen of perspiration on his face. He didn't need this.

"I don't need this shit, Eddie," he said. "Bring the Monte Carlo here, to the lot, or you don't get paid."

"No can do," Eddie said cheerfully. "Bank's a way better customer than you, Ronnie. You know where the old Belk's store was? Over there in Central Plaza? Meet you there in twenty minutes. And if you're not there, man, I'll just drop the Monte Carlo, leave it with the keys in it."

They both knew that any vehicle left unattended in the bulldozed former shopping center would be stolen or stripped within five minutes.

"I'm done with you, Eddie," Ronnie warned. "And I got friends in the business. You'll never snatch another car in this town again."

"Twenty minutes," Eddie repeated. "See ya."

Ronnie took a packet of bills out of the safe, took his own pistol, and handed Wormy his. "Let's go," he said with disgust. "I'm gonna take the blue LTD, you can bring the Monte Carlo back here. Then I gotta go deal with that bitch LeeAnn."

"You're paying her off?" Wormy asked. Were the pain pills making him hear things? Was Ronnie Bondurant getting soft?

"Get real," Ronnie said, showing Wormy the pistol he'd stuck in the waistband of his slacks. "Make sure your piece is loaded. After we get the keys from Eddie, get rid of him."

"What about the meet with Boone?" Wormy protested. "We can deal with that nigger repo man any time. Boone's a forty-five-thousand-dollar proposition, Ron."

"Busy night," Ronnie shrugged. "After this, people will start showing some respect. No more 'minority' partners, big-mouth whores, coked-up monkeys, or snotty repo men. Tonight, we clean house."

They heard a tapping on the glass in the showroom window. Ronnie looked out. It was Billy Tripp, peering through the window, the bandages on his face making him look like some white-masked orangutan.

"Just in time," Ronnie said.

He unlocked the door, clapped Billy on the shoulder, and watched with satisfaction as the kid grimaced in pain. "Billy!" Ronnie said. "You're early."

"Yeah," Billy said, looking around behind him. He seemed jumpier than usual, probably been sniffing some air freshener or whatever it was they sniffed these days.

"That's good," Ronnie said. "Got a little job for you and Wormy to do before we head out to Weedon Island. You go ahead with Wormy now, pick up that Monte Carlo and bring it back here. See you boys about nine, right?"

Ollie ran his hand reverently over the hood of Eddie's $40,000 customized repo truck. "Beautiful," he told Eddie. "How's it work?"

Eddie looked at Truman, who nodded. "I'll show you," Eddie said. "Hop on in."

It was after seven, and the sky was streaked shrimp pink and canteloupe orange with little grape-colored edges around the clouds. The temperature was still hovering at the ninety mark, the humidity at the bazillion level. Used to be, he and Nellie would take off for North Carolina at the tail end of a summer like this. Two weeks' vacation. They liked places like Bryson City and Franklin and Hendersonville and Highlands; cool, green places with mountains and clear-running rivers and waterfalls tumbling down through sweet-scented forests. They didn't stay in the fancy resorts, just mom-and-pop motels, the kind of places where the owners remembered you from year to year, and sometimes would sit outside with you, drink a beer and watch the sun sink into those mist-shrouded mountains.

Nellie used to talk longingly about buying a little place "to summer up there in those mountains after we retire."

Now he was summering the same place he wintered and he couldn't remember the last time he had watched a sunset on purpose. It wasn't so awful, now that he was used to it. It just wasn't what he'd expected.

"Do you think Ronnie and Wormy are still at the car lot?" Jackie asked as she and Truman drove away from the Fountain of Youth in the Nova. She'd talked a lot of brave talk in front of Ollie, but she still remembered her last confrontation with Ronnie Bondurant and Wormy Weems, and it still made her shudder.

"They're not gonna let that Monte Carlo get away. It's a matter of pride with Ronnie. And Eddie swears he can snatch a car in fifteen seconds," Truman reassured her. "Nothing can stop him. Eddie and Ollie can keep Bondurant and Wormy out of our way for at least an hour. That's probably all we'll need."

"Isn't this pretty dangerous?" Ollie asked anxiously. The neighborhood they drove through was one he had never seen before. Rusted-out mobile homes hunched shoulder to shoulder on lots with waist-high weeds. Junked cars were parked everywhere, and wild-eyed feral dogs barked viciously from every other yard.

"Well, yeah," Eddie said off-handedly. "It ain't Snell Isle." He pointed at a faded turquoise mobile home half a block ahead, on the right. A two-tone urine-and-iodine-colored sedan was parked directly in front of the front door, right in the middle of the yard, which looked to be mostly sand and scrub palms.

"Wesley Coombs ain't taking no chances now," Eddie said. He slowed and pulled the truck to the curb. It was growing darker, and crickets and cicadas hummed busily in the dusky recesses of the occasional oleander tree.

"What now?" Ollie asked. He dug in his pocket and brought out the snub-nosed .22 he kept in the cash drawer at the newsstand. "Want me to cover you?"

"Let's watch a few minutes," Eddie said, "make sure all the folks are inside watching TV, minding their own business."

So the cicadas hummed, and Ollie fidgeted, and Eddie sat with his forearms draped over the steering wheel. "You know those oleander bushes?" he asked Ollie. "They're poison. Flowers, leaves, branches, all of it poison. Like, if you was to stick somebody with a oleander branch, in the eye, something like that? Boom. Dead. And nobody'd know what happened."

"Is that so?" Ollie asked. "Pretty flowers, though."

"Yeah," Eddie said. "I had me a house, I'd have me a oleander hedge."

Lights flickered on along the street, and at least one faint blue aura projected out the window of every home on the street. Even Wesley Coombs's home.

"Let's go," Eddie said, starting up the truck. "Look under the seat there," he told Ollie.

Ollie brought out a flat, inch-wide strip of metal with a hook at the bottom. "What's this?"

"Slim Jim," Eddie said. "Coombs will probably have the Monte Carlo locked, with the parking brake on, thinking that'll stop me. You just stick that flat against the glass on the driver's side, fish it down in there into the door, hook it on the locking mechanism, and yank it up. Opens anything."

"Me?" Ollie said, panicky. "Uh, isn't that something you should do? I mean, I don't have any, uh, experience. And it's dark. How can I see?"

"Check in the glove box," Eddie said. "You're looking for a thing looks like a black snake, with a little old glass eye on the end of it."

Ollie got the snakelike thing out and held it up to show Eddie.

"Fiber-optic flashlight," Eddie said proudly. "Drop it right down in there with the edge of the Slim Jim, you can see perfect. Of course," he added, "mostly I do it by feel. But that's for professionals."

Eddie steered straight for the turquoise trailer. He made a sharp turn, cut the headlights, and started backing the truck into the yard, his tires spitting sand

and weeds in all directions. He had work lights mounted on the roof and rear fender of the truck, and these he switched on.

Now he was steering with his left hand, the right hand on a small metal box with various buttons and levers and a kind of joystick that sat beside him on the seat of the truck. There was a huge rearview mirror mounted at eye level, and he stared intently into it, only occasionally turning around to check his progress.

Ollie sat up on his knees and turned completely around to see what was happening. There was a hum, and a steel arm unfolded itself from the truck bed. Eddie's fingers worked the switches, and the arm dropped until it was maybe a foot off the ground. Now he had his thumb and forefinger working the joystick, and a pair of hinged jaws slid out from the arm and silently slipped under the front axle of the Monte Carlo, each set of jaws poised with a tire between it. Another switch, and Ollie heard, rather than saw, the jaws clamp down.

"Okay, Ollie," Eddie said. "Let's unlock her."

For Ollie, the distance from the truck to the ground looked suicidal. He clutched the Slim Jim in one hand, the flashlight in the other, and leapt into the darkness. He landed on his butt in the soft sand, scrambled to his feet, and was beside the Monte Carlo in an instant. His hands trembled as he twisted the On switch of the flashlight.

He glanced inside the locked car and groaned. Eddie stood just behind him, his eyes on the door of the trailer, which, so far, had not opened. "It's no good," Ollie whispered. "Look what's on the steering wheel. It's the club." He recited the slogan he'd heard so often on the radio. "'Your car won't budge if you've got the club.'"

"No problem," Eddie said, moving alongside him now. "You mind?"

Ollie handed over his burglary tools and stepped aside. Eddie stuck the flashlight in the back pocket of his jeans. The pro-am was over. In a second he'd majicked the lock, in a half second he was squirting the hinges with a shot of WD-40, then he was sitting in the front seat, one big, be-ringed mitt grasping either side of the red rubber-coated device locked onto the steering wheel. He wiggled first one end, then the other.

Behind them, a screen door opened, and a porch light snapped on, leaving Ollie half blinded in its yellow glare. "What the hell?" The voice was a man's.

Now a dog was barking from inside the house, jumping up against the door, and other dogs in other yards joined in. Ollie crouched down behind the open car door, grasping the edge of it to keep himself from giving in to the terror and running away. "Eddie, we gotta get out of here," Ollie said. "Leave the car."

"Ju-uuu-ust a second now," Eddie said. "See, like most people, this asshole leaves just enough slack in it, if you know how, you can pop it right off. Okay, it's done." He wrenched the emergency brake downward, popped the car into neutral, and slammed the door shut, just in time for both of them to hear the man shout at someone inside. "Bring the shotgun, Suzie, they're stealing my damn car!"

"Go," Eddie urged.

They dashed for the truck. Before both doors were closed, Eddie had doused the work lights, his thumb was on the joystick, and the hinged arm was moving upward, until the front end of the Monte Carlo lifted primly above and out of the grubby ground of Wesley Coombs's yard.

Ollie saw the man come running out of the trailer with a horse-sized brindle hound baying at his heels. Coombs slid three shells into a shotgun, racked it, and swung the shotgun to his shoulder.

"Go!" Ollie screamed, sliding down onto the floor of the truck. "Go. Go. Go!"

Jackie and Truman watched while Wormy and Billy Tripp sped out of the Bondurant Motors lot together in the liver-colored Pinto Billy had arrived in. Fifteen minutes later, Ronnie walked out quickly, locked the door, and left, not in his own gray Lincoln, but in the powder-blue LTD.

"What's up?" Jackie asked nervously.

The Nova was half hidden behind the Dumpster in the parking lot of the Vietnamese restaurant next door to Bondurant Motors.

"Don't know," Truman said. "Wormy and Billy probably went to get the Monte Carlo. Maybe Ronnie went along to deal with Eddie."

With all the unlit floodlights, red and yellow Christmas lights, and the flashing, rotating pink Cadillac on the roof switched off, Bondurant Motors looked forlorn, like a carnival after all the rubes had gone home. The coast was clear, yet neither of them made a move to get out of the station wagon.

"They'll kill Eddie," Jackie said suddenly. "Ollie, too. We should never have let them try this. It's idiotic."

"Eddie has the element of surprise on his side,"

Truman said, wanting to convince himself. "He's tough. A real street type. He's got a gun, he knows they're coming, they don't know he knows what they're up to. We talked it all over, Jackleen. Everybody knows the risks."

"Let's call the cops now," Jackie said, her voice shaky. "We can tell them where Eddie's meeting Wormy. They'll stop anything bad from happening."

"And arrest them for what?" Truman asked. "It'll be the same thing as before. Our word against Bondurant's. And nobody will ever find out what happened to Jeff Cantrell. Or your Corvette, or any of it. We'll call the cops the minute we find something inside. No heroics this time," he added. "No surprises."

They were winding their way briskly through the rows of parked junkers and rust buckets. "You never did say how you plan to get us inside," Jackie reminded him.

"I'm a trusted employee," Truman said. "Ronnie showed me where the key was hidden this morning."

Once inside, they hurried into the garage. Truman headed straight for the drum of solvents. The lid popped off easily after one gentle prying motion of a screwdriver. Jackie held the flashlight.

Truman had a mop handle, which he thrust down into the oily green muck. "Step back," he warned Jackie, not feeling the need to explain why.

She held her hand up to cover her mouth and nose, and looked away. "Jeff wasn't that bad," she said. "I mean, at first, I thought he was real cute."

The solvent was thicker than he'd expected, and some of it slopped over the sides of the drum as he stirred the mop handle in a series of agonizingly slow figure eights. Jackie was still holding her breath when he pulled the mop handle out. "Nothing here but toxic wastes," he said, relieved.

"Thank the Lord," she said.

She played the light around the walls and ceilings of the garage, and walked over to the lift, looking not upward, at Ronnie Bondurant's stacked-up storage shed in the sky, but down, at the rectangular oil-spattered concrete and steel grating beneath the rack. The grate was, to her eyes, disturbingly coffin-shaped. She kicked the edge of it with her sneaker.

"What's this? What's it for?"

Truman kneeled down and ran the screwdriver around the edge of the grate. "It's the grease trap. When they put a car on the lift there, they let the oil drain out into there. When the trap's full, a truck comes along, sucks it out through a hose, and takes it to an oil reclamation place. I didn't notice it before."

"You think?"

He tapped the metal with the screwdriver. "There's an outlet here, where they insert the hose, but I'm not sure the grate part ever gets removed."

"Unless you have a body to hide," Jackie said.

They got crowbars off the tool bench, and tugged and heaved and pried until their hands were blistered. But the grate didn't move. Then they got a handful of bolts and washers and worked them through the holes in the grate. But they only heard the hollow sound of metal pinging on concrete.

"Empty," Truman said. "Nobody's worked on cars in here for a real long time."

"This thing hasn't been moved either," Jackie agreed. "You want to try some of the cars out back?"

"Later," Truman said, looking upward at the lube rack. "Shine that light up there, will you?"

CHAPTER

TWENTY-SEVEN

"ID LIKE TO DO WHAT YOU DO," OLLIE SAID wistfully. "Out there, riding around in the middle of the night, just you and the outlaws, right and wrong, justice and evil. Kind of like the wild, wild west."

"You crazy?" Eddie lifted one eyebrow that said Ollie was. "It's just a job, man. Just a service I provide for people who can pay. I gotta mingle with the wrong element, get all nasty dirty, lot of heavy lifting. It ain't all that exciting."

"Better than sitting in a crummy newsstand all day," Ollie said. "Selling *TV Guide*s and making change for bus fare."

Eddie got his .38 out of the glove box and checked to see that it was loaded. He pulled another Slim Jim out from under his seat and laid it right beside the pistol. "You're a pretty cool little dude," he said. "You can ride shotgun for me any time you like."

They were parked in a rubble-strewn parking lot on the back side of Central Plaza. It had been a branch of a big downtown St. Petersburg bank not that long ago. Then the bank got gobbled by another bank, and that bank got gobbled by a bank in Atlanta, and then everybody got gobbled by an institution in Charlotte, North Carolina.

Now all that was left was this pockmarked patch of asphalt, chained off from the street, well lit to keep out felons who might steal a parking lot.

Ollie used the bolt cutters to take care of the chain and then Eddie walked around the perimeter of the lot, shooting out the streetlights one by one. Cars drove past on Central Avenue a block away, but nobody cared what happened on this bleak little spot.

When the lot was good and dark, Eddie showed Ollie how to use the controls to unload the Monte Carlo.

"Not as easy as it looks," Ollie remarked.

"Took me two weeks to get used to the controls," Eddie said.

Ollie looked at the clock on the truck's dashboard. "They're late."

"Dissin' me," Eddie said. "You ready now, Ollie? Could get ugly. Ronnie Bondurant jokes around, but he don't play."

"I'm all set," Ollie said, clasping a Slim Jim in each hand. "You just give me the signal."

"Here they come," Eddie said. Ollie gulped and slid down onto the floor. He was so small that he could hide there, up under the truck's capacious dashboard.

Wormy pulled his pickup truck alongside Eddie's. It wasn't until Wormy pushed a button and let the electric window roll down less than an inch that Eddie realized it was not Ronnie Bondurant, but some other man who sat in the front seat alongside Wormy. The other man was younger, wrapped in bandages. Maybe, Eddie thought, this was the monkey who was supposedly still in the hospital.

"Where's Ronnie at?" Eddie said, immediately suspicious. He moved his right hand onto his thigh, the .38 under it.

Wormy kept the window rolled up. "He's got better things to do than screw around with you," he sneered. "Where's the keys to the Monte Carlo?"

"Where's my money?" Eddie asked.

Billy Tripp held up a handful of bills. "Come and get it, bro."

"I ain't any bro to you," Eddie said levelly. He held up the keys to the Monte Carlo so Wormy could see them. And as he opened the door of his truck to get out, he slid the Slim Jim into the waist of his jeans. The .38 disappeared into his palm, no bigger, comparatively, than a peanut.

Wormy and Ronnie watched Eddie's approach warily. They did not notice when the other door of the truck opened just a bit, or see the small man who seemed to slither out of the truck and along the pavement, through the bits of broken streetlights and gravel, until he was alongside Billy Tripp's door.

Eddie tossed the keys through the opening in the window, aiming for Wormy's face. The window slid shut again, and then it was rolling down, and Wormy leaned out a little, smiled and extended his right hand, not with Eddie's money, but with his loaded .38.

"Repo this," he said.

Everything happened so fast that afterward, even Ollie had to admit he wasn't positive about the sequence of events.

"Now," Eddie shouted.

Two shots rang out, and glass and blood spattered everywhere.

Ollie popped up, terrified, Slim Jim in hand, ready to jam the truck door locked to keep the outlaws from escaping. But nobody in that car was going anywhere. Wormy was slumped over to the right, pitched across Billy Tripp's lap, a gaping wound in his left shoulder. Blood trickled down his limp forearm. Tripp's bandaged and battered face lolled, with his chin resting against his chest.

"I think he's dead," Ollie said finally. "I think they're both dead."

Eddie stripped off his T-shirt and held it against his left forearm. The white shirt turned red. "It was a setup," he said. "We gotta call the lot, get Truman and Jackie out of there. Bondurant's still out there, maybe headed their way."

"You're shot," Ollie said. "We've got to get you to a doctor."

"In the truck," Eddie said weakly. "Duct tape. I'll fix it. You drive."

Ronnie buckled the seat belt around the Styrofoam cooler full of bills. He always liked to keep his money safe.

He was on the Bayway, headed out for the Gulf beaches. Just a quiet little ride. Ronnie and $20,000. He threw two quarters in the basket at the tollbooth at Eckerd College, had the car nosed forward even before the green light was flashing.

The bridge was lined with losers. People with no money and no hope, nothing better to do with a hot summer night than spend it standing around sweating, waiting for a stinking fish to bite another piece of stinking fish. If Ronnie Bondurant wanted fish, he went into an air-conditioned restaurant, had it brought to him with a slice of lemon and a baked potato, and put it on his American Express Gold Card. That was Ronnie's idea of fishing.

He was in the outside lane and he could see the boats out on the bay. Big cabin cruisers and ski boats zipped back and forth, leaving luminous white trails of froth in their wake. When all this was over, Ronnie promised himself, he'd spend a day out on the Hydrasport, cruise Pass-A-Grill Beach, find some new talent who liked fast boats and a guy with money to spend.

In the meantime, he passed the Point Brittany condo tower and made the left to head toward Tierra Verde. Nice out here, he thought. More happening out at the beaches than at sleepy old Pinellas Point. Lots of babes out here. With the money he took off Hernando Boone tonight, maybe he'd buy a place out here.

First he needed to deal with a certain bitch who thought she was smarter than Ronnie Bondurant. She was out here, somewhere, on this second bridge. He slowed down and his eyes swept first one side, then the other, looking for the familiar curves of LeeAnn Pilker. Plenty of lights out here, plenty of people. People were strung along the sidewalks lining each side; retirees with leatherlike skin, family groups with little kids running up and down, and teenagers with their blaring radios and tackle heavy enough to catch Moby Dick, should he ever find a way to swim up the west coast of Florida.

Women? Yeah, there were some old black ladies, squatted on yard chairs, touristy types with sun visors and DisneyWorld T-shirts, all of them too old or too young or too ugly to be LeeAnn Pilker.

The LTD nosed over the bridge's hump, past the bridge tender's booth, and on down, maybe half a mile, before Ronnie turned around at the Fort DeSoto exit, and came back over the bridge to get another look at the setup.

LeeAnn's arms were getting pretty tired, holding that heavy bait-casting rod. She'd been bent over this damned concrete railing for an hour now. At first she'd just let the line drift in the water, then, out of boredom, she'd accepted the offer of a big, live pinfish from a retired steelworker from McKeesport who was set up four or five feet away.

The pinfish was out there now, swimming against the tide, when she saw the big, blue LTD on its first pass by. It didn't surprise her to see Ronnie was here early in a different car, checking it out, trying to catch her up. Wasn't she a woman? Didn't she have shit for brains, not to mention a saggy ass and a bump on her nose?

She didn't turn around after she saw Ronnie pass by the second time, either, knowing he'd have to go clear back through the tollbooth to turn around again. Montana, she decided. They had mountains in Montana, and snow, and trees. And moose. She'd always wanted to see a moose.

Ten minutes later, Ronnie swept by again. When he reached the sandy embankment up ahead, he pulled off and parked, like LeeAnn had told him. Told him. The bitch. He lifted the lid of the cooler, took a look at his cash. Not good-bye. No way. He got the cooler out and locked the car. He had to dodge between cars to get to the other side, the cooler heavier than he would have thought. When he was across, he pulled the red baseball cap out of his back pocket, set it on his head, and started lugging the cooler up toward the crest of the bridge. Goddamn, he thought. Twenty thousand was heavy money, literally.

When she saw the red cap come bobbing up toward her, she allowed herself a tiny, private smile. She could see Ronnie gasping for breath. It was a hike, in this heat, up an incline, weighed down with all that money. Her money.

"Something's got your line," the steelworker said, tugging at her sleeve. "Big one. Better pay attention, hon."

LeeAnn heard the monofilament line whirling out through the reel. Ronnie was five feet away from the light pole where she'd told him to set down the cooler. What was he doing? Now he was walking away rapidly, his back to her.

"Set the hook, hon," the steelworker shouted. He'd put his pole down and was bent all the way over the bridge rail, watching the line unspool into the blue-black water.

There was a loud splash down there, and a huge silver streak, slicing up through the air, gaping mouth, flared gills, like a prehistoric thing. "It's a tarpon," the man shrieked. "Hey, this gal's got a tarpon on. Reel it in some, get that slack out of your line." People were running toward her now. A tarpon? Out here?

LeeAnn thrust the rod at the steelworker. "You reel it in," she said, and she started jogging toward the light pole and her cooler of money. The red baseball cap was nowhere in sight.

She was thirty yards away when she heard a long, low blast of a horn that seemed to be coming from the underside of the bridge. Cars were slowing and stopping on both sides. Now a yellow-and-black-striped bar with flashing lights across it dropped down across the roadway.

"Oh, no," LeeAnn said to herself, speeding up to a run. She was so close.

The concrete roadway started to move and rumble beneath her feet. Now she was maybe five yards away, with the cooler just on the other side of that set of barricades. The roadway was inching upward, and the sidewalk beneath her feet was moving, too, and then she was sprinting, the heavy construction boots slowing her down. From under the bridge she heard the clanking of the gears winching the span up and open.

She jumped, landed and rolled, landing hard on her knees. But the cooler was there, right there. She crawled forward and clutched it to her chest, struggling to her feet, to get away from the moving bridge.

She was right in front of the bridge tender's booth when Ronnie stepped over the railing separating the sidewalk from the booth.

"Hi, sugar," he said, gripping her arm so tightly she screamed as loud as she could, in pain and in fright.

Behind him, in the tiny lit-up booth, she saw a slender, red-haired woman who seemed to be napping across the control switches. There was blood on her uniform blouse.

"You go ahead and carry the money," Ronnie said, poking the .38 in the small of her back.

◆   ◆   ◆

The Publix truck was pulled way off on the shoulder of the road at the place where the state planned to build the impressive new roadway into the county's untouched wilderness area.

Hernando Boone drove alongside the cab of the eighteen-wheeler, waved at the driver, and parked nearby.

The driver was short and dark and spoke Cuban-accented English. "You Orlando's brother?" he asked. "I am Ignacio."

"Orlando's my half-brother," Boone said testily. "You can call me Mr. Boone. Let's see those ribs."

It was ten till nine, and there was no sign of Billy Tripp, who was supposed to be his new assistant, but was probably huddled up with Bondurant somewhere figuring out new ways to rip off Hernando Boone.

Now he saw headlights, and soon, a black-and-tan Cadillac Brougham came jouncing down the road. And now, there were more headlights, more cars. Damn. These sisters must think he was running an early-bird special. He and the Cuban would have to run the store all by themselves.

Ignacio jumped up on the rear bumper of the trailer, which was humming from all that juice needed to keep all those BTUs chilling the $2.98-a-pound baby-back ribs. He threw back the locking bar on the trailer and slid the doors outward, disappearing momentarily in the blast of arctic air that came shooting out into the hot, fetid evening.

Cars were streaming down the road now, dozens of them, parking even in the middle of the road. People were spilling out, happy, excited, chattering, a real carnival atmosphere. Women sipped wine coolers and grasped their counterfeit Louis Vuitton and Yves St. Laurent handbags close to their sides, full of cash for those bargain ribs. Plenty of men, too, and they were opening up the trunks of their cars, making room, opening coolers and stacking bags of ice; regular customers, familiar faces.

Ignacio looked at the lines of people surrounding the tractor-trailer, then back at the mountain of waxed cardboard cases stacked inside the truck, all the way to the ceiling.

"Shit," he said in authentic English.

Hernando Boone pulled on a pair of thick, insulated gloves, hopped up onto the trailer, and let down the steel loading ramp.

Ignacio climbed the stack of cases, hefted one onto his shoulder, and, grimacing, handed it down to Hernando, who nearly fell from the weight of it. But then the steroids, better business through chemistry, proved their worth, and Boone held the case aloft, over his head, like an ancient warrior showing the rest of the tribe a prized beaver pelt. With his block-shaped head, beaded ponytail, and massive torso, he was a god of meat, standing shoulders above the rest of the throng.

"Who's first?" Hernado called out loudly. He was putting the case of meat down when he felt a searing pain in his shoulders, the trapezoids, maybe, and the pain ran down his back. He had to see a doctor for real. The case fell off the back of the truck and landed on the road with a dull thud. The fitted top fell off and greasy pink-and-white slabs of meat spilled out onto the roadside.

"Oooh," several women cried.

Hernando slid down the ramp and in a moment was beside the ruined box. A hand reached out to snatch up a nice, meaty, five-pound slab. Five-finger discount. Hernando grabbed the hand and twisted until the discount shopper, a white-haired, stoop-shouldered granny, screamed "Have Mercy, Jesus," and passed out from the pain.

There was a respectful silence for a moment.

"That meat ain't cut," somebody pointed out.

"I know that's right," a high-pitched woman's voice joined in. "Ain't cut, ain't wrapped. Ain't weighed. Look like half a side of beef he selling."

Hernando got back up on the back of the trailer. The voices grew louder, and people were drifting away, starting their cars to drive off.

Ignacio had seen how things were working. And he'd already dealt with one Boone brother before. He slipped away and faded into the throng of departing meat buyers.

"Just a minute," Boone called out loudly. He looked around, realized the Cuban was gone, and knew that he was alone with a crowd gone badder than week-old poultry.

"Hey!" he thundered. The griping and moaning subsided.

"This is a warehouse sale," he called out. "We told y'all that. Cutting and weighing and wrapping costs extra. That's how we cut out the middleman."

"Alma didn't say nothing on the phone about having to buy no whole cow," a frizzle-haired white woman up front shouted.

Hernando could see his $45,000 profit sitting in that truck behind him, thawing, disappearing like an ice cube in July. When he got done with this fiasco, he resolved he would kill his brother. Orlando was only a half-brother, anyway.

"Split the slabs with your neighbors or friends," Hernando said in frustration. "Sell them their half for four ninety-nine a pound. Make you a little profit off this thing."

The shoppers conferred among themselves, and many concluded that this would, after all, be a decent transaction.

Ignacio saw the crowds moving forward with their fistfuls of money and decided to make his final break for freedom, snaking out from behind the construction trailer. The last thing he remembered was a hand, closing off his windpipe, and a voice, very quiet, whispering in English and Spanish that he was under arrest.

"You think Jeff's body is hidden up there, in all that junk? Where? How do we get up there?"

Jackie played the flashlight over the makeshift platform atop the lube rack and shook her head doubtfully.

"Seven feet up, probably," Truman estimated. "Didn't you ever climb trees when you were a little girl?"

"Trees, yeah," Jackie said. "Not greased poles. I'm no lumberjack, Mr. K."

Truman pulled open the door to the garage bay. Two cars were parked inside the fenced-in area. The purple Colt he ruled out immediately, but the silver Blazer, despite its battered body, would work, he thought.

With Jackie at the steering wheel and Truman pushing behind the bumper, it was slow rolling.

Inside the showroom, the phone rang three times and then stopped, abruptly.

Whoever had decided a Blazer was a light-utility truck, Truman thought, grunting and panting, his whole body pitted against the thing, had never had to push one.

When the Blazer was lopsidedly angled as close to the lube rack as they had the energy to maneuver it, Jackie clambered up on the roof and reached for the platform. Truman climbed up, too.

"You hold the light," he said. "I'll go up, see if the footing's solid."

"I'm lighter," Jackie protested, but he was already swinging one leg up and onto the platform.

She held the light with both hands, pointed low so it wouldn't shine in his eyes up there.

The platform was so cluttered with junk there was only a four-foot-square clearing that remained unobstructed. The planking creaked underfoot as he stepped gingerly to one side. It was dark despite the flashlight's puny beam. He felt the cold porcelain of the toilet, bumped a knee against something sharp.

"I'm coming up," Jackie declared.

"This is hopeless," she said when she was crowded right beside him. "If we try to climb around on here, it'll all fall down. Us with it. Maybe they moved the body," she said faintly. "Maybe it was never here." The dark was closing in on her, and she coughed from the dust they'd stirred up. Something skittered across her right arm and she slapped at it and felt it fall lightly on her foot. Just a roach. Just a roach, she told herself.

"Maybe they faked the whole thing," she said. "Maybe Jeff is still alive, in on it with Bondurant and them."

"Shine the flash back over there," Truman said. "To your right there, over by that Pepsi machine."

"It's too small," she said, running the beam of light over it. The Pepsi machine wasn't even five feet tall.

"Back to the right," Truman said, squinting to see better.

"Right."

"There."

A metal handrail was bolted to the wall. Painted the same dull gray as the garage walls. Six rungs led upward, but to where?

"Shine it on the ceiling," Truman said.

She traced a rectangle with it and they both saw the barely discernible outline of a door.

"An attic?" Jackie didn't get it. "Nobody has attics in Florida. Besides, I've seen the outside. The roof's flat."

Truman was already inching his way toward the far wall, knocking aside a stack of folding metal chairs. They fell and banged loudly against the hood of the Blazer below, followed by a cardboard carton full of old files, the backseat of a '72 Pontiac Firebird, and a stack of aluminum window screens.

"Keep that light steady," Truman told her, reaching for the first rung of the ladder. "As soon as I'm up there, climb down and go across the street and call Weingarten at the FDLE. Tell him what's been going on, and ask him to get his people here now. Don't come back until you see police cars. I mean it, Jackie."

The top rung stopped about three feet below the ceiling. He had to coil his head and neck down to keep from knocking his head against what felt like solid wood. With one foot resting on the rung, he pushed the weight of his shoulders upward.

When he straightened up, he found himself looking out across the flat tar and gravel roof of Bondurant Motors. At the pink 1957 Cadillac. A flock of seagulls swooped and whirled in the air above it, crying out at the disturbance.

CHAPTER

TWENTY-EIGHT

OLLIE DROVE. THE BIG BLACK TRUCK LURCHED forward in fits and starts, veering from side to side, at times jouncing up over the curb, then sharply back over into the left lane. Eddie winced at every jolt, but with his good hand, he kept dialing the number at Bondurant Motors.

"That's four times," he said finally. "Hope they're out of there."

Ollie was trying to concentrate on driving, but he couldn't miss the blood seeping out from the duct tape strapped around Eddie's forearm.

"I should take you to the hospital."

"I'm okay," Eddie insisted. "The bullet's just up there in the fatty part, near my underarm. It ain't nothing, Ollie. I had girlfriends cut me worse than this."

The truck jounced up on the sidewalk again, and this time Eddie reached over with his right arm and jerked the steering wheel sharply to the left, narrowly avoiding a head-on collision with a concrete bus-stop bench.

"You can't see nothin, can you?" Eddie asked. "Your head don't even clear the top of that steering wheel."

"I can see a lot," Ollie retorted. "If it's, you know, big."

Eddie took the steering wheel with his right hand. "I'll look out for the big stuff," he offered. "You take care of the brakes and the gas pedal. This bad boy will do one-twenty, you know."

"Right," Ollie said. He stomped down on the accelerator as hard as he could with the tip of his toes, and the speedometer jumped up to seventy, then eighty miles per hour.

"Say. You got a driver's license?" Eddie asked.

"This is frontier justice," Ollie said, keeping one hand on the steering wheel, just in case. "A driver's license is the least of our worries."

The bar at the Taste of Saigon doubled as its phone booth. The phone itself was balanced on top of a stack of phone books on the shiny, black-lacquered bar top.

Jackie edged her way between two shirt-sleeved businessmen and put her hand on the phone.

The bartender was in front of her immediately. "Fifties cent for call," she informed Jackie.

"It's a quarter at the gas station down the street," Jackie said.

"You go down street," she said. "This private phone."

Jackie slid two quarters across the counter and dialed the number for Ed Weingarten at the FDLE with nervous fingers. It was nine-thirty. Ollie and Eddie had been gone a long time and there was no telling when Ronnie and Wormy would be back.

"You've reached the voice mail for Ed Weingarten," an anonymous female voice told her. "Please leave a message, or dial zero to reach the operator for further directions."

She dialed zero and got a recorded list of options, none of which included speaking to a human being.

Jackie clicked the disconnect button and started to dial again. There must be somebody at that office who could send help. The bartender held her hand over the dial pad. "Phone is for customer," she said, looking meaningfully down the bar at the customers who sat there, laughing, talking, drinking, and smoking. There was a lot of smoke.

"I paid you fifty cents," Jackie protested.

"For customer," she said firmly.

Jackie ordered a Coke she didn't want, put two dollar bills down on the bar, and dialed Weingarten again. "I'm calling for Truman Kicklighter," she said. "It's absolutely urgent that you meet him, right away, at Bondurant Motors. He's found the body of Jeff Cantrell, and Ronnie Bondurant is due back any minute. Please hurry." She ended by giving him the phone number at Taste of Saigon, which she read off the take-out menu posted on the wall. Then she sat down to wait.

The bartender zeroed in on her again. "You want food or drink? Bar is for customers."

"Another Coke."

The front side of the roof was dominated by the four-foot-high Bondurant Motors sign that ran the length of the building. From the back side of it, Truman could see the neon lighting coils outlining the letters, and the metal struts that held the sign upright. The sign was turned off. And the Cadillac was, too.

The flat tar roof radiated heat like a sizzling black-iron skillet. The tar was soft under his shoes and the sick, sweet rotting smell hanging in the thick, humid air told him he was in the right place. But this time he had to be sure.

Truman peered down over the edge of the sign. He saw the cars below, lined up neatly in the lot, and traffic whizzing past on U.S. 19. Across the street, the Taste of Saigon looked like a brick box on top of which somebody had placed a red plastic prefabricated pagoda. Right next door was the Candy Store, so brightly pink it seemed to throb and send off a weird rose-colored glow into the night. The nightclub's parking lot was full, and the overflow crowd was pulling into the restaurant's lot in search of empty spaces.

He hoped Jackie was safely inside the restaurant, telling Ed Weingarten the whole bizarre story. He wanted to get this over with. Up here on the roof like this, he was as vulnerable as a tin duck in a shooting gallery.

"Get on with it, Kicklighter," he said out loud.

The Cadillac had been mounted on a thick set of iron girders bolted to a plate on the roof of the showroom. Obviously, the original owners had used a crane to lift the car into place.

From up here, he could see the coil and gearbox mounted on the underside of the car's chassis, and the simple machinery that made the Caddie spin and dip six feet up in the air.

He'd noticed an aluminum extension ladder leaned up against the back side of the sign. He dragged it over to the base of the girder, and set it up.

Halfway up the ladder he wished for the flashlight he'd left with Jackie.

But the glow of the streetlights out on the highway would have to do. He climbed upward, forcing himself not to look down, willing himself not to think about what awaited him at the top of that ladder.

The first surprise was the Cadillac itself. When he pulled himself onto the top rung, he could stick his head inside the yawning hole where a window should have been. There was no glass in the windows or the windshield, and as his eyes became accustomed to the dim light, he saw that there was no dashboard, no seats, no steering wheel. He thumped the door. Instead of the ping of solid Detroit steel he was answered by a hollow, flat knocking. The car was just a shell, the original body covered in fiberglass to keep it from rusting out.

Hell of a thing to do to a great old car like a '57 Cadillac, Truman thought, although to his mind, the '57 Chevy Bel Air was the sportier of the two cars.

He boosted one leg up on the doorsill, then swung the other leg through, too, and wiggled the rest of himself right inside the car.

Almost before he'd landed on the floor of the car, someone was screaming. "EEEE-AHHHH. EEEE-AHHHH." Over and over again. Then something sharp was clawing at his face, digging into the flesh. He flailed at the thing, one-armed, trying to protect his face and eyes with the other arm. Then, as suddenly as the attack had started, it was over.

Truman crouched on his hands and knees and raised his head cautiously, opened his eyes and saw that the air around him was full of slowly sifting, downy white-and-gray feathers. The last seagull flapped out through the Cadillac's open windshield. Truman reared up his head and sneezed. Three times, rapidly.

Then he set out, crawling, to find Jeff Cantrell's body so he could get himself out of this Hitchcockian hell.

Except for an inch-thick layer of leaves, feathers, eggshells, and seagull dung, there was nothing to find. All that was left, he realized, was the trunk.

LeeAnn couldn't seem to concentrate on her driving. Other than that, she was amazingly calm. It was like somebody else was in this LTD, driving down the road with Ronnie Bondurant sitting right beside her, sticking a nickel-plated revolver into her rib cage. Like LeeAnn herself was somewhere else, on a cool, green mountain in Montana, looking down, seeing some other girl having a really shitty life.

The jabbing was real, though.

"Don't even try it," Ronnie said. "Face it, LeeAnn, your ticket to the circus was that body of yours, not your pathetic pea brain. The only reason I didn't shoot you back there at the bridge and throw you down to those sharks is I got some business to take care of. Work now, play later, right, sugar?"

"What are you going to do to me?" LeeAnn asked, trying to make herself concentrate on the road and the other cars. For once, she thought, why couldn't a cop be on her tail for speeding or running a red light?

"Right now?" Ronnie said. "We're going back to the lot and pick up Wormy. He had to run another little errand." He ruffled his fingers through her short hair. "Say, that's right. I almost forgot. Eddie was a friend of yours, wasn't he? The repo man? Wormy had to go show the guy what happens when people try to jerk Ronnie Bondurant around."

"You kill them," she said automatically.

"Sometimes."

"Like Jeff."

"And you're next," he said, avoiding the question. "Too bad. You're a real waste of talent, LeeAnn."

It was what all her teachers had said, all through school, that what-a-waste crap. LeeAnn had learned to tune them out, and now she tuned Ronnie out, too. Until she saw the pink glow up ahead. She knew that glow. The club. And across the street was Bondurant Motors. Last stop.

Jackie was almost out of money. She'd spent eight dollars trying to reach Ed Weingarten, four phone calls, three Cokes. In between calls, she ran outside and checked across the street.

She saw the LTD slow down, then pull into Bondurant Motors. Ronnie Bondurant got out and pulled a slender, short-haired girl out of the driver's side. His hand was extended, like he was pointing a gun at her.

Seeing the place unlit like that, Ronnie made up his mind. Wormy was history. Tonight. In fact, it would be a nice touch for Wormy and Hernando Boone to shoot each other.

He went to unlock the showroom door, but it was already open.

"Friggin' pillhead," he said, shoving LeeAnn inside. "Get in there," he said, pointing toward his office. He pushed her toward the office and she stumbled on the doorsill. He pushed her again, knocking her to the floor. "Don't move," he said. He locked the showroom door behind him.

The gray control box was on the wall, next to Wormy's desk. No telling how many folks had driven by his darkened business tonight, thinking Ronnie Bondurant couldn't pay his light bill. Or worse, that Ronnie Bondurant was out of business. No telling how many potential impulse buyers he'd lost tonight.

He started flipping switches. Now the red and yellow lights strung around the sales lot were ablaze. Now the custom-made billboard was a beacon to those in need of cheap transportation and one-stop financing. Now, he thought with satisfaction, the pink Cadillac that was the Bondurant Motors trademark, not to mention a Tampa Bay area landmark, was up there on the roof, its high beams flashing on and off, doing its slow dips and spins.

At The Taste of Saigon, Jackie saw all the lights switching on across the street at Bondurant Motors. Uh-oh.

Things got very bright very quickly. There was a series of clicks, and the car shuddered a bit. He knew instantly what had happened.

He had one leg out the window of the Cadillac when he heard the clang of the aluminum ladder hitting the roof below. For a split second, he considered jumping. Then he lost his balance and fell back inside the car. At least it was a shorter fall.

The first few rotations, the machinery seemed to be warming up. By the fourth or fifth loop, he had to grip the window frame with both hands to keep from being flung from side to side.

On one of the car's downward swoops he pulled himself to his knees and looked out the window, across the rooftop. Everything was a blur of light and color and motion. Just like the time he'd taken Cheryl up on the Tilt-A-Whirl at the State Fair when she was a little kid. Now he was the one who was dizzy and disoriented. His stomach churned violently. He hung his head out the window and threw up all over a Tampa Bay area landmark.

Ronnie rummaged around in his bottom desk drawer until he found what he was looking for. Only an eighteen-inch extension cord, but it would do. He stood over LeeAnn and pointed the pistol at her head. "Let's go."

LeeAnn stared up at him, wild-eyed. Last chance, girl. Ronnie was either going to tie her up and then shoot her, or strangle her with that cord. Either way, it would be a closed-coffin funeral. "Fuck you," she told him.

When he went to slap her, she curled her legs up to her chest and kicked, knees together, construction boots aimed right at his crotch. He sidestepped and she missed, catching him on the kneecap, not the nuts.

Ronnie howled with pain, whirled around and punched her, square in the mouth, with his closed fist. She screamed, but the cry was clogged with blood and broken teeth and it came out more as a high-pitched gurgle.

◆　　　◆　　　◆

Jackie remembered the keys as she was dodging the cars on U.S. 19. Truman had handed them to her after he'd unlocked the doors. She heard the howls and the faint cries from inside as she circled around toward the back of the lot, but she was too close to the building to be able to see the roof.

It was a tough call, but it didn't take much for her to make up her mind. She ran, crouched low, toward where she'd seen Truman last, the garage and the lube rack. LeeAnn Pilker would have to wait.

Eddie and Ollie parked beside Truman's station wagon at The Taste of Saigon. No sign of Truman or Jackie.

"That's Ronnie's car," Eddie said, pointing across the street at the Lincoln. "And that ain't good."

"I'm calling 911," Ollie said, reaching for the car phone.

"If my arm was okay, I'd say no, let's go in there ourselves," Eddie said grudgingly, "but I'm not a hundred percent right now."

Ollie put the phone down when he saw the yellow two-tone Monte Carlo come chugging up and turn into Bondurant Motors.

"Can't be," Eddie said.

"You shot them," Ollie said. "They were dead."

"One of 'em been resurrected," Eddie said.

Billy Tripp looked remarkably undead as he got out of the Monte Carlo. He stood there, checking the place out, making up his mind about something.

Eddie got his .38 and shoved it into the waistband of his jeans, and Ollie did the same with his .22.

Ronnie hadn't turned on the lights in the garage. Jackie could make out the outline of the Blazer, parked right where they'd left it in the garage, but where was the flashlight? Had she put it down somewhere? She'd never find anything up on that lube rack without a light.

There *was* light seeping out from under the door to the showroom. Maybe there was a better way, she thought.

It was so bright inside. She could hear Ronnie's voice, plain as anything, and a soft, hiccupping cry. LeeAnn.

"Shut up, bitch," Ronnie snapped. "I should have shot you back at the bridge and been done with it."

Jackie dropped to her knees. A good position for praying, or for crawling, unnoticed, she hoped, into the showroom. She could see the switchbox on the wall, not six feet away. He'd left the door conveniently open. But she'd have to crawl past Ronnie's office door to get to it, and it was open, too.

She was almost there, maybe a foot away, when somebody started beating on the front door. She dove under the kneehole of the nearest desk.

"Hey, Ronnie, it's me, Billy," a voice called. "Open up."

Billy Tripp darted inside when Ronnie opened the door. He couldn't have looked any worse than he had earlier in the day, but he did. His shirt was a collage of blood spatters and grease. The Monte Carlo had been a bitch to get cranked.

"What happened to you?" Ronnie asked. "Where's Wormy?"

"Shit," Billy said, disgusted. "That nigger repo man had somebody with him. It was a midget, Ronnie. Swear to God, a little old midget. Wormy popped the nigger, and I did the midget. Anyway, the Monte Carlo's out front. Wormy said, tell you he's taking care of things. He wants us to meet him in the parking lot of the Flora-Bama Motor Court, says you know where it's at. Hey, Ronnie, what's Wormy do with those bodies, anyway?"

Billy was never still. His eyes darted around the showroom, and he saw LeeAnn cowering on the floor of Ronnie's office. "Hey, is this Jeff's girlfriend?"

"Don't you ever shut up?" Ronnie said irritably. "We're late. Boone will be gone if we don't get out there right now. Tie that extension cord around her hands. We'll put her in the trunk."

Jackie had to bite back the tears. She was trembling all over, not from fear now, but crazy, blinding rage. Ollie was dead. Eddie too. She shot out from under the desk, kicking over a trash basket. Ronnie whipped around, pistol drawn. She yanked down on the master circuit-breaker switch, he fired, and the room went black.

The Caddie stopped spinning so abruptly that Truman was thrown sideways across the floor. He got unsteadily to his knees and looked out the window. The Bondurant Motors sign was off, the red and yellow lights in the lot extinguished. Had help arrived?

He didn't intend to wait around up here and find out. He crawled out the rear window and onto the trunk of the car. The fiberglass was so slick, he started sliding immediately. Somehow, he managed to reach out and grab one of the Caddie's outrageous fins. Still slipping, but not as uncontrollably, he flopped over on his belly. He found the rear bumper with the toes of his tennis shoes and put on the brakes. Bracing his sweating palms on the trunk, he hand-walked himself to a semierect stance. He pushed off hard with his toes and tucked his body inward, sort of a reverse of the way he'd seen high divers do back flips. Only they were aiming for water, forgiving, soothing water. Tar and gravel was the best he could hope for.

The landing was bad and hard. His chin hit the roof first, driving his teeth right up into his skull, it felt like. Elbows and knees were lousy shock absorbers, too, especially ones as old as his. He lay there for a minute, dazed and bleeding and hurting worse than he could ever remember hurting in his whole life.

Pain was all right, he reasoned, groaning and struggling to stand up. Pain meant you were alive, not squashed like a bug on the windshield of life.

CHAPTER

TWENTY-NINE

"**Y**OU'LL HAVE TO GET THE PADLOCK," EDDIE said, handing Ollie the bolt cutters and leaning heavily against the chain-link fence. His breath was coming short and shallow now, and in the floodlights of the back lot he could see that his arm was bleeding badly again.

"I can get it," Ollie assured him, clenching his teeth as he squeezed the bolt cutter's handles together.

"Hold it steady," Eddie coached. "Those bolt cutters are diamond-forged. Could slice a telephone pole in half."

"I . . . can . . . get . . . it," Ollie grunted.

The padlock fell to the asphalt. "I did it," he said, disbelieving.

Eddie didn't answer. He was sprawled out on the ground, blood puddling under his outstretched arm.

"Eddie?" He'd lost a lot of blood. But he's a big guy, Ollie thought. He's got a lot of blood. See if there's a pulse, Ollie told himself. He could feel his own pulse racing like a hamster on amphetamines. He put his fingers on Eddie's jaw, just under his earlobe. The beat was faint and slow, but it was there.

Ollie pitched the bolt cutters aside and yanked the gate open. He had to get to Truman and Jackie, get to the phone, get an ambulance, get the cops. He reached down and gently removed the .38 from Eddie's waistband. Ollie was alone now. He needed all the firepower he could get.

The garage door was open, but it was dark inside. This was the way Truman and Jackie must have gotten in. He was running toward the garage when the lights went out. A moment later he heard the gunshot. From inside somewhere. The showroom? Whose gun? Ollie froze. He needed to think. As far as he knew, Jackie and Truman didn't have weapons. That left Ronnie Bondurant and Billy Tripp.

Truman's equilibrium had been knocked for a loop, along with most of his joints and his eyeglasses. He felt around in the dark, found his glasses, then started inching toward the glow of the streetlights on U.S. 19. When he got to the fuzzy gray outline of the billboard, he stood and looked down at the parking lot. He saw the traffic on the highway, and the sales inventory of Bondurant Motors. And the gray Lincoln. Parked right beside it was a car he didn't recognize at first. Two tones of yellow. Late seventies, American sedan. With a sinking feeling, he knew it was the Monte Carlo, and that something had gone very wrong.

Looking down made him dizzier. He steadied himself and moved toward where he thought the trapdoor should be. He could almost hear his bones creaking. One minute he was taking a step, the next his foot met not solid footing, but thin air. He stumbled backward, nearly falling again, righted himself, and sensibly eased himself down to a sitting position, feeling for the edge of the trapdoor with his hands.

Finding it, he dangled his legs down into the hole until he found the top rung of the ladder and started the laborious climb down. Up had been a hell of a lot easier.

Faint voices were coming from the front of the car lot. Their words were indistinguishable. Maybe, Ollie thought, it's the cops, the good guys. But just in case it was the bad guys, he drew the big pistol, the .38. It was so heavy he had to hold it with both hands, the left hand clamped around the right wrist, and still he couldn't hold it any higher than waist level, not while he was crouched low, keeping tight to the side of the building, moving in on the voices like Elliot Ness and the Untouchables on the Chicago mob.

"Goddamnit," Ronnie was saying. "Didn't I tell you to tie her up? Didn't I? Did you look in the back like I told you?"

They were standing outside the front door of the showroom, so close Ollie could have hit them with a rock from where he hid. "I'm sorry, Ronnie," Billy said, shoulders twitching. "I'm real sorry. She was gone when I got there. I looked, but she ain't back there. She must have come out this way, huh?"

Ronnie trotted out to the sidewalk, paced up and down in front of the lot three times, then came back.

LeeAnn could have run across the street to her friends at The Candy Store for help. She could hide for a while, but she wouldn't get far. And she was scared of him now. Too scared to go to the cops, he'd guarantee that.

"Screw it," he said finally. "Let's get going. There's forty-five-thousand dollars riding on this thing. Bring that black chick out here. Wormy can take care of her after the thing with Boone is done. You said the Flora-Bama, right?"

"Yeah, Ronnie," Billy said. "Man, I'm sorry about LeeAnn getting away. Hey. You want me to get rid of the other one in there? Sort of make up for LeeAnn? I hit her a good one on the head. She's out cold. I can dump her in one of those canals out there on Weedon Island. By the time the gators and crabs get done with her, won't be nothing left to identify. I'll meet you guys at the Flora-Bama and we'll take down Hernando Boone. Right?"

Ronnie nodded irritably. "All right. Don't screw this one up, Billy. It's your last chance. Screw this one up and you'll end up in that canal right alongside the girl."

Ronnie got behind the steering wheel of the Lincoln and sped out of the parking lot.

Ollie let him go. It was Jackie he was worried about now.

Not three minutes later, Billy Tripp kicked the front door open and came out carrying Jackie in his arms. She was limp, but Ollie couldn't see how bad she was hurt. He aimed the .38 and actually had Tripp in his sights for a fleeting instant. Then he put the gun away. He was no sharpshooter. There was no way he could nail Tripp without hitting Jackie. He watched while Tripp dumped Jackie in the backseat of the Monte Carlo and waited until he saw Tripp head in the same direction as Ronnie Bondurant.

The showroom was still dark, but he felt around until he found a phone. Ollie called 911 like he should have done before. "We need an ambulance at Bondurant Motors," Ollie said urgently. "Send the police. There's been a shooting."

There was a loud clatter coming from the garage. He hesitated, then took out the .38.

Truman dropped down onto the hood of the Blazer and from there slid down to the garage floor. The tool bench was only a few steps away. Pity he hadn't memorized how many. He kicked something with his foot, heard it roll, reached down to retrieve it, and found the flashlight Jackie had set on the floor.

With the light he could choose his weapon. A tire iron seemed appropriate, but as he reached for it, he knocked a metric wrench to the floor. The ringing seemed to echo through the garage. It would bring Ronnie or Wormy out here to investigate, he knew. He pressed himself flat against the open door to the showroom, the tire iron raised above his head, ready to strike.

Ollie moved, catlike, toward the door to the garage. It was eerily quiet now, and even darker than the showroom because of the lack of windows. He stepped into the doorway, assuming his crouched gunslinger stance.

Truman saw only the toe of the intruder's shoe. But it was such a small shoe.

"Ollie?" he whispered.

"Truman?" Ollie's hand relaxed on the .22.

"For Pete's sake!" Truman said. "I saw the Monte Carlo out front and I just figured, uh, well, I figured it wasn't good news."

"It wasn't," Ollie said soberly. "Wormy pulled a gun, and he was going to kill us both. Eddie shot first. Wormy's dead, I think. But Billy Tripp, don't ask me how, he got away and came back here. Eddie got hit in the arm. He's lost a lot of blood, TK. He's passed out in back, right outside the fence. And there's more. Tripp's got Jackie. I saw him put her in his car. He said she was alive; but he was going to kill her."

"My God," Truman said. "I heard a shot. Was that what happened?"

"I don't know," Ollie said. "I heard it, too. That guy, TK, he's going to throw Jackie in one of those canals out on Weedon Island. There are alligators out there. Did you know that?"

"I know a little bit about Weedon Island," Truman said grimly. "Was that where Bondurant was headed, too?"

"They're supposed to meet first at some place called the Flora-Bama. I never heard of it before. Then they're going to Weedon Island, to rip off somebody named Hernando."

"The Flora-Bama's a tourist court. Out there by the dog track, right before you turn to go to Weedon Island," Truman said.

"Let's get out there then," Ollie said. He pulled the .38 out of the waistband of his sagging pants. "Here. Eddie's gun. I called 911, told them to send an ambulance and the police."

"I've got to talk to that damned FDLE agent," Truman said. "Jackie was supposed to call him. I've got to let him know what's going on. Bondurant is on the move."

They heard the wail of sirens coming close.

"I'd better get out there and show them where Eddie's at," Ollie said. "There was a lot of blood. And his pulse wasn't too good."

"You stay with Eddie," Truman said. "I'm going after Jackie. When the police get here, tell them what you just told me. Maybe they can put out an alert for that Monte Carlo."

Ollie tossed him a set of keys. "Take Eddie's truck. It can go a hundred and twenty an hour. And it has a phone, too."

Truman didn't waste any time with the operator at the FDLE office. "This is an emergency, life-and-death situation," he told her. "I know all these guys have beepers and car phones and all kinds of modern gadgets. I'm a taxpayer and I pay for them. You get Ed Weingarten on the horn and tell him to call Truman Kicklighter at this number."

The truck was humming along at seventy miles per hour, but it only felt like forty, which was the actual speed limit. The cell phone buzzed.

"Mr. Kicklighter?" Weingarten's voice crackled with anger. "Is this some kind of joke? I'm on an operation at this moment, sir, or I'd be talking to the state's attorney about obstruction of justice charges against you."

"Cut the crap," Truman snapped. "I'm on an operation, too. You'll find Jeff Cantrell's body in the trunk of the Cadillac on the roof of Bondurant Motors. St. Pete police and an ambulance are already there. Wormy Weems shot one of my associates earlier tonight, and he's in bad shape. Bondurant and one of his thugs, a young hood named Billy Tripp, are on their way to Weedon Island. Tripp has kidnapped a young woman, and she's in his car. They're planning some kind of holdup of Hernando Boone. I don't know too much about that part. I'm on my way out there right now."

"We'll take care of it," Weingarten said curtly.

"Wait a minute, damnit. Did you hear me? Tripp has Jackleen Canaday. She's been shot, I think. He's driving a seventies gold two-tone Monte Carlo. I don't know the license plate number. Tripp intends to dump Jackie's body in one of those canals on Weedon, then meet up with Bondurant at . . ."

"We're aware of the situation," Weingarten said, interrupting. "Stay away from Weedon Island, Mr. Kicklighter. You'll just be in the way. Go home. Watch the eleven o'clock news. Channel eight."

"You called in a television crew?" Truman was incredulous. "You idiot. I told you, Tripp has Jackie. We think she's still alive. And he could be anywhere on that island. If he gets wind that anybody's onto him, he'll finish the job and dump her. There are alligators in those canals, for Christ's sake."

"I've got to keep this line clear for official communications," Weingarten said. "Good-bye, Mr. Kicklighter."

"Son of a bitch," Truman said. He was going so much faster than the rest of the traffic, nobody could see him talking to himself. As if he cared now. He threw the cell phone on the seat next to him. "He'll get Jackie killed. And give an exclusive on my story. To a television station."

◆   ◆   ◆

Jackie's head felt like somebody had tried to chop it in two with an ax. It was the worst headache she'd ever had, and there was a place high up on the crown of her head that burned something fierce. She guessed the bullet had merely skimmed a new part in her hair. If there was a bullet lodged in her skull, she'd feel it, wouldn't she?

At first, after she'd been shot, she'd been sure she was dead. Then, when Bondurant grabbed her, all she could think to do was lie still and play possum.

Up in the front seat, Billy Tripp was mumbling to himself.

The back of the Monte Carlo was like a rolling garbage can. Beer bottles, paint cans, old shoes, dirty clothes, a big plastic bucket full of junk.

Jackie snaked a hand down to the bucket, keeping her eyes nearly closed, watching Tripp to make sure he wasn't watching her. She wondered where his gun was. The bucket was stuffed with rags, brushes, rollers, and a caulking gun. Too bad it wasn't a real gun. Her fingertips probed silently until they closed on something useful.

She sat up quickly and jabbed the knife blade into the base of Tripp's skull. "Don't turn around," she said fiercely. "Don't you move, boy, or I'll cut you ear to ear."

Tripp stiffened. "I thought you were dead. Don't cut me. Put the knife away. I'm not going to hurt you."

"You're not gonna get the chance," Jackie said, emboldened. "Take that gun of yours and toss it back here to me."

Tripp did as she said. The gun was black and it looked and felt real.

She looked out the window and tried to get her bearings, but everything she saw looked out of context until she saw a street marker and realized they were on Fourth Street North. Up ahead, she saw a big gas station with a little convenience store in the middle.

"Turn in at this Texaco," she said, jabbing at his neck. "And don't try to pull anything."

"What do you think you're doing?" he asked. But he signaled and turned into the gas station.

"Pretty snotty for a cracker boy with no gun and a knife in your neck, aren't you?" she said. "We're both getting out of this car now, and I'm going to call the police and tell them how you and your boss killed Jeff Cantrell and tried to kill me and toss me to the gators. Then we're going to sit and wait for your sorry butt to get put under arrest."

"I didn't kill anybody," Billy protested. "Ronnie killed Jeff Cantrell. They tried to kill me. They did kill Weems."

"Too bad they didn't kill you," Jackie said. "Anyway, I heard you tell Ronnie that Wormy was going to meet up with you at that motel. How's a dead man going to a motel?"

"There's no time for all this now," Tripp said, sighing. "You're screwing up everything. Look. I don't work for Bondurant. I'm an undercover FDLE agent."

"And I'm Aretha Franklin," Jackie said.

"I work for Ed Weingarten. Your friend Truman knows him. We've been investigating Bondurant and Boone for a long time. I've been undercover two months. Tonight's the night we bust them. Wormy is dead. If I don't show up to meet Ronnie at that motel, he could get suspicious and blow town. He won't go after Boone alone."

"How do I know you're not just making all this up?" Jackie asked, keeping the knife to his neck, but easing up a little, just in case.

"My service revolver is in a holster strapped to my ankle. My badge and ID are there, too," Tripp said. "And there's a microphone taped to my chest, under my shirt. I've been transmitting to our people. They're parked in a van out near the Boy Scout camp. Take that knife off my neck and I'll show you."

"Wow," she said after he showed her the badge and gun. "You could have shot me any time you wanted."

"You could have cut me ear to ear," he reminded her. "You called me a cracker boy."

"That was bad manners," Jackie said apologetically. "Anyway, it was only a putty knife. See?"

Truman reflexively eased off the gas when he saw all the flashing blue lights converging on the Texaco station at Sixty-second Avenue North. Probably another holdup, he thought, pitying the poor devils who had to work late nights at convenience stores.

He stopped at the light at Eighty-third Avenue and saw, out of the corner of his eye, a hideous yellow Monte Carlo go barreling right through the red light.

Tripp. It had to be. And if he really meant to dump Jackie's body at Weedon Island, he'd just passed the turnoff for the quickest way there. He was still headed north on Fourth Street.

Truman zipped through the red light, too. When he was two car lengths back from the Monte Carlo, he backed off the accelerator. If Jackie was still alive, he didn't want to spook Tripp. There was one other way to get to Weedon Island that Truman knew of. If the road was still there. It had been a long time.

Tripp made a sharp right onto Gandy Boulevard and Truman did the same. Now Tripp could do one of two things—turn right onto Sam Martin and the back way across Riviera Bay to Weedon, or keep going a few blocks east if he were headed to meet Bondurant at the Flora-Bama Motor Court.

The Monte Carlo didn't slow as it passed the turnoff for Sam Martin. One, two, three, four blocks, then it veered left across traffic and into the parking lot of the Flora-Bama Motor Court. Truman passed the motel at a sedate speed, wishing that Eddie's customized $40,000 tow truck wasn't quite so conspicuous.

The Flora-Bama had been built in 1950 and the red neon VACANCY sign had been flashing since the end of the Nixon administration. There were three cars parked out front, but only one was a gray Lincoln, air-conditioning running but failing to cool Ronnie Bondurant's temper.

Billy Tripp pulled up beside the Lincoln. The electric window slid open. "What the fuck took so long?" Ronnie demanded. "Boone isn't going to hang around all night. Did you take care of the girl?"

"Boone's still selling ribs off the back of that truck," Billy said. "I checked. After I dumped the girl back in those mangroves. Gators love mangroves. And dark meat."

"You sure she's dead? The last girl you were supposed to take care of is probably in Vegas by now."

Billy sniggered. "I cut her throat. Ear to ear. She's dead. Hey. Where's Wormy?"

"How the fuck should I know? Probably zoned out of his skull somewhere. Forget him."

Ronnie got out of the Lincoln and locked it up. "We'll take the Monte Carlo. Boone knows my car."

"Right," Billy said loudly, doing that freaky head-bobbing thing with his head. "Right, Ronnie. We'll take the Monte Carlo. Good idea."

The Save-Inn was right next door to the Flora-Bama Motor Court and more modern by thirty years. Its mildewing yellow-adobe facade and cracked red-tile roof weren't what filled up the parking lot on Friday nights. That would be the Save-Inn Lounge. Most of the vehicles were pickups. Truman parked the tow truck in a row of Chevys and Fords. He saw Bondurant climb into the Monte Carlo.

Truman eyed the other trucks. If Weingarten's men really were "on top of the situation," were some of them hiding in these trucks? Why didn't they move in on Bondurant and Tripp right now? Before Jackie got hurt. Unless they planned to wait and catch them in the act of robbing Boone. Television news crews loved that kind of live-action stuff. And if innocent civilians got caught up in the crossfire, they could score even bigger ratings points.

After the Monte Carlo passed, Truman followed. All the Chevys and Fords stayed right where they were.

It was getting close to eleven o'clock. Hernando Boone was in a murderous mood. All night he'd been dickering with these people. What did he have to show for it? Maybe $15,000 in cash, rolled up in the pocket of his baggy silk warm-up pants. Now there were four women left, huddled up over there between their cars, trying to make up their minds about whether they wanted to pool their money and buy the last ten cases of ribs for a stinking hundred bucks. It was almost as bad as giving it away, but Boone didn't care.

"Okay," he yelled at the stragglers. "Closing time. You want the meat or not? Let's go, folks."

The frizzle-haired white lady was appointed to be the payee. "All right," she said. "We'll buy it."

Boone held out his hand for the money and she started counting out the bills. "One dollar. Two dollars. Three dollars—"

"What's this shit?" Boone roared. "No way. I don't want no hundred singles. This ain't bingo night, lady. Nothing smaller than a twenty. And hurry up."

"Oh, dear," she said, and she shuffled off to consult with the others.

Boone walked up the ramp to start moving the packing cases toward the back of the trailer. He turned. "Cash and carry," he yelled at the women. "That means you gotta carry it off the truck. Or no sale."

A new car pulled up fifty yards from the trailer, its headlights extinguished. The driver honked the horn twice. Boone stuck his head out of the trailer. "I'm closed," he hollered, and he went back inside.

Beep. Beep.

"I'm closed, asshole. You're too late."

Beep. Beep. Beep.

Boone had been wanting to shoot somebody. Now he would. He came out of the trailer and started down the ramp, semiautomatic drawn.

◆　　◆　　◆

Tripp reached for his own gun.

Ronnie Bondurant knocked his hand away. "Wait. Let him come closer. The stupid fucker still thinks we want to buy meat."

"He'll shoot us, Ronnie," Billy whined.

"Give him the horn again," Ronnie ordered.

Beep.

Boone couldn't believe this fool. He kept walking, gun pointed right at the car. What was it, a Monte Carlo, something like that? The driver had long hair. A woman. With a man beside her.

"One more step," Ronnie said slowly. "Then hit him with the brights. Then you shoot."

"Okay, Ronnie," Billy repeated. "Boone takes one more step. Then we hit the brights and we kill him."

"What are you, a fucking parrot?" Ronnie snarled.

Truman had been driving without lights since the turnoff at Weedon Drive. He was running slow and staying back. At the marker for the Boy Scout camp, he pulled off the road, backed in a dozen yards or so, and left the truck with the motor running.

He stayed off the paved road, struggling to jog along the soft, sandy shoulder. Every step reminded him of his age and the night's events.

When he could see the lights of the construction site ahead, Truman swung wide to the right. It was slower going dodging around the heavy equipment and the stacks of materials, but this way there was less of a chance that he would be seen.

Now he could see a big white tractor-trailer rig, with green lettering on the side. A Publix truck out here? Somebody was honking a car horn. Two cars he'd never seen before were parked on the road. Fifty yards away, he saw the now familiar outline of the Monte Carlo.

Hernando Boone was yelling and walking straight toward the Monte Carlo, and he had a semiautomatic pistol aimed right at the car's windshield. Tripp, behind the wheel, kept honking his horn.

Truman's only plan was to keep anybody from shooting in or at the Monte Carlo. Jackie could be in the backseat, or even the trunk. He began running toward the Monte Carlo, Eddie's bulky .38 clutched tightly in his hand.

Suddenly, two shafts of blinding white lights snapped on and were crisscrossing the trailer, Boone, and the Monte Carlo. Four middle-aged women he hadn't noticed before were pulling short-barreled shotguns out of their phony Fendi handbags and now they were leaned across the hoods of their cars. One of the women, frizzy-haired, had a megaphone, too.

"This is the Florida Department of Law Enforcement," her voiced boomed, echoing in the dark, swampy night. "Put your weapons down. You are under arrest."

The door of the construction trailer burst open and six burly men wearing black commando gear came pouring out, brandishing yet more short-barreled shotguns.

Boone froze.

"Shoot, goddammnit," Ronnie screamed at Billy. "Shoot!"

When Billy didn't follow his orders, he pointed his own .38 at Hernando Boone. Tripp turned sideways in his seat and, incredibly, put the barrel of his gun right to Ronnie's temple.

"Hey, Ronnie," Tripp announced. "I'm sorry, man. You're busted."

Hernando Boone picked that moment to unfreeze. He made a lunging eight-foot dive off to the left and rolled off the shoulder and into a three-foot drainage ditch. The dive and roll part of the move was an old, hated football drill from his days at the University of Florida. The hiding in a drainage ditch was something his Miccosukee ancestors had done when Andrew Jackson sent his troops to wipe out the Indians in Florida. Or so he'd always heard.

Ronnie Bondurant's eyes never blinked. He was watching Hernando Boone. And he intended to kill every cop in Florida if it meant keeping Boone from living even one more minute.

He dropped his gun. Coiled. Waiting. Tripp gave that weasely snigger of his and took his finger off the trigger. Asshole.

Ronnie pivoted and sidearmed Tripp, catching him in the windpipe. Then again, harder. "Gaaagh." Tripp's eyes rolled up in his head.

Ronnie threw the car door open and turned toward the blank space where Boone had last been seen. Even before he was out of the Monte Carlo, he was firing, scattering shots in any direction Boone might move.

The FDLE commandos moved in closer and kept their shotguns aimed at the Monte Carlo, but with one of their own inside, they held their fire.

In all the confusion, nobody noticed the sixty-something gentleman with the tinted red hair who was running full speed toward the side of the Monte

Carlo. Truman's body remembered what he himself had not thought of since his days on the scrub squad at Kokomo High School back in the late forties. He tucked his head down, dropped his shoulders, and threw the whole weight of his torso against the open door of the Monte Carlo. The old body block.

Bondurant's forehead bounced off the roof of the car, and he would have dropped like a rock, too, except that Truman, out of adrenaline and ideas, was slumped on the other side of the door, pinning Bondurant in place.

"This is the Florida Department of Law Enforcement," the frizzle-haired woman called on the megaphone. "You are under arrest." She and half the other commandos rushed at Hernando Boone, cowering in the mosquito-engorged drainage ditch. The other half of the team veered toward the Monte Carlo. The operation went just the way they'd practiced in their SWAT team exercises. With stunning precision they grabbed Boone out of the ditch and then wrestled the bleeding, unconscious Ronnie Bondurant to the ground in order to subdue him.

When the Channel 8 *Action News* crew was ready, lights adjusted and cameras rolling, Ed Weingarten himself strode out of the shadows. He was wearing his own custom-designed official special-agent-in-charge black commando outfit. His uniform blouse bristled with embroidered patches, silver insignia badges, and half a dozen pockets and pouches loaded down with his portable battery pack, cell phone, beeper, pistol, and badge. The trousers snugged into high-topped lace-up black boots so new they still squeaked as he walked.

The other agents stepped respectfully aside while Special Agent in Charge Ed Weingarten personally snapped the handcuffs around Ronnie Bondurant's wrists.

Hustled off to the side, out of concern for his safety and, yes, community relations purposes, Truman recalled yet one more football move. What was it called? A dropkick? Whatever it was, it involved a kick and it made the cameraman drop a $26,000 Sony BetaCam.

At the studio in Tampa, the floor producer cursed softly when the live feed from Weedon Island suddenly went dead. There went his lead story. Luckily, the back-up lead was almost as good.

Action News anchorperson Sherri Lynn moistened her lips, took a cleansing breath, looked directly into the TelePrompTer, and started to read.

"Officials at the Lakeland-based Publix Supermarket chain reported today that they are gravely concerned over the theft of a tractor-trailer containing fifteen thousand pounds of tainted frozen babyback ribs. The ribs, Publix says, were discovered to be part of a shipment of beef smuggled into the U.S. from a now defunct English processor accused of selling meat from cattle believed to have been exposed to mad cow disease. The ribs were to have been destroyed today. Health officials warn that serious illness and, in some cases, death, can result from eating mad cow exposed meat. In other news . . ."